"You and the kids should live with me, Charlie."

"The offer's appreciated, Rose, truly. I'm just not sure. The kids and I are finally starting to…" I hesitated to explain how we were only recently adjusting to the family of three we'd become, because I didn't want to make her sound excluded.

She played her trump card. "I don't think you and I were ever as close as Tom would have liked. I believe this decision would help him rest easier, don't you?"

Yes, it would have made him very happy.

"We'll be like Stella and Louise," Rose said, sounding eager.

"Who?"

"Some movie." She frowned. "Weren't there two women who, I don't know, bonded?"

"Thelma. You meant *Thelma and Louise*. And that movie ended in joint suicide."

"Oh. You're sure?"

"They drove into the Grand Canyon." Whistling, I made a diving motion with my hand.

"What a silly way to end a film. Okay, then. Not like them! Some other pair that would make a good roommate analogy."

Felix and Oscar came to mind. Hard to believe Rose and I would be any *odder* a couple.

Tanya Michaels

enjoys writing about love, whether it's the romantic kind or the occasionally exasperated affection we feel for family members. Tanya made her debut with a 2003 romantic comedy, and her books have been nominated for awards such as *Romantic Times* Reviewer's Choice, Romance Writers of America's RITA® Award, the National Readers' Choice and the Maggie Award of Excellence. She's lucky enough to have a hero of a husband, as well as family and friends who love her despite numerous quirks. Visit www.tanyamichaels.com to learn more about Tanya and her upcoming books.

Tanya Michaels

DATING
THE MRS. SMITHS

DATING THE MRS. SMITHS

copyright © 2005 Tanya Michna

isbn 0373880685

TheNextNovel.com

 HARLEQUIN®

PRINTED IN U.S.A.

Dear Reader,

You know the expression that you can choose your friends, but not your family? Well, it's also true that you can choose your husband, but you can't choose *his* family, which are generally part of the package deal. But what if that husband was gone, and his family—specifically his disapproving mother—was all you had left?

These were the thoughts that led to the idea for *Dating the Mrs. Smiths*, a story in which widow Charlotte "Charlie" Smith and her two young children end up relocating to Boston and moving in with her mother-in-law, Rose, a woman with a good heart buried underneath all her strong opinions. Deep, deep underneath.

I'm very excited about my first book for NEXT, and hope you enjoy it! If you do, please drop me a note at t.michaels@earthlink.net. You can also visit my Web site at www.tanyamichaels.com for giveaways, book excerpts and all my latest news.

Wishing you happy reading and wonderful in-laws.

Tanya

Thank you, Jen and Pam,
for helping me figure out my NEXT step.
And special thanks to my parents-in-law,
Harvey and Sandra, for your support and
encouragement of my writing. I'm very thankful
that you raised such a wonderful son and that
my kids have such loving grandparents.

CHAPTER 1

"This isn't a time to panic," Martin assured me from behind his desk. "Only a time of change."

Considering some of the changes I'd experienced in my thirty-nine years, I didn't find the qualification particularly comforting.

"Think of it as two roads diverging," my boss continued with a paternal smile, "creating new paths for you, Charlotte."

Yeah. Well, I wanted to take the road most likely to pay my mortgage. After the months I'd struggled to recreate some sense of security for myself and my two children, Martin Kimble's informing me that the warehouse and office were being closed felt like a mortal blow. And he wanted me to dismiss it as just a flesh wound?

Despite his soothing tone, I noticed hypocritical traces of subdued panic behind Martin's wire-rimmed glasses. I didn't think he was worried about *his* mortgage, though. I think he feared having a hysterical woman on his hands. Or an angry woman who might staple his striped tie to his desk blotter.

Instead, what he had was a mostly numb woman. I would

have thought I was no longer naive enough to expect life to be fair, but I couldn't help my instinctive reaction, the denial welling up inside me, the inner protest that this really was unfair. Almost laughably so, if you had a sick sense of humor.

The kids and I were just starting to regain our footing, thanks in large part to Kazka Medical Supply taking me back. I'd worked here part-time for over a year before leaving to have Ben, never guessing I'd soon return, begging for a full forty hours a week. Forty hours that were about to be yanked out from under me.

"You have some choices," Martin added, nervously repeating the same phrase he'd used to open this Ides of March conversation. Okay, technically this was autumn—and I wasn't a Roman emperor about to be assassinated—but the sense of doom and betrayal seemed appropriate. Plus there's no great Shakespearean reference for the Ides of September.

Nodding to reassure my district manager I hadn't gone catatonic, I mulled over the options. All two of them.

Stay in Miami and hope like crazy that I found another job before the southeastern distribution center closed in October, or put in for a transfer and hope like crazy it was approved. Martin had said he was more than willing to recommend me for the latter and that he thought my chances were "quite good." Of course, a transfer would mean uprooting Ben and Sara, and praying Kazka's northern locations continued to do well and weren't shut down soon after I moved. Thirteen-month-old Ben would probably adjust all right. If he felt anxious in a new place, I could just put him in his playpen, where the world view was four navy mesh walls no matter what zip code we called home. But Sara...

A first grader whose biggest worries should have been subtraction and whether or not she'd like the sandwich in her sack lunch, she'd already been through so much in the last two years. After four years of being home with an attentive mommy all day, Sara had started pre-K, followed by kindergarten—the year Sara had learned she would no longer be an only child. At first we'd thought her frequent but vague complaints about not feeling well were cries for attention, but she had indeed been experiencing periodic viral throat infections throughout my pregnancy. Then, less than eight weeks after the baby and I had been discharged from the hospital, Tom had checked in. Sara and Ben's father, my late husband, had been scheduled for a "routine" and "low-risk" surgery.

Doctors had assured us that serious complications from angioplasty were quite rare. If we were going to experience a freak overturn of the odds, why couldn't it have been winning the Florida Lotto?

Sara was finally coping with her dad's death, and a month into the new school year, she'd yet to be out sick—her life was improving. What would a child psychologist say about my now removing her from a class she enjoyed and taking her away from the only state she'd ever lived in, destroying her barely recovered sense of stability? I had a quick, flash-forward image of my daughter as a black-clad, green-haired teenager with her pierced lip curled back in a sneer as she explained to a sympathetic talk-show host, "I never had a chance. My mother completely screwed me up when I was young."

Oh dear.

"I saved the good news for last," Martin said coaxingly.

I glanced up from the hands I'd been unconsciously wringing in the lap of my outdated broomstick skirt. "There's good news?"

"You haven't asked where we would transfer you." He beamed at me as if the relocation, hardly a done deal even if I wanted it, would take me to paradise on earth.

Hershey, Pennsylvania? I hear the streets there are paved with chocolate. Or at least named for it.

"Chicago is the first option," he said. "But the more likely location for someone with your sales and marketing experience is…Boston."

"The one in Massachusetts?" *No, genius, the one in Nevada.* My question was really just a rhetorical reflex—I'd forgotten we even had a location there. In my defense, I'd had a few other things on my mind.

Martin was nodding. "Home of the Red Sox, famous clam chowder and, if I'm not mistaken, some family members of yours?"

"My mother-in-law." Rose Fiorello Smith.

Technically several of Tom's relatives lived around Boston, but it was Rose who loomed large in my mind. Her visits to Florida had been rare during our marriage, but as last fall became winter, she'd made an unprecedented three trips here: to meet Ben, to bury her son, and to "celebrate" Christmas with us, that awful first holiday season without Tom. A closer mother- and daughter-in-law duo probably would have been a comfort to each other. But love for Tom was one of the few things Rose and I had in common; with him gone, the awkward strain between us was more pronounced.

"Rose is the children's only living grandparent," I told Martin, reminding myself of why it was important to try to make more time to call or visit her. Even if it was a subconscious relief to let months go by without talking.

"And she's in the Boston area? Wonderful!" Martin's shoulders sagged in visible relief. Obviously the possibility of my being near family made him feel less guilty about this afternoon's bad news. "You see? Where one door closes…"

Thank goodness he trailed off. If he'd added "another opens," or some quaint remark about windows, I probably *would* have stapled his tie to his desk blotter.

It wasn't that I necessarily disagreed with the unspoken sentiment, but I'd heard my share of well-meaning platitudes since Tom's surgery had gone wrong, leaving me a widow with two young children. People desperately wanted to say something to make the situation more bearable. *Time heals all wounds; everything happens for a reason; loved ones live on in our hearts. You're not alone* had been the worst. I knew intentions were good, but when I woke up at four in the morning, reaching for a man who'd shared my bed for twenty years and was now in the ground, it sure as hell *felt* like I was alone.

Inhaling deeply, I forced myself back to the present. "Do I have to give you an answer today?" I hoped not. My thoughts were too jumbled to form a rational decision, and I was suddenly so tired that just asking the question took effort. Truthfully, I was a little alarmed by the oppressive, foglike fatigue rolling in—a disturbingly familiar sensation.

Last year, the combined lack of sleep, postpartum mood swings and overwhelming grief had banished me to a hazy depression I hadn't fully escaped until spring. I thanked the Lord every day for my friend Dianne Linney. Sara adored "Aunt Di," and Dianne, a single young woman with no children of her own, had helped with my daughter during those long, bleak months I'd felt trapped in a dark hole. Dianne had also fielded more than a couple pediatrician's visits on days when I absolutely couldn't miss work.

"I wouldn't dream of pushing you for a decision," Martin said. "I'll break the news to the salespeople tomorrow, when I have them all in the office for our meeting—I'd appreciate your discretion in the meantime—and the official company-wide memo won't go out until next Monday. So take a few days to give the matter some thought, no reason to rush."

No reason except the office being closed in a matter of weeks and my inordinate fondness for being able to buy groceries. But sarcasm was never the answer. If it were, I could make a killing on *Jeopardy*.

I stood, smiling to show there were no hard feelings, and returned to the office that had been mine since my return and advancement to full-time status. Inside the building, we could only pick up one radio station with consistent clarity, so I listened to a lot of Spanish rock music at my desk. Its sassy beat sounded muffled now, distorted, and the rest of my day passed like a recording playing at the wrong speed.

By the time I pulled into the driveway of my one-story stucco house that evening, I had managed to shrug off the tentacles of encroaching depression—mostly by making internal, inappropriate jokes. But I still hadn't adjusted to the fact that my current job situation, our financial lifeline, was disappearing.

I exited the car, trying to ignore the warm humidity that plastered my clothes to my skin, and waved to our retired neighbor, Mrs. Winslow, who was out mulching her flower beds. Mrs. Winslow watched the kids for me on Fridays, but one day a week with young children was enough for her. I was fortunate that Dianne, aforementioned gift from heaven, could stay with Ben and pick up Sara from school on Monday through Thursdays, allowing them to play with their own toys and be in the security of a familiar environment. There were several good day cares in the area, but God knows how I would have afforded one of them.

And Tom, who had been raised by a doting and devoted mother, had always maintained that day cares were too impersonal for his children. If I was no longer the stay-at-home mom we'd planned for me to be, at least the children were with someone who loved them unconditionally. I insisted on paying Dianne a nominal fee, which she added to what she made as a performer in a ritzy Vegas-style Miami hotel on the weekends, but we both knew she was saving me a bundle. Sometimes it seemed comical that my best friend was a gorgeous twenty-four-year-old who shook her booty for a living, when I myself was a newly widowed almost-forty-year-old from the burbs, but I'd hit it off instantly with the younger woman when a co-worker of Tom's had brought her to the company picnic. She'd become the sister I'd never had.

If not for Dianne's generosity and the last few dollars of the life insurance settlement, I might have had to sell my body on street corners to make ends meet—not that I expected a high profit margin on the bod of a woman who's nursed two babies. Unless there was a trendy stretch-mark fetish I didn't know about.

The wind chimes hanging in the alcove at my front door greeted me with tinkling metallic cheer. Even nicer were the voices I heard as I turned the knob.

"Mommy's home!" A pink-socked Sara barreled in from the carpeted living room onto the slick square of tile just inside the door.

I caught her as she skated into me, nearly knocking both

of us back out into the front yard. "Missed you today, Sara-bear."

Behind her, Ben wobbled into view, grinning and drooling. He didn't have much of a vocabulary yet—I couldn't count *ma-ma* since he generally said it to the oscillating fan in the kitchen—but his high-pitched squeals made it clear he was happy to see me. From the screened sunroom at the back of the house, Gretchen added her woofs of joy that I'd returned. Gretchen is a German shepherd mix who joined us after Tom insisted that it was good for kids to grow up with a dog and that he'd feel better knowing a trained canine was helping to look after the family. Thus resulting in my ownership of a sixty-five-pound nervous condition with chronic shedding.

Since Gretchen was terrified of the geckos that frequently got in the house, I didn't consider her my go-to line of defense in an emergency.

I hugged both of my children tight, closing my eyes and breathing in the faint scents of baby shampoo and Play-Doh. Being away from the kids all day was a difficult adjustment. I'd loved being home with Sara for her first three years, doing things like Mommy and Me activity groups, trips to the zoo and playdates at the park. Somewhere along the line, getting outside the neighborhood had become a must. I don't remember the median age in our subdivision being sixty-seven when Tom and I had bought the house, but more and more I was feeling like the only one at the monthly potluck who still had all her own teeth.

"Hey." Dianne met us as we rounded the corner from the living room into the kitchen. I wore a skirt, blouse and pumps, yet my statuesque friend looked far more glamorous in her faded jeans and yellow Life's a Beach T-shirt. For all our superficial difference, she "gets" me and we share the same loyal streak.

She jerked her thumb toward the ivy-print kettle steaming on the stove. "I was just brewing some tea. How was your day?"

So many possible answers, so few of them appropriate in front of children.

I hadn't called Dianne because I'd worried that if I tried to talk about today's news before fully absorbing it, lurking despair might snatch me into its jaws. But I was home now and armed with my secret weapon against despair—kiddo-hugs and a mouse-shaped cookie jar stuffed to the rim with reduced-fat Oreos. I predicted significant cookie depletion by morning.

Dianne raised one red eyebrow when I didn't answer. She's boasted more than once that among the redheads in her act, she's the only natural one. "That bad, huh? Want me to stay and help with dinner?"

I glanced at the jar pushed back on the mauve countertop, theoretically out of Sara's reach. Which was silly, since my daughter was plenty enterprising enough to drag one of the table chairs toward her goal. At least the scraping of wood on linoleum gave me an opportunity to foil her plans. "I was kind of thinking six-course Oreos."

"Oh. So *really* that bad."

"Or maybe I should come up with something more representative of the four food groups?" I averted my gaze guiltily, remembering the gourmet meals made from scratch I'd proudly had on the table when Tom got home after a hard day's work. The carefully prepared casseroles I'd frozen toward the end of my pregnancy with Ben, so that nutritious dinners could be tossed in the oven with no thought or trouble once the baby came.

"P-i-z-z-a offers bread, dairy, meats and veggies," Dianne suggested with a wink at my daughter, knowing perfectly well that Sara could spell *pizza* and enough other words to make her one of the best readers in her first-grade class.

Sara began jumping up and down. "Pizza! Can we have pizza, Mommy? Please!"

Caught up in her exuberance, Ben began waving his sippy cup of apple juice, ostensibly in demand of a ham-and-pineapple deep dish.

"Okay." I reached for the kitchen drawer where I kept coupons for the local delivery place. "Pizza sounds like decent comfort food."

"You want to talk about why you need comforting?" Dianne asked.

"Maybe this isn't the best time." I jerked my head toward the kids, who were bouncing around the kitchen in time to Sara's whoops of excitement. Ben wouldn't understand the technicalities of Kazka's downsizing, but even he could pick up on that Bad News vibe children are sensitive to, no matter how casual adults try to keep conversation. And Sara was bound to take the threat of more change badly.

"After they go to bed, then," Dianne said.

"You sure you want to stick around that late?" I floundered between wanting to talk to another grown-up and not wanting to take advantage of my friend's constant kindness. It was Wednesday, which meant she worked tomorrow night on top of watching my kids during the day.

"I can make us rumrunners," she cajoled. Dianne mixed better drinks than Tom Cruise's character in that old 1980s bartending movie.

Which is why several hours later, I hovered between a pleasant buzz and that weepy feeling alcohol can induce when you're blue. Feet tucked under me, I sat at one end of the couch, wearing flannel pajama bottoms and a T-shirt of Tom's—I'd donated most of his clothes to charity, but had been unable to part with all of them. From the other end of the sofa, Dianne was regarding me with unconcealed worry.

"I'm just a little down now because the news is still fresh. I'll be fine once I have a few days to take it in," I insisted. Wanting to reassure us both, I managed a smile and conjured one of those clichés I knew by heart. "You know, that which doesn't kill us—"

"Sucks swamp water, nonetheless?" Dianne supplied, her eyes twinkling.

"Exactly."

* * *

Perhaps saying I would be "fine" in a few days had been unrealistic. After all, it had been a long time since I'd truly felt fine. But I was coping. The weekend rolled around, and I eyed the classifieds in Friday's paper as I browned hamburger meat for dinner.

As the person who coordinated all of Kazka's sales appointments for the Southeast, I had contacts within the pharmaceutical distribution and medical equipment industry. Several people had agreed to look at my updated résumé. I suspected, though, that most of these offers stemmed more from professional courtesy than an overwhelming need to fill openings, which didn't bode well for me.

I knew I could find a job, but one that would allow me to support the family? Not for the first time, I regretted that I'd never gone back to college to complete my bachelor's degree. My college career had been cut short by Dad's unexpected death and my marrying young, but I'd finished enough credits to earn my associate's. The degree didn't carry as much weight in the current job market, though, and it wasn't my only handicap. I'd quickly proven myself at Kazka before leaving to have my second baby and had been told a full-time position was mine if I ever wanted it. But as far as impressing prospective new employers went, the stay-at-home-mommy years I'd missed in the workforce could put me behind the competition.

I stirred the beef around, making a mental note to get

chicken or fish sticks into the kids tomorrow since we'd had cheeseburger kids' meals last night. Once I'd set down the plastic spatula, I reached for the newspaper, which crinkled as I folded it back. Pickings were slim, unless I wanted an exciting job in the field of selling condo time-shares to tourists. Would applying for the transfer to Boston really be such a bad choice?

For the last few days, my knee-jerk reaction had been that I didn't want to uproot the kids. This was home, the place Tom and I had made our life together, a place full of memories.

He and I had met while attending the University of Florida, where he'd been offered a football scholarship. I'd been a freshman away from my Georgia home for the first time, enchanted with the good-looking Gator receiver. We were both only children, both raised by single parents. And now I was the single parent.

If the kids were going to be stuck with just me, maybe I should move somewhere where they had more family. They loved Dianne, but she dreamed of one day moving to Las Vegas or New York to perform. In Boston, Sara and Ben would be closer to their adoring grandmother. Unfortunately, so would I.

It wasn't that I didn't like my mother-in-law. We got along, particularly when we were in different states. But Rose had been raised in a patriarchal family where the men were revered and waited on—when she'd lost her husband, she'd transferred her devotion to her teenage son. Her pride and joy. The focus of her entire being. The first time he'd brought me home, during a semester break in college, I'd had the distinct impression that she'd wanted better for him. Maybe it wasn't personal; maybe no mere mortal woman could have lived up to what Rose envisioned for him.

But that point was moot now. And the kids deserved people in their lives besides me.

Speaking of the children… I glanced around the corner into the too-quiet living room. Although it might seem counterintuitive to worry that silence signifies chaos, it was amazing what my cherubs could do covertly. They were like a little sneaky special-forces team, usually on search-and-destroy missions. For the time being, though, Sara was lying on her stomach on the floor, tugging at the carpet that needed vacuuming as she watched a video. Ben was stacking soft blocks in the corner, then knocking them down and clapping his hands. Gretchen was probably either asleep in the hallway or hiding under my bed from any geckos that had infiltrated the house.

If we moved to Boston, I definitely wouldn't miss finding lizards in the tub. Nor would I miss palmetto bugs so large they flew into the outdoor electric insect zappers just for the head rush.

Not wanting to disturb the kids when they were behaving so well, I tiptoed back into the kitchen, where I followed the back-of-the-box directions to finish preparing our meal.

I poured a cup of milk into the drained hamburger, then stirred in noodles and a powdered sauce mix. With dinner finally simmering on the stove, I picked up the cordless phone. All this pondering a move to Boston made me guiltily aware that I hadn't found time to call Rose recently. Tom would have been disappointed in me.

What were the odds she wasn't even home and I could just leave a dutiful "we're thinking about you" message on the machine?

She answered on the first ring. "Hello?"

"Rose, hi. It's Charlotte. Charlie." The informal name everyone else called me wasn't quite as comfortable with her; it had taken me years just to stop referring to her as "Mrs. Smith."

"What an unexpected pleasha to heah from you!" Though Rose and her tight-knit family were active in an Italian subcommunity, a lifetime of living in Boston had my mother-in-law sounding more like a Kennedy than a Corleone—at least to my ears. "It's so lovely you remembered, even if it is a few days late. But I always thought a birthday is better when you spread it out, anyway."

"Um...absolutely." Birthday. Last week. Damn. How could I forget when we were both September babies? Of course, I was in serious denial about turning forty later this month, so that might explain it. "Happy belated birthday! Did you do anything special to celebrate?"

"Had lunch with some friends, puttered in the greenhouse, spent the evening looking over old photo albums, thinking about the restaurant where Thomas Sr. used to take me on my birthdays. I don't even know if it's in business now. I don't believe I've been since he passed on."

The image of Rose alone in that big house, surrounded by pictures of her lost husband and son, made me feel like the worst daughter-in-law on the planet. The least I could have done was sent a card.

"While we're on the subject of birthdays," Rose said, "I saw something on sale I wanted to send you."

"Oh, Rose, you don't have to do that."

"Nonsense. What kind of family would I be to ignore your birthday?"

Ouch. Direct hit!

"Just let me know what size you are, dear. Still carrying around all that pregnancy weight you gained?"

Yes. I'd thoughtlessly ignored her birthday *and* I was fat.

After a brief pause, I lied, naming a size two digits smaller than I could comfortably zip. It wasn't as though I were likely to wear the gift even if it did fit. For herself, Rose has great taste in clothes. She knows exactly what colors and styles flatter her dark looks. Regarding my fair-to-the-brink-of-sallow blond complexion, she's a little less successful. Last September, when she'd come to meet her grandson, she'd given me an early birthday present. A thick wool sweater unsuited to the muggy Florida climate, in a shade of unflattering army-green.

That night, in the privacy of our room, Tom had asked, "You are going to keep it, though, right?" My reply of "Sure, you never know when the bilious look might make a comeback," hadn't amused him, but when I'd promised to have the sweater on hand for future holidays with Rose, he'd pulled me into a grateful hug. He'd smelled like his favorite bar soap—a "manly" soap he'd always teased, telling me he'd leave the sissy moisturizing stuff to me. Sometimes I still caught myself reaching for his soap at the grocery store before I remembered no one in the house used it.

I sighed, missing my husband. He would have wanted me to make more of an effort with his mother. "Rose, I really am sorry I didn't get a chance to call you on your birthday. Things have been so…" Description eluded me.

"Busy with that job, I imagine. How do you modern career girls do it, always on the go? It probably makes me something of a relic, but I was naturally the housewife type, with no outside ambitions. I believe a mother can do so much good at home with her children."

Well, if your precious son hadn't up and died on me—

Whoa. My heart was slamming and my vision swam in a red haze. I knew from the books on grief Dianne had badgered me to read that rage was just another expression of loss, but the unexpected flash of fury still sent waves of shock and guilt through me. Tom hadn't asked to abandon us. And I'd come too close to verbally lashing out at Rose. So much for my theory that I was more balanced these days, moving on to the next stages of acceptance.

I spoke slowly, keeping my tone neutral. "Being a stay-at-home mom is certainly a noble choice."

"I know it's what Tom always wanted for his children."

Since I had no honest response that didn't seem cruel, I bit my tongue. I could manage that for one phone call.

But on a more permanent basis?

I'd forgotten how tense Rose could make me. Oh, I knew it on an objective level, but I'd repressed the actual physiological reactions she provoked—stomach in knots, palms clammy as I wondered what I would do or say wrong next. Living near this woman wouldn't be in the best interests of my blood pressure.

I cleared my throat. "Why don't I get Sara and let you chat with her while I finish making dinner?"

"I'd love to talk to the darling girl! But isn't it a bit late for them to be eating?"

"It's not that late. Well, maybe it is. Traffic was—" I did not have to justify my children's eating habits. One look at them would assure anyone that I wasn't raising underfed waifs. And tomorrow was Saturday, so there was no harm in letting them sleep in a little if our evening ran behind schedule. For that matter, it would mean *I* got to sleep in a little, assuming stress didn't have me awake again in the murky predawn hours.

"I didn't mean to sound critical, dear," Rose said. "It takes time to properly prepare a good home-cooked meal, and I applaud you. Too many parents nowadays rely on fast food. What are you fixing?"

Glad I'd called her tonight and not after last night's take-out kids' meals, I glanced at the empty cardboard box and the plastic bags. "Um, lasagna." Lasagna-flavored, anyway. I saw no reason to elaborate and find out whether or not the fare met Rose's criteria for "home-cooked."

"Wonderful! One of Tom's favorites."

My stomach clenched again. I wasn't used to other people mentioning him so flagrantly, dredging up twenty years of memories each time his name was spoken. Dianne always waited for me to broach the subject. With the kids, I didn't *avoid* talking about him—it was important they knew their father loved them—but I didn't want to push, either. And, I admit, not discussing him sometimes made it easier for me to get through the day.

When I thought about him too much, wishing he were here to hug me and say everything would be okay, to reassure me I would somehow be enough for the kids, that I'd find the answers to the tough questions, that I'd—

"Mommy! Fire, Mommy, fire!"

I jumped at Sara's presence as much as her announcement. I'd been too lost in thought to notice her wandering into the kitchen, so her voice at my elbow came as a shock.

As Rose demanded to know what had happened, I glanced toward the stove. My pan of simmering food had boiled over just enough that some of the noodles had fallen onto the burner and ignited. Pasta flambé. But nothing that would require actual firemen at the scene.

"Everything's fine," I assured my mother-in-law as I turned off the stove. "No reason to worry. I just ran into a snag with dinner. We'll call you back tomorrow, if that's all right."

"All right? It will be the highlight of my weekend! *Two* calls, after months and months of not hearing from you? It's a grandmother's dream come true."

I hung up feeling thoroughly chastised, not realizing until I was loading the dishes later that, hey, wait a minute, Rose had a phone, too. She could always call us if she wanted to talk to the kids...or further criticize the way I was raising them. A pocket of resentment bubbled up in me, despite the noble intentions I'd had when I'd first dialed her number. Ten minutes of Rose went a long way.

What would weekly—or, gulp, *daily*—interaction be like? Oh, yeah. Moving to Boston was out of the question.

CHAPTER 2

"I can't believe you're moving to Boston!" Dianne, who'd waited until my daughter and her giggly best friend were out of earshot, looked suspiciously as if she might cry.

"No waterworks," I warned, feeling shaky myself. "If you start, we're both doomed."

Bawling in my kitchen was not how I wanted to commemorate my fortieth birthday. Giving Martin my final decision this morning had been difficult enough. Still, Di's recent announcement had made accepting the transfer a no-brainer.

Determined to be happy for her, even though I would miss her, I smiled. "You're moving on to bigger things yourself. I didn't even know lounge acts had talent scouts. And they want you to be headliner!"

"Yeah, but the cruise-ship thing is only temporary. I'm just subletting my place. And when I come back, you..." She turned away, unbuckling a newly scrubbed, fresh-faced Ben from his high chair. There for a while, it had been touch or go whether we'd ever find him underneath a layer of frosting.

"My son certainly appreciated your baking efforts," I

teased. When I'd come home for the evening birthday celebration we'd promised the kids, Dianne had greeted me with the announcement that she'd made a cake but doubted it was edible.

"Ben mistook it for face paint and didn't know it was food. You were kind to have a slice, but face it, I lack your domestic-goddess skills."

I thought about the accumulated fast-food dinners in the past few months and the fact that my bedroom had become a wildlife refuge for dust bunnies. "Fallen domestic goddess, you mean."

She set Ben down, her gaze sympathetic. "Don't be so hard on yourself, babe. You're doing the best you can."

That's what worries me. What if it didn't get better? Or, what if moving to Boston made things even worse?

I obviously didn't hide my concerns very well because Dianne's expression filled with guilt.

"It's all my fault you have to go."

"You're not responsible for the company's falling profits of the last two quarters and Kazka being edged out by the competition here in Florida."

"No, but my being away for six months leaves you without a much-needed babysitter. Maybe if—"

"I'm sure you spent all those years in dance class so you could become an inadequately compensated nanny. Besides, you might have noticed I'm also without a much-needed job."

She bit her lip. "There is that."

In the two weeks since Martin's "road diverging" speech, I'd been on several interviews with varying degrees of success. Two companies expressed polite disinterest, one company had offered a salary that wasn't going to cover mortgage and child care, and the last interviewer was a sleaze who'd stopped one suggestive question shy of my reporting him to the Equal Employment Opportunity Commission. Luckily, our office in Boston sounded happy to have me. In diametric opposition to their Floridian counterpart, Kazka's northeastern division was doing so well that they'd expanded the sales force, promoting the woman who'd served as sales coordinator, the position I'd held here and would fill for them.

Moving was the logical step, even if I hadn't yet found a place to live…or the courage to tell the kids. I'd put it off as long as possible, not wanting to upset them until I'd exhausted every option. The thought of telling Sara she'd have to leave the only home she knew filled me with dread.

You can't shelter her from everything. Isn't that what I'd told Tom on more than one occasion?

Rather than be faced with his daughter's tears of frustration, he practically offered to tie her shoelaces until she was in high school. Like me, Sara had been blessed with a father who absolutely adored her. I'd never known my mom—her post C-section infection had been fatally complicated by diabetes—but my protective dad had tried hard to be the perfect parent. He'd done an admirable job, yet there were pains and losses from which even he couldn't spare me. Especially after the stupid fall that had killed him while he'd tried to help a neighbor patch her roof.

I swallowed back a lump of emotion and jerked a thumb over my shoulder. "I'd, um, better check on the girls. All I need for them is to get lipstick all over the carpet before we put the house on the market."

Ben grinned up at me, cherubically unalarmed by the words *house* and *market*. As Martin had cheerfully pointed out today, I had a ton to do, and finding a real-estate agent was at the top of the list. I would also need to tell Rose about the move and probably beg her to help us find a place in Boston. Assuming anyone wanted to buy *this* place and that I could get us all packed in less than a month.

I'd barely finalized the decision to transfer and was already wondering how to accomplish it all, how to find a good school for Sara, wondering if I'd given up the job search here too early. It was funny—in that decidedly unhumorous way—how I'd been the one to make the bulk of day-to-day parenting decisions when Tom had been alive, but now that he wasn't here I keenly felt the burden of responsibility. What if Sara never got better at math? Who was going to teach Ben to pee standing up? If either of them grew up to be a serial killer, guess whose fault it would be?

I supposed I could look into some sort of single-mother support group for my occasionally neurotic thoughts, but how was I going to find the time and energy to commiserate with other moms about my lack of time and energy?

With a mental shake, I poked my head into Sara's room. She and her friend Callie both wore the traditional cardboard cone party hats, held in place with elastic chin straps. Sara had also placed one on Ellie, her beloved pink stuffed elephant.

"Hi, Mommy." My daughter beamed up at me, pink lipstick smeared around her mouth and green shadow circling her eyes. "Callie doesn't hafta go home yet, does she?"

"No, I was just checking to see if you were still playing beauty parlor."

Sara shook her head. "Nope. We got pretty for a princess ball, and we're going to that now."

I grinned, glad Callie's mom wouldn't mind the "princess makeup" when I took her daughter home. "You guys have fun. I'm going to go say goodbye to Dianne."

My friend had to work tonight, but it had been sweet of her to stay to have an early dinner and cake with me and the kids. I found her on the back patio, pushing Ben in his outdoor toddler swing. Even though we'd reached the end of September, it was still warm outside. Yesterday, the air-conditioning window unit in my office had crapped out and I'd felt as if I'd been trying to finish filing in a sauna.

"You know," I said slowly, "it might be nice to live somewhere where they have actual seasons."

Dianne sent me a comically blank look. "What are those?"

We definitely didn't get a lot of white Christmases in these parts, and while I had nothing against palm trees, they don't provide spectacular autumn foliage.

I snapped my fingers, remembering Rose's birthday gift last year. "And sweater weather!" Just not army-green ones, no offense to those who were being all they could be.

Unflattering colors aside, I'd much rather be seen in a soft knit turtleneck than a bathing suit. Sure, some women looked good in swimsuits even after multiple pregnancies, but clearly they'd struck some sort of Faustian bargain.

Switching places with Dianne, I took over swinging my laughing son. "Boston won't be so bad. Rose will lavish affection on the kids. And I'll be fine, learning the ropes in the new office."

"Who's worried about *you?*" She sniffed. "I'm thinking of myself. When I come back, you won't even be here!"

"Yes, but you'll be rich and famous by then and can afford to visit me. Besides, you're never gonna meet hot young guys if you spend all your time around a widowed suburbanite."

Her lips curled in an appreciative grin. "Ah, hot young guys. Now there's a topic that perks me up. Maybe you should give guys some thought, too."

"What?" My head snapped in her direction, and I was so startled I let my hands drop to my sides. When I didn't catch Ben's swing on the rebound, it hit me in the midsection. "Oof."

Dianne glanced down, and I didn't know if it was because

she was trying not to laugh or because she was hesitant about broaching the subject. "I know you've been through…more than I can imagine. But moving to a new city is like a fresh start in a lot of ways. Full of new opportunities."

"You sound like Martin."

"He tells you to think about dating, too?"

"No."

Dating? An interesting idea, but interesting in the same way as me being an astronaut—unlikely and surreal. I'd been with Tom for half my life, almost all of my adult life. Would I even know how to date?

"I know I'm butting in," Dianne said unrepentantly, "but that's what best friends do. You'll be meeting people, and Rose might be available for some weekend babysitting. You call yourself a widowed suburbanite—"

"Which part of that statement is inaccurate?"

"I'm just saying there's more to you than that. A lot more."

I didn't know what to say, so I merely nodded. Theoretically, I wasn't opposed to dating someday, but it was at the bottom of my very long list of concerns right now. Still, I was touched that my younger friend with the comparatively exciting life saw more to me than I suspected my sympathetic neighbors and co-workers often did. There was a brief silence as we recognized that we'd gone from playground chat to one of those girlie bonding moments often portrayed in commercials for yogurt and International coffees.

She gave a sideways little grin. "All I'm saying is that you should consider dating, and if you should meet any good-looking younger guys, feel free to tell them about me."

"Who said I don't want a younger guy?" I was kidding, of course, but one of the things I adored about Dianne was how I never had to explain that.

"You might need one to keep up with you. I've heard women really hit their stride at forty, get empowered and stuff. These will probably be your bad-ass years."

Charlie Smith, bad-ass at large. I laughed, despite knowing in that moment how keenly I would miss her.

Encouraged, she continued. "I hope when I'm forty, I've still 'got it' enough that strange men risk sexual harassment suits just to hit on me." Her joking helped take the edge off the awful interview I'd had early in the week.

"You're deranged," I said affectionately.

"Yeah, and I can't bake a cake to save my life. When you start making new friends in Boston, try to trade up, would you?"

"Not possible."

Her expression sobered. "Are you going to tell them tonight? I could stay if you want."

"Your boss refused to give you the night off," I reminded her. "You should probably be leaving now."

"True. But I'm starting a new job in two weeks anyway. What's he going to do, fire me?"

I sighed, torn between wanting her there when I broke the news to the kids, and being afraid that when they realized they wouldn't see her anymore, the conversation would go even worse. "No, you get to work. I'm not going to tell the kids tonight, anyway. Sara's been insistent about celebrating my birthday, and there's no reason to bring it up before morning."

Maybe by then, I would have found the right words and the confidence to assure them that everything was going to turn out great.

Nights were the worst. It's so much easier not to worry during the day, not to remember, but when it's dark and still, the things you don't want to think about have a way of finding you. Especially if you're alone.

It was a little pathetic, the way I wished Sara were here to stay up and watch movies with me, but Callie's mom had invited my daughter to spend the night. Since I knew Sara and Callie wouldn't be seeing much of each other in the months to come, I'd instantly agreed.

Ben was asleep in his room and I was doing my best to fall asleep in the living room watching television. Our powder-blue couch was nubby and going threadbare in the arms, and so many of the pillows were stained that I had to turn them backward when company came. The sofa was comfortable in a favorite ratty sweatshirt kind of way, though, and I didn't think I could sleep in my room tonight.

When I'd turned thirty-nine, Tom and I had celebrated alone together, our first big night out since I'd had Ben. Tom had joked that the romantic dinner was for me, but that our having sex afterward was more like a present to him. Since it's not always easy to work up enthusiasm for intimacy when you're the mother of a newborn, that night had been the last time we'd made love. I wished now that there had been something unique about it, something special that stood out that I could hold on to in my memory. *Like what, rose petals strewn across the comforter?* But it had just been us, my husband and me, coming together as we had hundreds of times before. No more, no less. We'd had no idea that we didn't have many nights left.

Tom had been hale and hearty in that macho "I don't need doctors" sense, proud of how few sick days he'd taken at the construction firm where he'd worked his way into management. Although fiercely protective of his wife and kids, he wasn't by nature a worrier and refused to stress over intangibles like his cholesterol count. I was the one who'd nagged him into that last checkup, reminding him that his own father had died of a stroke when Tom had still been in high school. Though he'd humored me by eventually making the appointment, he'd pointed out not unkindly that my dad had been perfectly healthy before the fall that had killed him, so there was no sense in obsessing over what we couldn't control.

Even when the doctors had concluded that Tom needed the angioplasty and could no longer dismiss the chest pains he'd tried to downplay, my husband hadn't seemed concerned. He'd told me everything would be fine—a frequent reassurance I missed but that had turned out to be hollow in this case. He reminded me that angioplasty wasn't even considered a surgery anymore but just a procedure, that's how low-key it was. He'd still been chiding me about it before they'd wheeled him away, before the arterial spasm that had caused damage, leading to an emergency bypass and freak fatal heart attack.

You worry too much, baby. Haven't I always taken care of you?

He always had. But now here I was, my first birthday without him since I'd been eighteen—a lifetime ago.

The children had each had birthdays over the summer. The night Ben had turned one, after the kids were in bed, I'd sobbed until I threw up. Earlier in the day, well-meaning Gladys Winslow had assured me Tom was witnessing the milestone in heaven. My spiritual belief that he was indeed in a better place hadn't stopped me from briefly wanting to shake my elderly neighbor by her frail shoulders and scream, "How is watching from some ethereal distance doing the kids and me any good?"

Anger was supposed to be one of the early stages of grieving, followed later by depression and eventually acceptance, but I seemed to experience them in a random and sometimes repeating jumble.

For Sara's sixth birthday, I'd thrown an all-out bash, even scrimping and saving beforehand to rent a pony. There had been brief, teary moments that day when I knew she'd been thinking about her father, but, mostly, the sugar-charged five- and six-year-olds running and screaming through my house had served as a decent distraction. Maybe I should have invited them all back for *my* birthday today. Even if I had, I'd still have to deal with now, the night, and the realization that I was forty and alone.

Forty was fine, in theory, this just wasn't where I'd planned on being in my life. When Tom and I had married right after his winter graduation, I'd been young and uncertain in some areas. Moving away from the shelter of the small Georgia town I'd grown up in had been a huge change; losing my dad had been devastating. But I'd had Tom at my side to help me work through it, and I'd possessed lots of youthful optimism. Convinced I'd become accomplished and assured as I grew older, I took a part-time job as a receptionist and threw myself into efforts to be the perfect wife and, one day, mother. I'd had visions of hand-knitted booties, future PTA presidencies, the day when Tom would brag to an unhappy coworker on his second marriage to a petite trophy wife that I was more than enough to keep a man happy at home.

I'd thought that by forty, Tom and I would be raising teenagers. I hadn't counted on the two miscarriages before having Sara and being over thirty when I had my first baby. I had imagined we'd be financially secure after wisely investing for several years, maybe sneaking off for the occasional romantic cruise. I hadn't expected to be dashing around town trying to find a job, second-guessing the decisions I had to make for myself and my children.

That was what really pissed me off about this birthday, about my age. Not the wrinkles, which were so far mostly limited to the laugh lines around my blue eyes; not the streaks of silver, which didn't stand out too much yet in my pale hair; not even the sagging boobs, which I could claim to have earned nobly by nursing two children. No, what grated my cheese was the fact that I'd pictured having a stable life by forty, one in which I knew what the hell I was doing.

Boy, had I been off the mark.

After breakfast in the morning, I still had a few minutes before I needed to pick up Sara. Deciding there was no time like the present to take proactive steps toward our new future, I phoned a woman who had been in Sara's and my Mommy and Me group. Having heard through the grapevine that Lindsay and her husband had sold a house not far from us a few months ago, I was curious to know if she'd recommend her agent. If so, it might save me from randomly sorting through the 340 Realtors in our area. If not, I could at least cross the guy off the list and narrow down prospects to the other 339.

Lindsay was the proud mother of a seven-year-old little boy, four-year-old girl and their six-month-old baby sister. As we talked, all three of them seemed to be clamoring for Lindsay's attention, along with her husband—who, she informed me, was packing for an overseas business conference and not a lot of help with the trio of noisemakers.

"So you're serious about selling the house?" she asked over someone's crying and her husband demanding to know if she'd seen his other brown belt. "I don't envy you. That whole process was such a pain, I'd…oh, but I'm sure *you'll* have a much better experience."

Definitely. Because I'd been the poster child for good luck lately. "Well, I have a great job waiting for me in Boston and family there, so I think the move will be healthy for me and the kids."

"I'm glad to hear it. I—did you check the closet? What about the hook behind the bathroom door? Sorry, Charlie, I was talking to Mark there, not you. Anyway, I'm thrilled you'll be closer to helping hands. I've always felt so awful that there wasn't more I could do, but with the pregnancy and everything…"

"I understand, Lindsay." And I did. But understanding hadn't eased the sting completely. After Tom had died, I'd felt as if I'd not only lost him but the circle of friends we'd had, which was made up primarily of other married couples.

At first, people had invited me over, but it had been awkward, like being the only unicorn on an ark full of paired-off animals. I don't remember if the invitations stopped first or if I'd started making excuses not to go. Maybe the gradual distance was my fault, but I got the impression everyone had been relieved when they didn't have to tiptoe around marital subjects anymore. I wondered with sudden insight if this was part of the reason I was so comfortable with a woman over a decade younger than me who didn't even have a serious boyfriend, much less impending nuptial plans.

"Just know that you're in our prayers and our hearts," Lindsay added. "You give me a holler if there's ever anything I can do for you."

"I would be grateful for that agent's name and number," I reminded her cheerfully.

"Oops. Right, sorry." She'd just finished reciting the information I'd called for when she was interrupted by her husband again, this time because he couldn't find his cell phone. "Oh, for… I can't believe they let this disorganized man plan their budget at work! I'd better run, or he's going to end up missing his flight. You know how husbands are."

There was a sharp silence, followed by immediate apologies I was too slow to stem. "I am so, so… I shouldn't have said that, Charlie. Honestly, I don't know where my head is. The last thing you need is to be *reminded*… I didn't mean to—"

"It's okay, Lindsay. Tell Mark I said hi." On the bright side, I told myself as I hung up, compared to that conversation, telling Rose about the move this afternoon would be a breeze.

Except that hours later, after spending an active day at the park and getting the kids tucked in for a short nap, calling my mother-in-law didn't seem any easier. Why was this so hard? *Because it'll be real then. This chapter of your life will come to an end.*

Then again, once it did, maybe I could move on. Maybe I'd reach a point where my emotions weren't hovering so close to the surface, like bruises just under the skin, where tiny reminders weren't around every corner, catching me off guard and evoking a fresh sense of loss. People assured me I'd adjust to the grief; mostly, to my extreme shame, I just wanted it *gone*. How terrible was it that sometimes I wished I could just forget the man who'd fathered my children and spent half his life with me?

Maybe my guilt was what made talking to his mother even more difficult.

But stalling wasn't helping anyone. I sat on the sofa with the cordless phone, propping my feet on the coffee table and sinking down in the cushions. Then I made the call.

To say Rose was startled to hear from me would be an understatement. "Yoah stahting to worry me, Chahlie."

I wondered absently if the kids would one day speak with Bostonian accents.

"So many calls in such a short time!" she exclaimed. "Oh, but you're probably calling to say thank you."

Belatedly, I recalled the sunshine-yellow blouse that had arrived yesterday. My own fault that it was too small and, if buttoned across my chest, would probably get me arrested. "Well, yes, thank you for the shirt, but—"

"You don't like it?"

"Oh, no, it's, um…bright. Very cheery. I was just going to say that I have an additional reason for calling."

"Are you unwell? The children?"

When Tom had died, I'd felt I should be the one to tell her. The conversation was a blur to me, except for Dianne taking the phone when I couldn't get through the words, but the sudden panic in Rose's voice gave me a moment of déjà vu, a flicker of repressed memory.

"Everybody's fine," I rushed to assure her. "Actually, I have good news."

"This is what you sound like when you're happy?"

"Well. It's the kind of news that's good in the long run but chaotic in the short. The kids and I are moving. To Boston. Kazka is closing the warehouse and offices here and sending me up north."

"Boston? Why, that's fantastic! How soon will you be here? I have a friend with a granddaughter just Sara's age, they'll get along famously. And there are a couple of private schools we might still be able to get her in, even though the year's started. Thank God you have plenty of time to put Ben on all the right waiting lists. You'll just need to—"

"Whoa, slow down!" I hadn't even told the kids yet, and she'd already yanked them out of the public school system? "I, uh, appreciate your enthusiasm, but I'm still feeling a little overwhelmed by the impending move. Just getting there is going to be an ordeal." I didn't relish a road trip with toddlers and a German shepherd, but paying for airfare was out of the question. Besides, how else would I get our van to Boston?

"You didn't breathe a word of this last time we spoke. Were you holding out until you had a definite buyer?"

I meant to tell her that this had all been rather sudden, but instead echoed, "Buyer?"

"When do you close?" she asked. "Did they meet your asking price? I hope you're not letting yourself get taken advantage of with all kinds of silly demands like recarpeting the place or giving them your washer and dryer."

I couldn't imagine anyone actually wanting my laundry set, which dated back to the Paleozoic, but it was all too easy to picture new occupants demanding carpet untouched by kid, Kool-Aid or dog. Thoughts like that were rather cart before the horse, however. I needed people to come see the place before I started worrying about haggling over the contract.

"We haven't sold the house quite yet." Or put it on the market, if one wanted to get technical. "But I'm absolutely confident it won't be a problem."

"Oh." Her dubious tone didn't reflect my confidence, not that I blamed her. Mine was fake, anyway. "Well, I'm sure it will be all right, dear."

It would be, eventually. After I'd told the kids and we'd all adjusted to the idea. "I'll keep you updated on the specifics, but I should run now—wake the kids up and figure out what to do for dinner."

"Goodness, if you let them sleep so late in the day, how on earth do you get them to bed at night?"

I sighed. "Talk to you soon, Rose." Was it already too late to change my mind about the move?

CHAPTER 3

As I walked down the hall to get the kids, I heard murmurs and rustles from Ben's room, along with the familiar annoyed cry as he realized he was waking up to a wet diaper. Even that tugged at my heart. I loved my kids so much and I just wanted to make the right decisions. Sometimes when I opened the door, where Sara and I had stenciled his name in animal-themed letters, I felt a jolt of happy anticipation at seeing him, snuggling him close. I knew that as they grew, snuggling opportunities became more rare.

Ben was standing in his crib, holding the cherrywood rails and bouncing slightly as he began chanting "Mmm-a, mmm-a." Maybe I was finally pulling ahead of the oscillating fan in the "Are you my mother?" race.

Once I had Ben changed, I carried him into Sara's room and sat on the edge of her twin bed, smiling at the way her dark hair was spread across the Barbie pillowcase. How odd that she could be so feminine and tiny and delicate, yet still look so much like her father. Ben had darker hair than mine, too, but he had my blue eyes, not Sara's and Tom's deep brown ones. I gently shook her shoulder. My daughter woke up in stages, and it usually took at least ten minutes before she was alert enough to do more than stare blankly into space and hug her floppy-eared pink-and-white elephant.

When she was more awake, I asked if they wanted to go talk on my bed. About half the time, I keep the baby gate latched in the hall to give Gretchen the back half of the house as refuge from Sara's attempts to put lipstick on the dog or to make her the horsey in a game of cowgirl. Also, keeping the gate up meant that the children couldn't breeze into my room whenever they wanted and destroy it in a matter of seconds, like a swarm of locusts dressed in OshKosh. The kids loved the rare treat of cuddling in the master suite on special occasions such as rainstorms, story time, or when I felt whimsical enough to let them jump on the bed for a few supervised minutes.

I'd already lumped the pillows into a mound against the rounded oak headboard, and a blue leather photo album sat on the nightstand. I was hoping visual aids would keep Sara in a positive mindset.

I hugged the kids close. "You like talking to Nonna Rose on the phone, right?"

Sara had enjoyed the Saturday call following the night of the pasta fire. Long-distance charges meant nothing when you were six, and she'd sung her entire repertoire of songs, from "Alice the Camel" all the way to "If You're Happy and You Know It," which is Ben's favorite because he likes to clap along.

My daughter nodded, her face lighting up. "Can we call her again?"

"Even better, wouldn't you like to see her in Boston?"

"You mean, visit Nonna?"

I wondered if she remembered the trips we'd taken when she was younger. We'd spent the Christmas before Ben was born in Boston but hadn't been back since.

"More than just a visit, pumpkin. You know how Billy from across the street moved?" The house had promptly been bought by a couple eager to retire here before another Milwaukee winter set in. Would that God sent such retirees my way. "And Mommy explained how people go to new homes sometimes? We could get a house near Nonna."

"No, thank you, Mommy. We don't need a new house. I like this one."

"But I need a new job, Sara-bear. There's a place where I can go to work there. And lots of fun things for you to do." I flipped open the photo album in my lap, holding it up so both kids could see the pictures of Rose's house. "You remember? We had such a good time."

"Will I get to stay in my class and see Mrs. Bennings every day? Will Callie still get to come over?"

"You won't see them every day, but maybe we can visit sometimes. And you'll have a new class, meet lots of new friends."

Ben was sucking on the side of his hand, taking this with the nonchalance I had anticipated. Unfortunately, Sara was also reacting pretty much the way I'd expected. Her doe brown eyes grew large and her bottom lip quivered. She squeezed Ellie hard enough that I feared for the fuzzy pachyderm's seams. I'd tried to make *new* sound exciting— Sara loved new books and new toys and new movies—but she wasn't buying it.

She scrambled off the bed, her eyes welling with tears. "I don't want to move. Don't work anymore, stay home with us. Like you used to!"

The slurping sounds had stopped and Ben looked up with an anxious expression, as if he were trying to calculate where this fell on the uh-oh meter.

"Sara, I wish I could, honey, but I've got to have a job."

"Why? *Daddy* didn't want you to have one. Everything was better before!"

She was right about Tom not wanting me to go back to work when she'd started school, but I hadn't realized she'd been aware of our disagreeing on the subject. "Sara, sometimes things change, and even if we don't really want them to, that doesn't mean the changes won't be for the best." Great. Now I was the one spouting the inane clichés, which weren't going to do a damn thing to lessen her worry about leaving home and losing the people close to her. How could I ask her to give up Dianne, her friends, the neighbors she'd known since she was a baby, when she was still coping with the loss of her adored father?

"No!" Sara shrieked, wild-eyed. "Nononono!"

Well. Not much chance of refuting that logic.

I let her run out of the room, and didn't follow to scold her when she slammed her door. By then, Ben had started to cry in earnest, so I sat for a few minutes comforting him. Should I have been easing them into the notion over time instead of just dumping it on them?

Ben's tears subsided to hiccups a few minutes later, and I carried him toward Sara's room. Heaven knows sitting on my bed wondering if I'd completely mishandled this wasn't accomplishing anything. I knocked once, opening the door when Sara didn't answer. I didn't dare set Ben down because he'd toddle over to help himself to her toys, and something told me she wasn't in her most magnanimous sharing mood. Trying to carry on this conversation while my children beat each other with LEGO blocks wouldn't be an improvement.

As it was, I was reduced to talking to a pink lump. She was sitting on the floor of her room, her bed comforter pulled over her head, with only Ellie's skinny plush tail visible.

"Sara, I know you don't want to move, but we have to. If you just give it a chance, I think—"

"What if Daddy came back?" The comforter slid off, her earlier anger replaced by a deep sadness that looked out of place on a child. "What if Daddy came back, and we weren't here?"

Oh, God. My heart clenched painfully. This never got easier, no matter how many times we went through it. "We've talked about this, pumpkin. You know Daddy can't come back. But he can watch over you, and he'll never stop loving you. He'll watch over you no matter where we live."

"You promise?" Her voice trembled.

"I promise. We'll find a house you and Ben really like. And you can help me decorate it. We'll make lots of good memories there, just like we have here."

She thought it over. "I can have a pink room?"

"Any color you like." I rearranged Ben enough that I could press my daughter close to me, her tears warm and damp against the front of my blouse. "It will be okay, bear. You'll make lots of new friends in Boston. And I bet we'll see snow in a few months."

There was silence as she considered the benefits of playing in snow—not that she'd had much experience with the fluffy white stuff, but she'd seen it on television.

I pushed my advantage. "We can celebrate our moving to a new house by ordering pizza tonight."

"Pizza!" Sara bounded back. "Yay!"

Ben rocked in my lap, also shrieking with delight. Crisis averted.

What were the odds everything to come could be dealt with so easily?

Despite suffering my share of headaches in the past, I didn't think I'd ever experienced an actual migraine such as I'd heard other women describe. Turns out, trying to move to another state is one big migraine, complete with blinding pain and the urge to curl up quietly in the fetal position.

During my initial meeting with the real-estate agent, the day after I'd called Lindsay for his number, the man had informed me that if I would just add a half bath at the front of the house, we could dramatically increase both the chances of selling it quickly and the asking price. Skipping over my skepticism that there was sufficient space for another room, no matter how small, I patiently explained that I had neither the money nor the time to worry about plumbing renovations.

We hustled the house onto the market, stipulating in the paperwork that I had two small children and a dog, so interested parties and their agents needed to call ahead before coming to look. Two nights later, my Realtor let himself in with his lockbox key on an unannounced visit to show the house to a middle-aged couple with a teenage son. Toys were strewn all over, the dinner dishes were still sitting on the kitchen counter, and Sara and I were having a heated discussion about her decision to "improve" her room by coloring flowers on the wall with a marker. Gretchen was so unnerved by the sudden appearance of strangers that she'd thrown up— a crackerjack watchdog, that one. Worse, since I hadn't had time to prepare Sara for the walk-through, she'd decided that these invasive strangers were the problem, that they wanted to take away her home. She'd commanded them to stay out of her room and punctuated the order by slamming a door.

Why the man who actually worked for me didn't understand that the call-ahead commandment applied to him as well as outside Realtors, I have no idea. It would have given me a great deal of temporary satisfaction to fire him, but then I'd have to pay listing fees out of pocket now instead of them coming from his six-percent commission after the sale. I had nothing out of pocket. I barely had pockets.

In the week and a half since, we'd only had a handful of viewers, and none of them had called back. My ever-helpful real-estate agent seemed to think that getting someone to fall in love with the house would be easier if the kids and I weren't actually here when people came to see it. So we were living in a DEFCON four state, diaper bag always at the ready so we could leave on a moment's notice. Oddly enough, my mother-in-law's increasingly enthusiastic, near-daily calls to see if we had found a buyer yet weren't helping. Nor was Sara's anxiety over Halloween. While doing some sort of holiday creative-writing unit at school, my daughter had become fixated with the idea that our move might prevent her from trick-or-treating. I promised her, repeatedly, that no matter what state we were living in at the end of the month, she would be in costume and begging door-to-door for candy.

At least I knew we could stay with Rose while I house hunted in Boston, a daunting task. I was due to be there the fourth week of October to start my new job. In other words, I had nine days. Dianne, with her typical graciousness, had spent a lot of time here over the past couple of weeks, helping me repaint over crayon marks and grubby handprints. I was trying not to think about her shipping out tomorrow afternoon. Saying goodbye to the person who had helped me cope with the most devastating change of my life was far more daunting than moving to another state.

Other than some minor house maintenance, I had hardly rounded up all the boxes I would need, much less begun packing. Martin had promised I'd receive half pay during the transitional, out-of-work interim between my positions. Thank God, or we'd be living *in* boxes instead of labeling them Bedroom, Kitchen and Kids. Apparently, preparing for the move, working full-time during the office's last week before shutdown and trying to calm Sara out of hyperventilating every fifteen minutes wasn't a full enough schedule for me. Because I'd also decided to go in with Mrs. Winslow and throw a "jewelry party."

She'd recently rediscovered her inner entrepreneur but lacked a good-sized living room for cramming in a semicircle of attendees. So, we'd invited the little old ladies of the neighborhood to my house for chips and dip and the chance to watch us model jewelry manufactured by Mrs. Winslow's parent company, ZirStone. She and I would each get a cut from any sales. It just so happened she'd mentioned the business deal to me on the same day I'd been getting cost estimates from moving companies, catching me in a weak moment when I'd been contemplating hocking the television and VCR for cash.

Today was the party. I'd bribed Sara with a rented video I was allowing the kids to watch in my room. Ben was viewing the movie from inside the comfort of his playpen, accompanied by a few of his favorite toys. Now, if I could just get someone from the neighborhood interested in some of the quality synthetic gemstones we had available, perhaps I could justify losing half a Saturday of potential packing. But fifteen minutes into my sales pitch, a real-estate agent called wanting to show the house.

"I wanted to know if this afternoon would be good," he said.

I peeked around the corner of the kitchen, where Mrs. Winslow was opening a gray box of earrings with a flourish Vanna White would have envied. "Approximately what time were you thinking?"

"We're looking at a place the next subdivision over, so about ten minutes."

"Ten minutes?" I could barely get both children properly strapped into their respective car seat and booster in that amount of time, much less empty the living room of guests.

Following my shrieked question, the buzz of conversation in the next room stopped abruptly.

There was also silence on the other end of the phone, but the man recovered quickly, sounding a tad defensive. "Look, if you don't *want* prospective buyers to come see your house—"

"No, it's not that." I couldn't afford to turn them away.

How could I possibly make two monthly house payments? The mere thought prompted me to plead, "Please bring them by. But you have to understand that I wasn't expecting to show the house today."

"Oh, so there haven't been many visitors?" *Oh, so there's not much interest and we can whittle down the asking price?*

"Plenty! Just none scheduled for today," I clarified. "I have a few people over, and you didn't give us much notice—"

"We don't want to disturb anyone," he interrupted, back to the smoothly polished salesman's voice with which he'd started the conversation. "We'll have a quiet look around, and you and your guests will hardly notice we're there."

I got off the phone wondering how much of his estimated ten minutes were left and whether or not I should try to shoo the ladies out of the house. But they weren't exactly in an age demographic known for speed and agility. Besides, it would look odder for people to view the house with empty folding chairs in the living room and a sideboard of half-eaten snacks than for them to just walk through while we concluded the jewelry show. Heck, if the potential buyers didn't want the house, maybe I could still talk them into a faux black pearl bracelet.

I quickly updated the ladies, letting them know visitors would be walking through but that we should carry on as scheduled. I didn't have to worry about wrangling the dog outside because I'd already let her into the sunroom before the jewelry shindig, but I did rush back to my room to check on the kids. God bless 'em, they were behaving perfectly. Ben was sitting in his play area flipping through a board book about fire trucks, while Sara was cuddled with Ellie on my bed, focused on her movie.

She barely glanced in my direction. "Is your party over, Mommy?"

"Not yet, but there are some people coming to see the house."

"Do we have to leave again?" She did look at me then, annoyance clear on her young features. "I haven't watched my favorite song yet."

Though she'd stopped viewing potential buyers as The Enemy, she resented her life being disrupted for the convenience of others.

"Nope, just stay back here in Mommy's room. Don't even get off the bed, okay?"

Her brown eyes narrowed thoughtfully. "What if I have to use the bathroom?" The way she was always looking for loopholes, I figured she had a brilliant future as an attorney.

"Why not go use it now?" I suggested. "Hurry, because they'll be here soon."

I went back to the living room, suspecting Mrs. Winslow would try to cut me out of my half of the profits if I didn't actually spend a few minutes helping her. I was explaining, as per the instructional brochure, why jewelry should be the last thing you put on before you go out when our doorbell rang. The Realtor let himself in before I got there, however. Either he'd only rung the bell to prevent startling anyone or he'd remembered after doing so that I had guests and didn't want to interrupt.

Behind the agent, there was a harried-looking couple who wore matching we-stopped-being-able-to-tell-floor-plans-apart-twelve-houses-ago expressions. They had three kids in tow. I wasn't sure this house had enough space for a family of five, but the youngest child was a girl who appeared to be about four, and I suspected she'd appreciate the girlish decor in Sara's room, hopefully causing her to remember this as a house she liked. In case they gave the four-year-old a vote.

Yeesh, I really *was* desperate.

"Hi. Come on in, and please look around," I invited. "Don't feel like you're imposing, just take your time."

I barely resisted the urge to tack on, *And we have some lovely blue topaz earrings that would match your eyes, ma'am.*

The four-year-old made a beeline for the refreshment table, only to be scolded by her father, at which point she burst into tears. The middle child, a boy wearing a black T-shirt and a scowl that made me recall every time my dad had ever teased, "Your face is gonna freeze like that," declared, "I don't like this house. It smells funny."

I chose to believe that any odor came from the combined eight or nine perfumes and numerous arthritis relief creams of my guests.

The Realtor cleared his throat, meeting my gaze. "Um, kitchen's this way, is it?"

I nodded, but they hadn't yet turned the corner when there was a cry from the back of the house. The realty party froze in place as I strode toward the hallway.

Sara catapulted out of my room, screaming, "Snake!" She was moving with astounding speed for someone who had Dora the Explorer panties down around her knees beneath her denim skirt.

I met her halfway, scooping her up and probably giving her a wedgie as I hurriedly tugged her undies into proper place. "Are you all right?"

She nodded. "But there's a snake, Mommy!"

In all the time we'd lived in this house, we had never once had a snake in the house—if we did, Tom was smart enough not to tell *me* about it—so why now? Why today? This was way beyond simple Murphy's Law. This was more like Murphy's Magna Carta. I instinctively muttered a phrase under my breath that I sincerely hoped Sara hadn't heard.

With Ben still at the back of the house, I jogged down the hall, not acknowledging the buzz of alarmed comments behind me. "Where was it?"

"In the bathroom." Her voice was shaking. "I was sitting on the potty, singing 'Catalina Madalina,' and I looked down and seen it. Saw it."

"Okay. I'll take care of it." *How?*

Maybe it was just a little bitty garden snake, the harmless

kind that could be tossed outside. Not that I particularly wanted to get close enough for tossing, but as the only adult in the family, these things fell to me. *And if it isn't harmless?*

Ignoring that thought, I lifted Ben out of his pen and set him down in the hallway, letting him crawl for freedom. *Save yourself, son.* Sara, dragging Ellie by the trunk, followed me so closely that if I stopped, she'd bang into me.

"Stay back," I told her as I approached the master bath. When I glanced at her to make sure she understood I was serious, I saw that the Realtor and the family touring the house were all hovering in the bedroom doorway. The preteen daughter looked as if she might lose consciousness. The sullen boy was actually smiling now. Figured.

There was no closet in my bedroom, but the bathroom was spacious enough to make up for the deficiency—equipped with the standard toilet and sink vanity, a shower/garden-spa tub and a walk-in closet with its own lights. I'd better find the damn snake, because I didn't relish wondering if it would slither out at me every time I opened the closet door for the next week.

The Realtor cleared his throat—a habit of his, I'd noticed. "So why again are you trying to get rid of this house?"

"We're selling the house because I accepted a job in Boston," I said, wondering what part of my tense body language made it look as if now were a swell time to chat. "Sara, where did you see it?"

"Under the sink. It's green." She was climbing up on my bed as she answered, her eyes wide.

Green. Most harmless garden snakes were green, right? I peeked into the room, my gaze coming to a screeching halt when I saw the thin green line across the tile, curling slightly. It was only a couple of inches long, but it disappeared beneath the edge of the vanity, so I wasn't sure how much more there was. I executed a leap that would have qualified me for National Champion Long Jump status and then reached into my closet for a shoe box, dumping out a pair of strappy silver sandals I'd last worn to a holiday party with Tom.

As I crouched down to make the capture with shaking hands, I blinked, realizing the only reason I'd thought even for a millisecond that I was dealing with a snake was because I'd been told—by a hysterical six-year-old—to expect a snake.

Relief ballooned inside me. "Sara, there's no reason to be scared. It's just one of those lizards that are always getting into the house."

At the sound of my voice, the gecko disappeared the rest of the way beneath the sink. I found out a moment later that he wasn't the only one startled. I came out of the bathroom with a smile that vanished as soon as I saw the expression of the woman who'd been considering the house.

"*Always* getting in?" she asked, her face pasty.

"Cool," her son said.

"Well, not always," I amended, "but Florida does have a lot of lizards. They're, um, good for eating the bugs."

Her eyes darted from side to side, as if she expected giant winged insects to swoop down and carry her off. "The bugs?"

Somehow I got the impression these nice folks weren't going to be making an offer this afternoon. Maybe now would be the time to see if I could send her on her way with a lovely parting purchase of earrings and matching pendant. But I never got the chance to ask because the doorbell rang.

If it was another real-estate agent, I was going to smack him in the head with his own cell phone…just as a gentle reminder to call ahead next time. But it was more likely to be one of the neighbors who had RSVPed that she might attend late. I opened the door with a cheerful, welcoming, "Hi!" and almost passed out on the spot.

My mother-in-law beamed at me. "Chahlie, deah!"

CHAPTER 4

Carrying a small suitcase in each hand, Rose Fiorello Smith swept into my house. A short woman with a solid build, dark bun and tidy appearance, she radiated authority despite her small stature. I wasn't sure whether her entrance reminded me more of Mary Poppins or Napoleon.

"H-how did you get here?" I saw neither a flying umbrella nor mounted cavalry.

"Plane, rental car. Who *are* all these people? I hope it's a packing party, you don't look nearly ready to go. There they are, my beautiful babies!" She'd spotted her grandchildren, not that they were hard to pick out of the crowd since Sara was rushing toward us.

Ben hung back, quietly watchful in contrast to his sister's running narrative.

"Nonna!" Sara tugged at the sleeve of Rose's red blazer. "Come watch my movie with me. You can hear my favorite song, only we hafta rewind because I missed it when I went pee-pee and there was a snake in the bathroom. Mommy said a dirty word. I can't say which one, because it was real bad."

And there went all *my* motivation for ever encouraging Ben to talk.

"It wasn't a snake, just a lizard," I said. "Harmless gecko. Gone now. Um, Rose, can I offer you something to drink?"

With her eyebrows arched toward her dramatically white-streaked hairline, Rose moved farther into the house—a good thing, since the prospective buyers looked as if they would shove her out of the way to escape this loony bin.

Except for the boy. I distinctly heard him mutter, "Cool," one last time as his parents hurried down our sidewalk. The Realtor followed, making assurances that the next home would better suit their needs.

"They were looking at the house," I said weakly.

Rose drew the obvious conclusion. "I believe they've decided to pass. You know, dear, your living room would appear a lot more spacious if it weren't full of folding chairs and whatnot."

Mrs. Winslow glared at me. Apparently, I was testing the limits of her graciousness with the constant interruptions to her business venture.

"Rose, this is Gladys Winslow. We were in the middle of showing the ladies some of ZirStone's fine merchandise. Mrs. Winslow, my mother-in-law, Rose Smith."

The two women shook hands and Rose stepped forward, Sara still at her side. "Lovely to meet you. Would you mind if I took a look at those earrings, Gladys? Oh, these are fabulous. Do you take out-of-state checks? I hate to cut your party short, but I haven't had the chance to visit with my grandchildren in almost a year. I'm sure you ladies under-stand. Oh, did you see this pendant?" she asked a woman sitting to her left. "It would be beautiful on you. Such a graceful neck."

She somehow ushered my neighbors out of the house and made four sales for Gladys at the same time. "Did you see how this brooch is the same style as your bracelet, dear? You should splurge on yourself. We all should, before the busy holiday season starts and our time and energy is devoted to others. Goodbye, it was wonderful to have met you ladies."

I just stared, belatedly moving into action as Gladys closed her jewelry case and turned to gather up her dishes. My business partner was whistling cheerfully when I shut the front door behind her. And then it was just me, Rose and the kids.

My mother-in-law was seated on the couch, Ben nestled in her lap as Sara sat next to her, showing off one of her favorite books. Rose glanced up with a reproachful smile. "If I'd known how much you needed my help, dear, I would have arrived sooner."

"Tell me again," Dianne urged, grinning over the rim of her mimosa. She was dappled in the sunlight spilling through mini-blinds we'd half closed because of the glare off the water and sand.

"So glad to provide the entertainment," I said dryly.

The original plan had been for the kids and me to take

Dianne to breakfast before she left this afternoon. With Rose unexpectedly available to babysit, Dianne and I had grabbed the rare opportunity for a more elegant brunch in the restaurant of a five-star beachfront hotel. We didn't often get to sit down just the two of us, adults only, without being interrupted or having to dice someone else's food. When we were done here, we'd go to the house so Ben and Sara could say their goodbyes.

Between Dianne's interruptions and unfeminine snorts of laughter, it had taken me almost forty minutes to relay the full story of yesterday's events.

She cut off a piece of Belgian waffle. "I'm just glad we got this chance for a girls' morning out before I left. Although it is weird not to have the munchkins here."

"'Weird' is relative. After yesterday, this hardly qualifies. I still can't believe she showed up out of the blue like that."

At least Rose had tempered her declarations that I clearly couldn't handle the move by myself with the admission that she'd been so excited about seeing her grandbabies, she just couldn't help herself.

Dianne raised an eyebrow. "Showed up and took over, from the sounds of it."

It was true that Rose had assigned Sara packing tasks within half an hour of arrival, but I was too tired to resent offers of help.

"It's her way. You know how she is." They'd only met on a few occasions, but it didn't take long for Rose to make an impression.

"Yeah. That, I know. What I don't know is whether I feel less worried about you because you'll have her help in Boston or more worried about you and whether or not you're going to end up needing strong prescriptions for antipsychotics."

I laughed and we managed to joke our way through the rest of the brunch. Neither of us wanted some weepy, sentimental goodbye, even though we both knew that our friendship wouldn't be the same after today. Driving separately back to the house kept me from saying anything that would sound like a badly written greeting card. I parked next to Rose's rental car, Dianne behind it. When my friend stepped out onto the driveway, she held packages in her arms.

"Don't get your hopes up," Dianne teased. "Neither of these is for you."

"Somehow I suspected as much." I nodded toward the Disney-themed wrapping paper featuring some of my kids' favorite animated characters.

The kids met us in the foyer, Sara's cries of "Aunt Di" quickly changing to "Presents!"

Rose hung back in the living room, her lips pursed. "Now, Sara, that's hardly good manners. Let the ladies at least get into the house before you bombard them."

"Oh, I don't mind the bombardment." Dianne hugged the children close to her. "I'd better stock up while I can!"

This reassurance didn't really help with the lip-pursing. One of the sources of tension between my mother-in-law and me was that Rose had never warmed to Dianne. When I'd first heard Tom's co-worker was dating a woman half his age who danced in skimpy costumes at a club on the weekends, I'd formed a premature impression, too—and learned a valuable lesson about rushing to judgment. But no matter how much the kids and I raved about Dianne, Tom's mother had always seemed annoyed that the children's closest "family" was the off-Broadway version of a Vegas showgirl. Deep down, though, Rose was probably envious of how little *she* got to see the kids in comparison.

Either she was respectful enough of my friendship with Dianne not to have made any snarky comments about my splurging on a leisurely brunch when I should be packing, or she was too glad to have an excuse to be alone with her grandkids.

We all adjourned to the living room, where Dianne, the kids and I squeezed onto the couch. I glanced up with the guilty realization that Rose probably felt excluded. Just because I hadn't expected her to come down right before Dianne's departure didn't mean I should be inhospitable.

"Would you like a seat?" I asked. "I actually have something I should go get from my bedroom, anyway."

Rose shook her head. "Thank you, dear, but no. I'll go finish up in the kitchen."

She'd informed me yesterday afternoon that she was here to chip in, and we'd begun the labor-intensive process of wrapping dishes and other breakables and boxing them. It had been a relief that someone besides me could pack the wedding china Tom and I had registered for all those years ago, for use on Thanksgiving and our April wedding anniversary. Whenever I handled the gold-rimmed plates, I was assailed with memories: our first Christmas as a married couple, when I'd overcooked the duck and Tom had assured me it was delicious; my teasing the strapping macho football player about helping me with the bridal registry; the expression on his darkly handsome face when he'd proposed beneath our favorite tree on the UF campus.

With practiced effort, I pushed away the achingly bittersweet past, determined to focus on the present. More important, the future. Though Tom and I wouldn't have one together, I still had to raise our children with as much love and enthusiasm as I could. After my months of depression, Sara particularly worried when she noticed me looking unhappy.

Summoning a smile, I watched as both kids engaged in frantic tearing, shredding little bits of wrapping paper onto the carpet. Ben had uncovered a soft-to-the-touch choo-choo train that made all kinds of noises when you pressed various places and even lit up. One of the sounds was the urgent "ding! ding! ding!" of a railroad crossing.

Dianne's eyes were bright with affectionate mischief. "I'll bet you'll think of me the whooole ride to Boston."

"I'll bet the batteries will have mysteriously disappeared by then," I kidded in return.

Sara unwrapped a purple cardboard box with a clear plastic front that showed dress-up accessories inside. Squeals of anticipation escaped her as she tried to get to the pink feather boa, sparkly tiara, plastic high heels and translucent purse full of makeup.

"Look, Mommy, look!"

While Dianne dutifully helped Sara into her new finery, I slipped out of the room and down the hall. Finances weren't much right now—I'd pretty well blown any mad money I had on our extravagant brunch—but I'd put together a little something for my friend. I was grinning, thinking about the calendar gag gift, but my mouth dropped open in astonishment when I stepped inside my room.

My clothes were not where I had left them that morning. Dresses lay across the bed, sweaters dangled from plastic hangers on the door, and every pair of shoes I owned was lined up in front of the bureau. *Rose.* I knew she wanted to help with the packing process, but that's why I'd given her the kitchen to tackle. I wasn't wild about the idea of her going through my personal things when I wasn't around.

If Tom were here, he would have told me she was just trying to make herself useful and I should let it slide; then again, if Tom were here, I wouldn't be moving to Boston in the first place. Since I was, and Rose and I would presumably be seeing a lot more of each other, I thought it would be best to get certain boundaries clarified *now*. I sucked in a deep breath, prepared to call her in here, but then reminded myself that she was my mother-in-law, not my six-year-old. We could talk about it after Dianne had said her goodbyes to everyone.

When I returned to the living room, Sara and her brother were both wearing pink lip gloss that Sara informed me tasted like strawberries. Sara was teetering in her new heels, with the boa thrown over her shoulders, and Ellie sat on the couch, the "jeweled" tiara perched drunkenly between her plushy elephantine ears.

"I have a little going-away present for you," I told Dianne, handing over a flat package wrapped in staid paper, a pattern of mauves and muted gold. "Nothing much, just something you can remember us by while you're at sea."

Dianne smiled at me and peeled away the curly ribbon and tape to expose a calendar with modern dancers posing on the cover, in contorted yet somehow still graceful positions—except that I'd stapled another calendar entirely inside the cover. She flipped it open, and a green-eyed hunk grinned up at her from February. His naked biceps were flexed as he prepared to shoot an arrow from a bow, and only the fact that he was standing behind a large red heart on a waist-high white column allowed the calendar to be sold in family-friendly stores.

Surprised, Dianne let out a short bark of laughter.

"I'm sure you'll have a great time onboard," I said. "But I figured, by that last month, you might be counting the days until you're permanently on dry land and back to your own place. Might as well have something fun to look at while you're counting! But here's your real gift to remember us by."

I handed her a two-sided, five-by-seven hinged frame that folded shut. On the left was a picture of Dianne and the kids at the beach; on the right was a picture of Dianne and me. We'd been at a bachelorette party for one of Tom's secretaries. It was before he'd died, before I'd known I was pregnant with Ben. In the photo, I was a lot thinner and I hadn't developed the matching baggage under my eyes yet. Dianne and I were grinning foolishly at the camera. God, it seemed like a long time ago.

She hugged me fiercely for just a moment, then let me go. "Well. I have to run. But I do have one thing for you first." She reached into the beige purse resting against the corner of the sofa and pulled out a glossy brochure. "Here."

"What's this?"

"A day spa I researched in Boston. I'm booking us some decadent treatments for August. I plan to come up for Ben's birthday." She turned to Sara. "When I come up, we'll celebrate yours, too, princess. Which is cool because that means you'll get presents in June *and* in August. Deal?"

"Deal!" Sara gave her an enthusiastic high five.

Dianne scooped up both kids for noisy kisses, then stood, looking at me with an unspoken warning in her eyes. I was not allowed to tell her how much I was going to miss her. "See you soon?"

I nodded, a lump in my throat as I thought about how

much she'd done for us. "See you soon. Is 'break a leg' the appropriate term for dancers? I know it's what we used to say before all the plays when I was in high school."

"It'll work." She held up the calendar with sixteen months worth of beefcake and grinned. "You just keep this sense of humor, and you'll be fine. Boston will love you."

"Are you kidding? I'm not worried at all." I squared my shoulders. "When you hit forty, you become a bad-ass, remember?"

Sara's jaw dropped. "Nonna Rose! Mommy said a bad word again!"

Once the kids had fallen asleep at nap time, I sought Rose out in the kitchen. She was unrolling a strip of packing tape for a box teeming with paper-wrapped glasses.

"You want to take a break?" I asked her. "I could pour us some tea and break out a couple of those brownies left over from the jewelry party."

Rose shot me a sidelong glance, ripping the tape against the roller's metal teeth with a loud tear. "I'm surprised you would suggest a break with so much to be done. Or brownies. Are they low-fat?"

No, they were triple fudge. And they'd been an attempt to start this conversation on friendly footing, even if the last thing my hips needed was chocolate.

I gnawed my bottom lip. "The truth is, I thought we should talk for a minute."

She repositioned the roller to reinforce one of the box's corners. "I can talk while I work." *Rrrip*.

"Okay. First, I want to say I really appreciate your help. I can use it, especially with Dianne leaving."

"Does she normally give Sara presents like that?" *Rrrip*. "High heels and makeup and feathers?"

"Sara's a little girl. They love high heels and makeup."

"Hm. I suppose I should just be glad your friend didn't get her a pole."

With fishing being such a popular hobby among people I knew, it took me a befuddled moment to register what kind of pole Rose meant. I slapped my hand down on the table. "Look, I'm not blind to the fact that you and Dianne never really took to each other, but she's a wonderful person. The stage show she's part of is at a nice place and has been written up as part of Miami's performing arts revival in the last few years. But even if she danced at Louie's Girls, Girls, Girls, it wouldn't change how grateful I am to her. Without her help, there's no way I could have... I wouldn't have made it. You don't have to like her, but you sure as hell aren't going to speak badly about her in front of me or the kids."

She set down the roller and crossed her arms over the navy sweater she was wearing. "Did you always swear this much?"

I had an insanely juvenile impulse to answer, *Yes, dammit, I did*. Maturity won out. "Sorry, it's just been a frustrating time."

Even before having kids and needing to watch what I

said, I hadn't been one to curse often. My protective father had been an old-fashioned Southern guy and had considered it completely inappropriate to swear in front of me. When I'd later blushed at some of the language of Tom's college football buddies, Tom had found it endearing, telling me I was such a lady. I remembered his look of shocked disapproval when I'd sworn at him during a highly uncharacteristic argument, then his relief when we'd discovered I was pregnant and therefore wildly hormonal.

"Well." Rose's arms dropped to her sides. "You're frustrated because you're overwhelmed. But you have my help now. Speaking of which, before I forget, I did you a favor and called a groomer for Gretchen while you were out."

"What?"

"She has an appointment on Tuesday. Looks like it's been weeks since the poor thing had a bath."

More like months. Most of Gretchen's irregular baths took place in the backyard when it was warm. I wondered what a professional charged.

"You've probably just been too busy to take her in," Rose continued. "But I know you wouldn't want Tom's dog to be neglected. And we certainly don't want to drive all the way to Boston in the car with a stinky German shepherd."

All the way to Boston...*we?* Last night, between active packing and Rose spending as much time as she could rebonding with her grandchildren, I hadn't double-checked my assumption that her airline ticket had been round-trip. Now

I realized she meant to make the drive with me, which was sensible from a certain standpoint. Two adults to split the driving, a second pair of hands to help with the children. But fifteen hundred miles with Rose?

Aiyee.

Okay, one thing at a time, Charlie. I took a deep breath. "You're definitely, um, proactive about helping. I noticed you'd pulled my clothes out?"

She nodded crisply. "While I was packing kitchen items, I noticed there's plenty here you don't need to take with you. One pot looks like it's practically falling apart, but the wok is brand new. Have you ever even taken it out of the box? If you never use it, why not leave it? I was thinking a garage sale would cut down on what you have to pack and maybe give you a little extra cash for the trip."

I'd be lucky to make enough to cover Gretchen's bath. My neighbors were seasoned hagglers and nothing devalued a household item faster than life with small children. "So this garage-sale idea led you to my closets?"

"You have outfits in there I'm sure you…" Her eyes narrowed critically as she surveyed me. "Never wear."

"You mean outfits I don't fit into?"

She reached out to pat my hand, which was clasped on the back of a kitchen chair in a death grip. "I think it's refreshing that you're not one of those women starving herself to be a toothpick or obsessed with boycotting carbohydrates. After all, one of the benefits of getting to be our age is a certain comfort within ourselves and realizing appearance isn't everything."

I wanted to scream, only that would wake up the kids.

Ever since Tom had first introduced me to his mother, Rose had been doing this to me. She'd say something that on the surface sounded innocuous, even complimentary, but still left me feeling as if I'd been criticized. Tom, whose protective nature definitely extended to his mom, had told me I was oversensitive, probably hyperconscious of wanting her to like me because I'd never had a mother.

Granted, I *was* sensitive to the fact that I owned at least a dozen outfits that no longer fit my small-boned frame. Anyone who hadn't known me before Ben was born might not classify me as overweight at first glance; Rose, however, made me acutely aware of the extra twenty pounds. My metabolism had slowed down a lot in the years since I'd had Sara. Some people under-eat during depression and lose weight, but missing Tom certainly hadn't made me gaunt. I'd been too inert to kick-start any weight loss, and, since going to work full-time, I'd fallen into the habit of eating whatever was effortless, from a drive-through burger at the kids' favorite fast-food place to a handful of cookies baked by a compassionate neighbor.

But defensive weight-reaction aside, I still took exception to the "getting to be *our* age." The woman was in her early sixties!

"I'll...think about the garage-sale idea." I was thinking about it now, wondering when the heck she expected me to organize one when we were leaving next week. "But I wanted to mention, I'm not wild about people going through my belongings when I'm not here. It's just a personal-space thing. I'm sure you understand, having lived alone for so long."

The words I'd meant to bridge the gap between us obviously didn't have the intended effect.

She stiffened. "If someone came into my home with the express purpose of helping me, I rather think I'd be grateful, relieved not to have to do everything by myself for a change."

This from the same woman who practically chased people out of the kitchen at ladle-point when they tried to assist? I'd learned years ago not to encroach on her territory.

But arguing wasn't going to dispel the tension our conversation had generated. "Why don't I just let you get back to what you were doing? I wanted to finish packing some living-room boxes before the kids wake up, and then I should start supper." Last night, Sara had convinced us to celebrate Rose's arrival by ordering a pizza, but I planned to reassert my culinary prowess with a tasty chicken casserole.

"No need, I've had a roast marinating in the refrigerator since this morning. I'll go ahead and put it in the oven now."

Nice to see everything was under control—dinner, the dog, which of my possessions weren't fit to go to Boston with me.

I suddenly remembered the half-empty bottle of rum in the bottom of the china cabinet. Maybe I should consider putting it to good use over the next week. After all, it would be one less thing I had to pack.

* * *

I'd forgotten.

I sat straight up in bed, jolted by whatever subconscious reminder I'd had in my dreams, awaking to a tangle of emotions that had half formed while I was still asleep. A sense of melancholy, guilt that I hadn't remembered sooner…of course, it's not as if it was an occasion you mark on your calendar. I recalled Rose's snippiness this afternoon, her bad mood during our roast dinner, and was certain that Tom's mother hadn't forgotten. I was surprised she hadn't mentioned it.

Running a hand through my hair, I noted that my bangs were damp with sweat. I should probably get used to that, as hot flashes were no doubt in my near future. Tonight, however, they weren't my main concern. There was a brief, strangled sound over top of the lulling white noise of Ben's baby monitor, and I realized I'd choked back a sob. It was like waking upset from a nightmare you don't even really remember. Or awaking *to* the nightmare. The times I dreamed of us together were the worst; the images so real that waking was like losing him all over again.

Taking a deep breath, I tried to clear a mental path through the thoughts and emotions clouding my sleep-fogged brain. I could at least cut through the darkness. After bumping a book and knocking my reading glasses to the floor, I reached the bedside lamp. A small ray of light illuminated the room, making me feel less vulnerable. Gretchen glanced up from where she lay in front of my dresser, her ears straightening in an alert, curious manner.

Sara slept with three night-lights in her room. Maybe some parents would deem that excessive, but who am I to tell her she has to face her fears in the dark? There are some things I'd rather not dwell on without at least forty watts glowing near me. I pushed aside the sheet and climbed out of bed, tugging on the hem of my green cotton sleep shirt. After using the bathroom and splashing some cold water on my face, I stood at my dresser, holding Ben's baby monitor for a few moments until I heard the rustling of him turning over in his crib, followed by a soft dreamy sigh. Then I padded barefoot down the carpeted hallway to my daughter's room, Gretchen trailing me. I only stepped far enough inside to watch the rhythmic rise and fall of Sara's pink comforter as she inhaled and exhaled.

Pausing to listen, I noted gratefully that there was no snoring or wheezing. At the height of her throat infections last spring, she'd been a restless sleeper and her pediatrician had wanted me to keep tabs on her breathing at night. I turned to tiptoe away, but accidentally kicked Ben's Alpha-Orb, which sang the ABCs as it rolled. The perky robot voice I'd triggered got to F before I could grab the ball. Rose would have been proud of me—I managed not to swear at the plastic sphere as I located the off switch.

"Mommy?"

"Go back to sleep, Sara-bear," I whispered over my shoulder. "I didn't mean to wake you."

She lifted her head partially off the pillow. "Kiss?"

I obligingly went to the side of her bed, kissing her sleep-warmed forehead and tucking her dark curls behind one ear. "Sweet dreams."

Her eyes were already closed again, but she lifted one arm, raising her favorite stuffed animal. "Ellie, too."

I dropped a kiss on Ellie's trunk and pulled the comforter over both of them. Sara was asleep before I even made it to the hall. The German shepherd was sitting where I'd left her, panting in a somewhat anxious manner. Better let her out since I'd disturbed her sleep.

Hoping not to encounter any more stray toys, I tried to keep my movements stealthy as we headed toward the living room. Ever since the first time she'd visited us, Rose had slept on the sleeper sofa. Tom had tried to get her to take our bed, but she wouldn't hear of it. "Kick my son out of his own room? You need rest so you can get up in the morning and get to that job refreshed, provide for your family."

I needn't have worried about waking her, however. As Gretchen and I reached the end of the hall, I noticed a faint blue light and muffled sound—the television. Rose was sitting on the fold-out bed, the long black hair she normally wore up twined over the shoulder of her yellow robe. She looked small somehow, sitting alone in the center of the queen-sized mattress.

Her gaze flicked toward me and the dog. "Couldn't sleep, either?"

She sounded so tired, I hated myself for how annoyed I'd been with her all evening. I still couldn't believe I'd forgotten. Was that a bad sign or a good sign?

"With everything else going on, I didn't even realize the date," I admitted. "But suddenly I just woke up thinking about it. Are you okay?"

The Idiot Question. Under different circumstances, I would have laughed at my own unthinking impulse. How many times after Tom's death had I forced myself to smile and assure someone that I would be all right when deep inside, I was thinking, *No, you moron, the other half of me is gone. I'm not okay*.

"I woke up thinking about it first thing this morning," she said. It was too dark for me to see any tears, but her voice was thick with them. "My baby's been gone a year."

Deciding Gretchen could just hold it a while longer, I sat on the mattress next to my mother-in-law. I'd so often thought of Tom's death in terms of his immediate household, in terms of the people who had counted on him day-to-day. How the kids would cope, whether or not I was doing it all wrong, whether or not there would ever come a day missing him wouldn't cause this stitch in my chest. I hadn't spent as much time considering Rose, who had seen Tom only a couple of times a year for most of his adult life.

Now, picturing Ben in his crib and Sara curled up with Ellie, I couldn't imagine a greater hell than burying my child. No matter how old the child had grown.

"I'm sorry for your loss," I said. "I don't think I ever told you that." But it was important to acknowledge. Not just our loss, as two people who'd loved Tom, but hers. As a mother.

There was a surprised pause before she answered, "Thank you."

We sat in silence that was more companionable than almost any conversation we'd ever had, an old black-and-white spaghetti western playing softly on the television.

Then she spoke, sniffling a little. "I'm sorry for yours. Losing a husband…"

"Sucks swamp water?" I supplied over the sounds of someone robbing a stagecoach. While losing Tom hadn't brought the two of us any closer, it occurred to me now that she knew what it was like to be a widow. Would she understand the conflicting emotions I'd have trouble articulating even to Dianne?

Rose's pause this time was a lot more shocked before she laughed. "I'm not even sure what that means, exactly, but it sounds accurate."

"It was hard when I lost Dad," I murmured, thinking of my own children who would grow up minus a parent. "But Tom and I were already dating then, and leaning on him helped. A lot."

She nodded. "When his father passed on, Tom really stepped up to being the man of the house. He took care of so much for as young as he was. He used to tell me that living in Florida was only temporary. He was going to accept the scholarship, then come back to play for the Patriots and provide for me when he was rich and famous."

A grin tugged at the corner of my mouth. It sounded like the confident sort of plan my husband would devise. I wondered how disappointed Rose had been that he'd never moved back north. And whether she'd seen his marrying me as the reason he hadn't.

"You know," I told her, "Tom's affection for you was why I agreed to go out with him. He was older than I was, a jock, and so good-looking it was hard to imagine he would truly stay interested in me for long, not with so many other girls on campus yearning to date him. I'd heard stories about how some of the guys tried to take advantage of freshman girls— mostly from Dad, who called every half hour to check up on me. But Tom and I were talking about my birthday after class one day, and he mentioned yours was in September, too. He spoke about you with such sincerity and respect that I immediately trusted him."

She smiled. "He was a good boy."

"He was a good man. I hate that the kids won't grow up with him, but I promise you they'll know how much he loved them." With that, at least, I had some experience. Dad had always found ways to work the mother I'd never known into our family traditions, without making it maudlin.

"You and the kids should live with me," Rose said suddenly.

The surprised pause this time was mine. "Well…it was the plan that we'd stay with you while we looked for a place."

I'd already had Sara's paperwork forwarded to a school near Rose's home. The Kazka office in Boston was close enough that I could probably keep the kids in that school district. I'd called for information on some of the apartment complexes in the area, but no one had seemed enthusiastic about having a German shepherd as a tenant. Actually, one landlady had sounded *quite* welcoming, as well she should have, since the nonrefundable pet deposit she'd quoted could probably support her into old age.

"What's the rush to find something?" Rose asked. "After all, who knows how long it will take for your broker to sell this house after you've left?"

"My agent is optimistic."

He'd said that sometimes homes sold faster when prospective buyers weren't tripping over the current residents. We'd scrub everything clean, then get out of the way, leaving behind furniture essentials until we found a place of our own. I had the inane thought that I was going to miss this couch in the interim.

"That's wonderful, dear—I hope you sell the place immediately. Even so, the house Thomas Sr. left me is obscenely big for one person, and we just agreed that it's easier to cope with loss when you have someone to share it with. You could help me with a few monthly bills and save up money for you and the kids at the same time."

"True." I did wake up from occasional nightmares about what college tuition would be by 2017.

"They won't grow up with their father, but they can grow up somewhere rich with his past, maybe connect with him that way. I've…appreciated our conversation tonight," she added haltingly.

"Me, too." While ordinarily, I might have said Rose and I didn't see eye to eye on much, we had weathered similar, unfortunate circumstances. She'd first lost a husband, then years later a son. I'd lost a father, then a husband. Unlike some of the people prone to patting my arm and murmuring, "I know just how you must feel," Rose probably did.

"What had you planned to do about child care?" she pressed. "I could help with that."

"The offer's appreciated, truly. I'm just not sure. The kids and I are finally starting to…" I hesitated to explain how we were only recently adjusting to the family of three we'd become, because I didn't want to make her sound excluded.

She played her trump card. "I don't think you and I were ever as close as Tom would have liked. I believe this decision would help him rest easier, don't you?"

It would have made him very happy. And her idea did solve a lot of logistical problems, such as how would I pay for a new place to live, much less day care, if my agent's optimism didn't pan out and I was still sending monthly checks for this house?

"We'll be like Stella and Louise," Rose said, sounding eager.

"Who?"

"Some movie." She frowned. "Weren't there two women who, I don't know, bonded?"

"Thelma. You meant *Thelma and Louise*. And that movie ended in joint suicide."

"Oh. You're sure?"

"They drove into the Grand Canyon." Whistling, I made a diving motion with my hand.

"What a silly way to end a film. Okay, then. Not like them! Some other pair that would make a good roommate analogy."

Felix and Oscar came to mind. Hard to believe Rose and I would be any *odder* a couple.

CHAPTER 5

I felt like the unseen narrator of one of those half-crazed survivor journals.

Day 38: The sun is beginning to drive me quite mad, and at night, there's an unholy cry, almost a howl, in the distance. Beast, native or someone who was once like myself? Difficult to say.

All right, a slight exaggeration.

For one thing, there was no sun—just dreary autumn drizzle that had turned the afternoon a slate-gray outside our blue minivan. Also, it was only day two—aka Friday—but it was no exaggeration to say the trip already seemed a lot longer than the three days it was scheduled to be. From one hour to the next, I couldn't decide whether I regretted not having Rose here to help with the kids, or whether I was grateful I'd had the forethought to send her and Gretchen ahead. After our discussion on the anniversary of Tom's death, Rose and I had agreed we would all become one big happy household, until at least next summer. I didn't have to worry about possibly making Sara change schools *again*, and we could decide in June what we all wanted to do.

Intuition told me that hours and hours in the car together wouldn't be the best way to start off our new living arrangement. Besides, Gretchen got carsick. So, I'd convinced Rose she would be the most help to us by flying back to Boston on Wednesday and taking the dog with her, via pet cargo.

Since the kids and I had driven off Thursday morning, our van full to bursting with our belongings, I'd had several moments where I'd pondered the feasibility of airlines instituting a *child* cargo hold. Well, not in the underbelly of the plane and certainly not in cages, but maybe children should have their own seating section. They could watch cartoons and ask each other, "Are we there yet?" four zillion times while the adults sat elsewhere, napping or possibly even engaging in intelligent conversation. Conversations that didn't revolve around "Ew, what's that smell, Mommy?"

A win-win situation.

So far, Sara's chief role on this road trip—other than kicking the back of my seat and begging to stop for McFood every single time we passed a billboard featuring a pair of golden arches—was alerting us to unpleasant aromas. Stagnant water and exhaust fumes as we made the long trip north through Florida, paper mills and pig farms inside Georgia, where we'd stayed last night, and most recently a few industrial plants as we passed through the Carolinas. Then there were the dozen times she'd announced her brother had a dirty diaper, some of which had turned out to be false, but understandable, alarms.

"Mommy?" Sara said now, an urgent tone to her voice.

I glanced at her in the rearview mirror. "What is it, pumpkin?" While I didn't smell anything, she'd proven over the past eight hundred miles to have some sort of bionic nose, detecting a new odor to complain about long before I noticed anything. I also hadn't seen a fast-food sign for the past couple of miles, but maybe she'd picked up the scent of salted French fries from inside a passing car.

"I need to go potty."

"Again?" Somehow, I managed not to give in to the impulse to bang my head repeatedly on the steering wheel. "You're sure?"

It had been my plan to stop in Baltimore tonight and push through the last leg of the trip tomorrow, giving us Sunday to rest before I took Sara to see her new school and I went to my new office. Apparently, I hadn't reserved enough hours in the itinerary for the three thousand pit stops a six-year-old's bladder would require.

"Yeah, I really need to go, Mommy. Quick!"

Naturally. Because Ben, who had decided around noon that he was tired of being strapped into his safety seat and had expressed his vocal displeasure for about a hundred miles, had finally fallen asleep. No way was I letting my six-year-old daughter go by herself into the bathroom at an interstate rest stop, and it was equally unthinkable that I'd leave my baby in the car. This meant he was almost definitely going to wake up…and cry the rest of the way to Baltimore. A course of action I could identify with more each passing moment.

Which is why having Rose along would have been a good idea. She could stay in the van with Ben while you took Sara inside. She could drive for a bit while you sobbed quietly.

I sighed, reminding myself to look on the bright side. All things considered, the kids weren't being bad. They were just being…kids. And the trip could have been worse. Sure, it was raining, but there hadn't been any serious storms along the way. No vehicle problems, either, such as flat tires or engine trouble. Big Blue, Tom's name for our van, had a lot of miles on her but had always proved to be reliable. I should've been counting my blessings.

But driving gave me way too much time to think. To worry about where we were headed and to miss what we were leaving behind.

Pulling out of our driveway for the last time had been easier than I'd anticipated, maybe because not having a buyer yet had kept it from seeming like a true goodbye. Or maybe because I'd just been too frazzled by the effort to get all the remaining foodstuffs in the house to Mrs. Winslow and load up the kids and all of the personal effects and small furnishings we weren't leaving behind. After a few hours on the road, though, leaving had sunk in. I would probably never again set foot in the house where Tom and I had celebrated a decade of Christmases together, the house where I'd thrown company dinners that Tom had boasted made him the most popular man at the firm, the house where Tom had held me in his arms as I'd wept over losing a baby, and the house where we'd finally brought two beautiful babies home. That was what I would miss, not "the house," but our home.

"Mommy! I gotta pee."

"Just a few more miles, I promise." Maybe the potty break would be just what the road-trip doctor ordered—a chance to get some fresh air and to stretch our legs. Although driving long distances consists of sitting in one place, it was a lot more physically grueling than one would think. My whole body hurt.

To distract both of us, I reminded Sara of our grand plans for Halloween: a fabulous princess costume. I'd found some inexpensive royal purple polyester velour that would make a nice cape for her and help ward off the chill while she trick-or-treated. We talked about what the dress should look like and she announced she wanted to use the tiara from Dianne's gift set as her crown.

The conversation worked for a few minutes, but by the time I veered off the highway into the rest-stop parking lot, Sara had her hands pressed to her lap and panic in her eyes. I got Ben out of his car seat as fast as I could, while Sara unbuckled herself. As I stopped to shove a fallen sippy cup and road atlas back into the van, she hurried up the sidewalk.

By the time we finished in the restroom, the rain was pouring down. When we passed the vending machines on our way out, Sara brightened. "Can I get a drink, Mommy?"

Not a chance in hell, o ye of the thimble-sized bladder. "Maybe later, pumpkin."

While we were inside, a car had parked too closely to us on the right side, so I urged Sara to climb in on her brother's side and buckle up. I was antsy to hit the road again since the unscheduled stop and worsening weather were really going to put us behind schedule.

At least Ben drifted off to sleep a few miles down the road while Sara and I played the alphabet game as I navigated increasing traffic outside Fredericksburg. We hit a second patch of bad weather, though, and I had to turn on *Travelin' Tunes* again, to keep Sara entertained while I concentrated on driving.

Nothing breaks your concentration faster than your distraught daughter suddenly screaming, *"Mommy!"*

This was not an "I gotta pee" tone. It was more like "A flaming asteroid is crashing toward the van." Even though asteroids were improbable, there was enough panic in Sara's voice for my foot to shoot instinctively toward the brake. I had only slightly decelerated before coming to my senses and realized that stopping in the middle of I-95 would be a terrible idea.

"You scared me," I told her over the rustling of Ben's waking up. "What on earth is wrong?"

"Ellie! Ellie's not here."

My heart skipped a beat. Despite getting dressed and eating a meal of chocolate milk and banana-berry breakfast bars, Sara had only been about half-awake when we'd left the hotel in Georgia that morning. I remembered trying to get her to move a little faster so that we could get our start for the day; had I made sure Ellie was secured in the van? If we'd left the fuzzy elephant behind in my haste, my daughter wouldn't speak to me again until college. And probably only then to ask for money.

Relief swamped me when I recalled Sara's requesting at lunch that Ellie come in to the restaurant with us. I'd said no, figuring it would be a bad idea to spill ketchup and other substances on the stuffed animal when we still had hundreds of miles between us and Rose's washing machine.

Sara sniffed and a quick look in the mirror confirmed fat tears were spilling down her cheeks.

"It's all right, bear. She probably just slid behind your seat. I'll pull over and check, okay?"

"O-k-kay."

I steered toward the shoulder and turned on my hazards.

A few moments later it occurred to me that this is what it truly meant to be a parent. I was standing in a downpour, further delaying an exhausting cross-country journey, to madly ransack my van for a stuffed toy that had cost about eight bucks. Within moments, I had to admit that Ellie wasn't here. Trying to think what to say to my hiccupping daughter, I knelt down to pick up an umbrella and Sara's sweater that had fallen out of the van.

Damn. Ellie had probably tumbled out at the last stop. We'd been in a rush to get inside the bathroom, and when we'd come back out, we hadn't gone around to Sara's side of the van, where we would have noticed our fallen friend.

I squeezed my temples, conflicting thoughts and impulses bombarding each other to create instant headache. Would the stuffed elephant even still be there? What if she'd disappeared at some potty break before that? I couldn't very well backtrack to every stop we'd made since lunch; when you're traveling with two small children, those pit stops add up fast. I had to be at work in a couple of days, and we still had hundreds of miles to go. Besides, what if the weather or traffic had ruined Ellie?

Deep inside, a voice whispered that the elephant was just a toy. It could be replaced. But listening to Sara's sobs, I knew that wasn't true. Just as I knew we were going back.

As an adult, I acknowledged that my father had been overprotective of me and I couldn't shield my kids from every possible hurt—that sometimes it wasn't even healthy to try—but Sara had lost her dad, her home, her school and her friends. There was only so much a six-year-old should have to deal with at once. In an alternate "fair" reality, anyway.

"Pumpkin, I think Ellie fell out of the car when we stopped earlier. Do you want to go back and look for her?"

She nodded, voicing her agreement incoherently.

Forming our plan was a lot simpler than executing it; you can't just whip a U-turn on the interstate. I found an exit and drove to the nearest on-ramp, going in the opposite direction. I ground my teeth together and pressed down on the accelerator. Why was traffic moving so slowly here? The obvious answer, of course, was universal conspiracy. While the rain hadn't kept most northbound travelers from going five to ten miles over the posted speed limit, it now seemed as if everyone around me was driving five under. If we had any hope of making it to Baltimore tonight before my sore back and cramping knees called it quits, I needed to get back to that rest stop *now*.

I flicked on my blinker, passed several cars and then changed lanes before zipping past a red Volvo. My foot grew heavier on the gas pedal, all my focus on hoping Ellie was still there, and in good enough shape that it wouldn't further my daughter's hysteria. Suddenly, over the discontent inside our van, I heard the unmistakable screech of a police siren. In the side mirror, I saw headlights flash on, illuminating a car on the median that had been semi-hidden in the dusk.

Ah, speed trap. That could explain why everyone else had been driving so slowly.

Red and blue flashing lights snapped into action as the car came toward me, the discordant siren growing progressively louder and startling Ben into shrieks of his own. Sara probably would have thought they were cool if she weren't already so upset. I clenched my jaw, squeezed my fingers into rigid vises against the steering wheel and bit back every swear word I'd ever heard one of Tom's construction buddies use.

I pulled over, suddenly very conscious of the line of cars I'd been attempting to pass. I remembered the feeling of vindication I'd had once, watching a member of the Miami Highway Patrol pull over a couple of teenage kids, soon after the hooligans had cut me off in traffic.

But I am not a sixteen-year-old joyrider! I'm a single mother in a big blue minivan, just trying to do the right thing, dammit.

As the police officer took the time to call in my out-of-state license plate, I tensed. Finally, the man approached. He had light hair and a dark uniform, and he came bearing a pad of paper and a vibe of stern reprimand.

"Good evening, ma'am."

I don't know if it was his tone or the seizure-inducing lights still flashing behind me, but I couldn't contain my frustration. "Good? *Good?*"

In response to my snarl, he took a reflexive step backward. At least he didn't reach for his gun.

"I'm sorry," I said. "Things are…not going well, so if we could just move this along?"

Wrong thing to say.

"Ma'am, I don't care where you're going or how badly you want to get there, it's not worth driving recklessly. You know why I pulled you over?"

"Because I was going thirteen miles over the speed limit."

"Are you taking Mommy to jail?" Sara wailed. "Don't take Mommy to jail! Then I won't have a mommy, a daddy *or* an Ellie."

His blond eyebrows shot upward as he peered into the van, at my two squalling little ones. "Your mommy's not going anywhere, honey—she just needs to slow down some."

Her lip quivered. "But we have to save Ellie!"

"Is there someone in danger, ma'am?"

"Pink elephant," I muttered.

For just a moment, I could've sworn the corner of his lips twitched. "Don't tell me I have to give you a Breathalyzer, too."

"My daughter," I began, trying to form words calmly and dispel any notion he might harbor that I was a crazy woman. Even if I did feel like I was becoming one. "She has a pink elephant that means the world to her. And we think we left it at a rest stop."

He considered this. "You've got Florida plates. Where are you headed?"

"Boston, ultimately. We're moving."

"My daddy went to heaven and Mommy lost her job," Sara announced. "And now my Ellie is *gone!*"

The man's features softened and he looked back at me. "I think we can let you off with a warning this time, just try not to drive too fast."

"Thank you, thank you so much." Hotels and restaurants were straining the budget; I didn't even want to know what speeding tickets cost these days.

"I'd offer a police escort for the mission," he said, finally allowing a grin, "but I'm afraid you're headed a little too far away from my beat."

I smiled at the image of his clearing a path through traffic, sirens blaring as we hauled ass to rescue Ellie. "It's a nice thought, anyway."

As we headed back down the highway, I thought to myself that the world may not always be fair, but at least there were some decent people in it. A notion reinforced when, not quite an hour later, we found Ellie, sitting up at the building's main entrance, beneath the overhang where someone had placed her safely away from rain and traffic.

Thank. God. We arrived later than I'd anticipated, but at least we had finally reached Boston. The city, an interesting tangle of different neighborhoods, had always been a geographical puzzle to me. Tom and I had been married for years before I'd realized the South End and South Boston weren't the same thing. When we'd driven here with Sara, he'd teased that the Big Dig—a massive highway and tunnel project—was the Boston natives' little joke on tourists, keeping them confused about where they were going. I'd heard him laugh over the seemingly endless construction, predicting in mock-grim tones that he'd probably be long dead before they got around to finishing the project.

My stomach twisted at his unintentionally accurate forecast. It was exactly these stupid memories that hit me the hardest—silly things that now took on a sadder meaning.

As I navigated our way around the city, I caught occasional glimpses of the water beneath the twilight sky, but instead of sandy beaches dotted with tourists, there were industrial fishing boats and white-capped currents brisk with the breeze. In Miami, it wasn't unusual for iPod-carrying pedestrians to zoom by on their in-line skates, wearing shorts and bathing suits. Here, even though the weather was moderate for a Boston autumn, it was far too cold for anyone to consider a bikini public wear. Instead, when we snaked by several parks and squares in slow-moving traffic, we saw people in light jackets and university sweatshirts.

After at least three wrong turns, we entered Rose's nearly forty-year-old subdivision, lit by streetlamps now that the evening had grown fully dark. We were here. I might've burst into grateful tears if I'd had the energy to cry.

I thought absently of Dianne. Unlike me, her television viewing habits weren't dictated by a six-year-old, and she'd always filled me in on grown-up TV, including a couple of reality shows where contestants had to pit their strength, endurance and wit against one another. If the networks were interested in *really* finding out who had survival skills, they'd film a show where lone men and women were sent on a road trip with little kids…in a van whose cruise-control function had stopped working somewhere in north Virginia.

People would beg to be eliminated.

"We're just about there," I promised Sara, who had been claiming she needed to go to the bathroom for the last few miles. "Look, there's Nonna's house."

I stared at the brick two-story situated at the curve of the cul-de-sac. Déjà vu jolted me like static electricity. How often had we pulled into that very driveway? Tom had first brought me here the summer after my freshman year, although we'd flown since neither of our parents had wanted us stopping at roadside motels. Having already met my father during Dad's UF visits, I think Tom had wanted to introduce me to his mother and get her approval before proposing to me the following September, on my birthday. I'd been terrified of Rose before meeting her. And not much less terrified afterward.

"Do you remember playing here?" I asked Sara.

"No." She looked out her window. "Is this where Daddy lived before he lived with us?"

"It's where he grew up, yeah."

"Ben and I are going to grow up there, too?"

"Um…sort of." I doubted she would be going through adolescence in this particular house, but figured she could only process one move at a time.

She thought this over, then sighed happily. "Cool."

So it was with her blessing that I parked the van in front of our new home. The house only had a single-car garage, but Tom and his father had constructed a carport during Tom's teens, and I parked beneath it, as far to the right as possible, hugging the side yard so that Rose could back out around me if needed. Sara was wrestling impatiently with her seat belt when I opened Ben's door.

"Eager to go check out Nonna's place?" I asked her.

She shot me one of those "grown-ups are so stupid" expressions I hadn't fully expected until she hit puberty. "I gotta pee."

Right. At the moment, all other concerns were secondary. We followed a small stone path through dead grass toward the rickety wooden front porch—me carrying Ben, Sara clutching Ellie. She'd taken no risks since the rescue mission yesterday. There were neatly trimmed bushes up by the house, and I expected lots of flowers in the spring. Rose was as passionate about gardening as she was the women's charity organizations to which she belonged.

The front door swung open as we reached the top step, the screen clattering exactly the way it always had. Rose stepped out, beaming and brushing her hands on a pale mauve apron she wore over a long-sleeved denim house-dress with cranberry accents.

"Welcome!" she told us.

"Where's the bathroom, Nonna?"

Raising her eyebrows at my daughter's greeting, Rose pointed over her shoulder. "Go past the staircase, straight down this hall, and there's a bathroom just past the kitchen."

Sara sprinted off in that direction, calling a "thanks" over her shoulder and dragging Ellie behind her.

I shifted Ben to my other hip. "Sorry, she's had to go for a little while, and I just couldn't bring myself to stop again so close."

"Of course not." Rose ran her gaze over me. "And no reason to go out in public looking like that if you can help it."

Frankly, I hadn't given my appearance much thought…or effort, beginning with the lack of makeup before loading everyone up that morning. Under my mother-in-law's scrutiny, I grew more conscious of the strands of hair that had escaped my ponytail holder, various stains that bore testament to trying to eat or drink while driving, and the fact that my soft button-down shirt was half-tucked out of my jeans—I would've untucked it completely, but there was a tag in the back of my pants that rubbed against the skin above my cotton undies. It got annoying after several hours of sitting in the same position.

I stole a quick look at Ben to see if he looked any better; he didn't. His hair stuck up in wayward spikes, and apparently his nose had started to run sometime after our last pit stop.

Rose followed my gaze, then whisked a tissue out of the pocket of her apron. "The important thing is, you made it."

"*Finally.*" The word came out far more telling than I'd intended.

"You almost sound surprised, dear. It couldn't have been that bad?" This from the woman who made the trip in a couple of hours with the benefit of in-flight beverage service.

But since I was the person who'd put her on the flight and had insisted the drive would be no trouble without her, I simply shook my head. "It was fine."

No doubt she'd find out the truth from Sara soon enough.

"Well, come in, come in. I have a lovely beef Stroganoff waiting for you in the Crock-Pot. And Gretchen's out back. She'll be so happy to see you and the children!"

Maybe. It was equally possible the shepherd had enjoyed her time away from small kids. Ben and Sara loved the dog, but to the untrained eye, love from a toddler can occasionally resemble animal cruelty.

"What's sto-go-noff?" Sara asked as she walked back toward us. "Is it like pizza?"

Lips pursed, Rose shot me a don't-you-ever-feed-these-children-real-food glance.

"No, but it's yummy." I pulled the front door shut behind me and Ben. I knew there were things I had to unload from the van sooner rather than later, but right now even standing was draining. My eyes felt unnaturally heavy from hours of staring at the road, and I wanted to nap...for about five months. Those bears who hibernate until spring are on to something.

Since Ben was even heavier than my eyelids, I bent down, intending to set him on the entryway tile, but thought better of it. To our left was a room with matching pristine ivory brocade love seats, perched on delicate-looking round wooden legs. There was also a glass-fronted curio cabinet with Rose's eclectic collection of china teacups, a brass étagère with a slotted in-box for mail and bills and two green leafy plants that Ben would probably reduce to piles of dirt and broken pottery in under a minute. When Tom and I had brought Sara here in her early years, we'd never spent much time in the small but formal front room. Now I remembered why.

To our right was a sunken living room. Ben could probably manage the three steps with no physical danger. The knitting needles poking out of a basket next to Rose's favorite chair were another matter. At the moment, it would take less energy to just carry him than it would to corral him away from all the things he couldn't touch. Childproofing rocketed to the top of my to-do list tomorrow.

We retraced Sara's steps down the hall, past the stairs to the second-story bedrooms, and toward Rose's spacious kitchen. As we rounded the corner, I was struck by the insane certainty that Tom would be sitting in one of the four straight-backed chairs at his mother's table.

Everything looked untouched by time, exactly as I remembered—copper-bottom pots hanging over the kitchen island, daisy-printed tablecloth, and the plain, utilitarian set of enclosed shelves hanging on the wall that served as Rose's spice rack, filled to the brim with different sizes of assorted jars and tins. Higher up, on the flat space above her kitchen cabinets, cookbooks accumulated what was probably the only dust in her otherwise immaculate house.

I'd asked Tom once if he'd ever actually seen her open one

of those books, but he figured she'd long since memorized the recipes she wanted and tweaked them to suit her own taste. That and a hundred other trivial conversations came to mind as if they'd taken place yesterday. His presence was so strong here. I'd never been to Rose's house without him, and only now, with my surreal expectation that he'd walk in at any second, did I realize how accustomed I'd grown to his *not* being in our Miami home.

On the other hand, the memories were different here, vacation memories. It wasn't like sleeping in the bed we'd shared for twenty years and trying to get used to waking up alone; it was more like a field trip into my past, remembering fun, isolated moments. Tom's sitting in that kitchen chair by the window, looking every bit the proud new father as he gave Sara a bottle, his teasing me about something as we washed dishes after dinner and my swatting him with Rose's daisy-printed towel, a quick make-out session in the backyard greenhouse, where he'd ostensibly taken me to see prize-winning hydrangeas.

"Charlie?"

Blushing as if I'd actually been caught in that decades-old stolen embrace, I darted my gaze toward my mother-in-law. "Hm?"

"You were smiling."

"B-because we're so happy to be here."

"Uh-huh. Well, I'm thrilled that you'll be moving in, too. I should show everyone their rooms so that you can unpack the van while Sara and I set the table."

I smiled weakly, my muscles protesting. "Sounds great."

"I put you in the master suite," Rose said. "As we discussed."

When she'd initially suggested that she move out of her own room to the downstairs den/office converted into another bedroom behind the kitchen, I'd protested. But we couldn't figure out another solution that made sense, considering the children would be sleeping upstairs.

"It will be perfect," she'd told me. "The second bathroom's right there, anyway, and not any smaller than the one upstairs. When you get a few years older, you'll find you're not always excited about the prospect of going up the steps to bed or having to go all the way back down for a glass of juice in the middle of the night. I'll hire my neighbor's teenage hooligan sons who do my landscaping to come over and move some furniture before you arrive."

Since she not only invited the teens into her home but paid them, I knew she didn't truly think they were hooligans. They probably just didn't measure up to the golden boy Tom had been at their age. No one could, in Rose's estimation.

Even though her plan made the most sense, I knew it would take me a while to adjust to the idea of taking over Rose's room. Besides the kitchen, bathroom and converted bedroom, the only other space at the back of the house was the laundry room and a small tiled area overlooking the backyard that Rose had always called the mudroom. As we passed by it now, I saw that a large, fleecy dog bed had been purchased. Blinking, I also realized that there was a red dog bowl that had Gretchen's name printed on the side in gold cursive lettering.

Sort of made me nervous as to what to expect in the rooms she'd designated for the children. If the dog got a personalized bowl, would there be a pink canopy princess bed for Sara? I couldn't really imagine that, though, even in my exhausted, fanciful state. Sara would be getting Tom's old room, the one that had scarcely changed since he'd driven off for college. On the majority of Tom's and my visits, we'd been in the converted bedroom Rose was now moving into, and his room had just sat empty, a shrine to his high-school years. It was difficult to picture it as suddenly different now.

We all filed upstairs, and I made a mental note that one of the first things I needed to do was set up baby gates. I had one in the van, but we'd probably need a couple more.

There were only two real bedrooms upstairs, the master and the slightly smaller bedroom down the hall, with a full bathroom between them. But adjacent to the master suite was an old-fashioned offshoot, a circular area with its own door meant to be used as either a nursery or sewing room. Rose had pushed her sewing supplies to the side to make room for Ben's crib.

"The hooligans had their hands full moving bedroom furniture up and down the stairs, we didn't have time to resituate all this yet," she told me. "But I thought the room would work for Ben."

"It's perfect," I assured her.

She glanced down at Sara, her voice tremulous. "And you, beautiful little lady, you get your daddy's old room."

If the kitchen had looked unchanged to me, Tom's room was even more so. *Frozen* was the thought I had. I had expected all the familiar touches that had been the same since he'd left for college—same navy curtains, same old records stacked in the carved shelf beneath the window seat, same plaid comforter on the twin bed, same sports trophies lining the narrow wooden shelf that ran the length of the room, at what would have been about eye-level for my husband. Unless she'd taken it down during the past year, the same *Charlie's Angels* poster still hung on the inside of his closet door. Original Angels, naturally—pre-Barrymore, Diaz and Liu.

What I hadn't expected were the little traces of Tom's visits home through the years. There were a couple of audiocassette tapes still sitting in the opened cellophane package on the window seat. He'd bought the pack of four on one of our trips so that he could use Rose's turntable to record some favorite old songs. The two tapes he hadn't used were just sitting there, as if he might be coming back at any moment to record some more Blues Brothers or Boston songs. We had stayed in this room once, as newlyweds, when we'd come here for a cousin's wedding and an older couple had used the double bed downstairs. I'd brought a little rectangular travel clock with me and hadn't really noticed on subsequent visits that it still sat on the scarred wooden nightstand he'd never finished restoring.

It would be easy to believe Rose didn't even set foot in this room when Tom wasn't around, except that it was too clean. Not a smidge of dust on any of those old sports trophies, no accumulated lint on the vacuumed tan carpet, no wispy traces of webs anywhere, where an eight-legged guest might have tried to move in to the vacant room.

Yet there was still a crumpled-up piece of yellow paper next to the navy-lined wicker waste basket, probably one of the sketches Tom had liked to doodle on whatever legal pad was handy, then balled up and tossed at the trash years ago. I honestly believed his mom had been in and out of this room dusting and occasionally washing the linens to keep them from getting that musty, unused smell, and she'd left the paper there, as if Tom would come in and correct his bad aim. Or smooth out the drawing and decide he wanted to keep it, after all. He'd had a good job as senior manager in one of Miami's construction firms, but I'd always thought deep down that he was a frustrated architect, that maybe one day he'd go back to sch—

Damn. It's this room. Makes you feel like there are "maybes" in his future. The future he didn't have.

I did another hip shift with Ben to give my supporting arm a break, and reached down to ruffle Sara's hair. "I know it looks like a boy's room, but we can—"

"I like it," she said quickly. She turned to her grandmother. "Are those Daddy's trophies?"

"Mmm-hmm. He was something else on the football field,

a real dynamo. I'll bet Ben will grow up to play as well as his dad did. Thomas Sr. was quite the athlete, too."

Sara wrinkled her nose. "Can I be an ath-lete?"

"You can be anything you want to be," I told her firmly. "If you set your mind to it and work hard. But first, we have to get some dinner in you guys! Athletes need their energy, and they always eat their vegetables."

My daughter groaned at this edict, but she followed us downstairs, agreeing to at least try what Rose had made for dinner. I don't know that I set a very good example since most of my meal went untouched—I was busying myself with getting Ben's booster seat and other paraphernalia out of the van and then making sure he actually got some food in his mouth, not just smeared around it. Why do all toddlers seem to think they can take in nourishment through their skin, as if it were some kind of topical ointment? I can vouch from experience that they're perfectly willing to stick everything *else* in their mouths, from pen caps to the occasional nugget of dry dog food.

I was too exhausted to notice any hunger as I unfolded the playpen Ben would sleep in until I assembled his more complicated crib. Rose helpfully herded the kids into the upstairs bathtub, and I could hear them splashing and playing as I worked to get us settled for the night. The sounds of high-pitched giggles and Rose's lower, less-used chuckle were reassuring. I'd done the right thing bringing the children here. If we were going to move forward, we all needed to heal, and this seemed like a better spot for that than anything I could have come up with on my own.

By the time we shuttled the kids into bed, I felt dead on my feet. I almost said as much to my mother-in-law before revising my thoughtless wording and just saying, "I'm about to fall over. Thank you so much for dinner, and making room for us here. I think we're going to have to tackle everything else in the morning."

She nodded. "You should definitely get rest—you look terrible."

"Yeah, you made that clear earlier." I was too tired to censor the sarcasm, but the delivery was without bite.

There was a pause, then she just gave me a small, unreadable Mona Lisa smile. "Good night, Charlie."

"Sleep well," I answered. Once I was in my new room, however, I wondered if I would.

My surroundings represented the only real change in the whole house. All of Rose's knickknacks that I'd glimpsed over the years were gone now, presumably moved down to her new bedroom. The queen-size bed she'd shared with Thomas Sr. had been exchanged for the double, covered by a lavender-and-violet afghan I'd never seen before. The armoire and vanity were gone, leaving room for the small dresser still strapped into the back of my van. Even the walls were bare, with only faint outlines bearing testimony to the pictures that had hung there for so long. It was almost eerie, after the rest of the house had been so painstakingly preserved, to find the past erased from this one room.

How hard had it been for her, to take down that wedding portrait, to find a new place for the clay sculpture—some unidentified animal—Tom had made her a lifetime ago as a Mother's Day present? Recalling the way I'd felt wrapping my own dishes and pictures and the spray-painted gold macaroni jewelry box from Sara, I had a pretty good idea of how Rose had felt. It's never easy to say goodbye, even if you are just moving downstairs.

Then again... I looked at the naked walls, just waiting to be decorated with new pictures, new memories. Maybe neither one of us should look at this as a goodbye, just a badly needed fresh start.

CHAPTER 6

"Good morning."

Someone was chirping at me—why? I was used to being the first one awake in the house, except on the occasional Saturday when Sara got hungry watching cartoons and wanted to know if I would make her pancakes. Only this voice wasn't Sara's, it belonged to…?

Rose, my tired mind supplied. *She's visiting, remember?*

I opened my eyes slowly and the surroundings that met my bleary gaze were an immediate correction. She wasn't visiting anymore; we were at her house. As I squinted my mother-in-law's face into focus, I realized she was wearing makeup. And pearls. An entire ensemble of her Sunday best.

"Will you and the children be joining me for church?" she inquired cheerfully.

"Uh." Any chance I could send the kids along with her and sleep for another three or four hours? "Probably not."

I expected the pursed-lip disapproval, but instead she nodded. "I know you have a lot to do. I'll be home this afternoon after service and my weekly visit to Aunt Velda. She's at the same home Mother stayed in, a very nice place. You should bring the kids one Sunday, Velda would love to see them. If you'd like I can stop by the grocery store for you on my way back, just let me know what you plan to fix for dinner tonight."

"Dinner?" I sat up, blinking. Breakfast was currently the extent of my foggy mental grasp.

"It's your night," she said with the exaggerated patience she might have used to explain fractions to Sara. "To cook. But don't feel as if you have to do anything as fancy as the Stroganoff. Not while you're first getting on your feet."

"My night?" I distantly recognized that I had a bad case of the echoes, but I was too tired to follow her subject changes from Velda's home to my cooking skills.

"I wanted to show you the calendar last night, but you were just so wiped out, dear. We'll alternate dinner responsibilities each night, and I have our laundry days charted."

"Chart—" Abruptly, I bit off my instinctively parroted question. "You assigned us each specific laundry days?" I'd assumed we'd just toss our stuff in together as needed.

"Well, it will keep everything running more smoothly to have a schedule. And I knew you'd want to be responsible for your share of things and not be dependent on me." She beamed proudly. "You thought I was going to be territorial, didn't you? Look at it as my kitchen, do things my way, but see, I'm a wonderful roommate. We'll split errands and times. I put together a color-coded notebook."

"Um…thanks, Rose." I thought having my couch rather than the pristine antique armchairs would go a lot further toward making the kids and me feel at home, but I greatly appreciated her efforts.

A cry from the room next door drew both of our attention.

"Would you like me to get Ben so that you have a chance to wash up?" Rose offered.

"That would be great." Especially if I could get my sore legs to make it as far as the bathroom.

Ten minutes later, hobbling like Rose's aunt Velda, I made it downstairs to the kitchen. Velda had to have been at least seventy the first time I'd met her, but she'd always been a live wire. She'd been at Tom's and my wedding, very put out that the women in his family hadn't thrown me a bachelorette party. I'd assured her I hadn't minded, and she'd countered that she felt cheated out of seeing a stripper. Apparently, a woman's chances of seeing live naked men diminished once she was over sixty-five.

Tom and I had just had Sara when Rose had put her mother in the home; she'd gone every Sunday to visit Mrs. Fiorello and Velda. I knew that statistically, women outlived men, but it was odd, being at the retirement home—seeing the community of white-haired women, mostly Irish and Italian, widowed and reminiscing. Now, I'd lost Tom and I was dimly aware that last year, Mitsy, one of Tom's once-removed cousins had lost her husband. Were she and I the next generation of widows? Would there come a day when the kids and I would be visiting Rose every Sunday?

Rose sat at the table, reading the children a picture book Sara had carried in from the van.

"Mommy!" Sara bounded up to me for a hug. "Can we have breakfast now? Nonna has to leave soon for church. I told her we haven't been to ours in a long, long time."

Oh, good. I'd wanted to advertise that I was a slug who couldn't bring herself to get up early and put on pantyhose that one extra morning a week, and, consequently, was raising heathen children.

"So what do you want for breakfast?" I asked, deciding that the sooner I had Sara's mouth full of food, the better.

"Chocolate cake!"

My eyebrows shot up. I could at least redeem myself here, before Rose got the impression I loaded my kids up with dessert to start the day. "You know we don't have cake for breakfast."

"Oh." Her lower lip pudged out. "Nonna Rose said she stayed up and baked us a cake last night. I think she worked *really* hard on it, Mommy."

I managed not to roll my eyes at her dramatic announcement, which somehow made Rose sound like Cinderella, toiling in the wee hours. No doubt who the evil stepmother was in this scenario. "I'm sure she did, but I don't think she meant for us to have cake for breakfast."

"My homemade cake from fresh ingredients can't be any less

nutritious than some of the chocolate-covered breakfast bars I've seen them eat," Rose said in an oh-so-reasonable tone.

Sara shot her grandmother a look of melting adoration. "See? Nonna doesn't think it would be bad for us."

"We have some more strawberry toaster pastries in the box I brought with us," I said. "I'll go get those. Rose, could I talk to you for just a minute?"

"Uh-oh," my astute daughter said. "Are you in trouble, Nonna? Mommy, you'd better not yell at Nonna Rose."

"I don't 'yell' at anyone, Sara. Why don't you sit at the table and finish your milk while I talk to your grandmother?"

"What about Ben?" Sara wanted to know.

Sure enough, now that Rose had set my son down so that she was free to stand, he'd already toddled toward the nearest unsecured drawer. The kitchen stretched before him…a mecca of cabinets and knobs with zero baby-proofing.

I scooped up my son, jerking my head in the direction of the foyer. "Rose?"

She muttered something under her breath, probably a reminder that patience was a virtue.

Once we were in the hallway outside of the kitchen, I forced myself to smile, even though that expression didn't start occurring naturally until at least 9:00 a.m. "It was very thoughtful of you to bake the cake for everyone, and I'm sure it's delicious. But you kind of usurped my position in there."

Folding her arms across her chest, she frowned, little lines of perplexed confusion appearing above her aristocratic nose.

"I didn't tell Sara she could have the cake. I simply pointed out that most of what they get to eat for breakfast isn't that healthy, anyway. But then, I've never read the nutrition panel on a box of strawberry toaster pastries."

Maybe it was my lingering fatigue confusing me, but had she somehow just found a way to simultaneously condemn me for not feeding them healthy enough food *and* for not letting them have cake for breakfast? Talented.

"I didn't mean to step on your toes, dear," she added, patting my arm. "I forget sometimes how sensitive you are."

I started to voice an instinctive denial, then stopped, struck by how much she reminded me of Tom right then. He had never been comfortable admitting that the two women he loved most and felt so protective of didn't actually get along that well, and he'd insisted on downplaying it. I'd respected how important his mother was to him, but the few times I'd been upset enough to vent to him about her, I hadn't appreciated his telling me I'd probably just misunderstood her or might be overreacting. I hadn't wanted him to intervene, just listen, be supportive. Tom had seen me as the worrier and himself as the comforter, an accurate reflection of our partnership, but during our twenty years together, there had been a few times he'd been more patronizing than reassuring. It was damned annoying.

An uneasy sensation rippled through my stomach, kind of wiggly and nauseating, as if I'd swallowed tadpoles—guilt that I could feel anger toward a man whose ashes I'd scattered. That I could be so petty as to remember those minor irritations after so many wonderful years together.

Life's too short, I reminded myself, vowing to do a better job of shrugging off little things Rose said or did that rubbed me the wrong way. Besides, this was only our first morning living together. No doubt it would get easier with time.

Or one of us would kill the other—our problems living together would be solved either way. It was exactly the kind of warped thinking Tom would have scowled at, but it was enough to make me grin. "Have a nice time at church, Rose."

"I'll say some prayers for you, dear."

Good. I needed all the help I could get.

"I feel like I'm living in Alcatraz." Rose's glare swung from the newly latched kitchen cabinets to the baby gate I'd put up between the kitchen and foyer. "It'll take me forever to figure out how to work the little doohickey that opens it."

"Mommy just steps over the top of the gate," Sara offered helpfully, sitting in the chair next to her grandmother.

"Yes. Well, that gets difficult to do at a certain age. Especially in a skirt," Rose said.

"You could wear jeans," my daughter suggested.

Rose in jeans. Now there was an unlikely occurrence, I thought, rinsing more lettuce leaves at the sink. Although dinner tonight wasn't the height of culinary ambition, I could honestly claim that bacon, lettuce and tomato sandwiches on wheat represented some legitimate food groups.

"The latches are easier than they look," I assured my mother-in-law. In fact, Ben himself would probably get the hang of every safety mechanism I'd installed today before his second birthday. For the moment, however, he was sitting safely on the kitchen floor, playing with Tupperware. In retrospect, it's amusing how much importance anxious mothers place on a baby's mobility milestones:

He isn't crawling yet—shouldn't he be crawling?

Oh, look, Junior just took his first steps, isn't that fabulous?

There was something to be said for the halcyon days when the kid stayed where you put him. Chasing after Ben in the nonchildproofed environment this morning had probably added new gray to my hair. Now at least, I could finish making sandwiches without his pulling out the knife drawer or running into the front parlor to play bull to Rose's china shop.

"You really think those are necessary?" Rose asked, watching me open one of the plastic coverings over the stove knobs.

"With a gas stove? Absolutely." I was an advocate of kitchen safety even when we'd lived in a house of all electric appliances, but Ben could turn one of these dials and conjure actual flame.

"But they didn't have half of this stuff when Tom was a baby," she protested. "It seems to me that if you just kept close watch of your children—"

"I didn't install all of this because I'm *lazy!*" I took a deep breath, tried to make my tone more reasonable. "You're right, keeping an eye on the kids is important, but wouldn't you agree that when it comes to their well-being, better safe than sorry?"

"Of course." Coloring slightly, Rose lowered her gaze, fiddling with the painted wooden napkin holder that sat on the table. "I suppose I was selfishly thinking about my arthritis."

Oh. This was the first I'd heard of it. She carried herself with such powerful presence that it was tough to imagine her suffering any physical weakness. I glanced at the special doorknob coverings you had to squeeze *just so* to open. Definitely not arthritic-friendly.

"I'm sorry, Rose, I didn't realize you had problems with arthritis." I actually knew surprisingly little about her day-to-day life, considering how long Tom and I had been married.

"I don't talk about it much. And there are some days when it doesn't bother me at all." She added the last bit almost defensively, lest anyone think her decrepit.

Whereas I'd begun to feel like a needy whiner for turning so frequently to Dianne or Martin for help, my mother-in-law had the opposite problem. She never asked for help. I remembered how frustrated Tom would get on our visits here, when he saw things that could have been—should have been—taken care of, if she'd just let someone know.

"I have cousins that are occasionally in this area," he'd fumed once. "You'd think one of them could have replaced that step for her, or trimmed the tree that looks like it's going to fall onto the carport."

But Rose was prickly about accepting assistance. I took it as a promising sign that at least she was willing to hire the "hooligan boys" to do some occasional work. Still, it was funny that Tom could criticize a characteristic so prevalent in himself. He'd loved to be the protector, the provider, the Big Strong Man. I was beginning to realize it hadn't been a gender trait so much as a genetic one. He'd been terrible about admitting there was something he didn't know how to do, or that he was feeling under the weather. If I hadn't forced him to go to the doctor...

Would things have been different if I'd been able to get him in for a physical sooner? I knew Dianne would smack me for thinking like that, but it was tough to avoid. I made an on-the-spot promise that if Rose ever needed my help, she'd get it. Whether she wanted it or not. I almost laughed— maybe her full-steam personality was rubbing off on me.

Having dropped the subject of her new prisonlike decor, Rose turned back to the photo album on the table. She'd pulled it out for Sara, to show her pictures of Tom when he'd been our daughter's age.

"Here's one of his birthday," Rose pointed out. "Though he's hard to see underneath all that frosting he got on his face."

"Daddy looks silly!" Sara laughed, then eagerly turned the page.

I was relieved to hear her talk about her father without the brittle pensiveness that had been present just six months ago, as she'd continued to ask me when he was coming back and why he had to leave. Eventually, she'd accepted that he was dead and that he hadn't abandoned us voluntarily; unfortunately, she'd then become preoccupied with wanting assurance that *I* wouldn't die. During those many years Tom and I had struggled to have children, I don't think I'd ever truly understood what a heartbreaking undertaking parenthood could sometimes be. There would be even more questions as the kids grew older, and Lord knew how I would find answers for all of them.

"Mommy, come see this one," Sara said.

I glanced away from the bacon I was probably burning. "Just a minute, honey. Let me get dinner finished."

"This was at a Halloween party," Rose said to Sara. "Do kids still bob for apples? I made the cowboy outfit, except for the hat we bought him at the five-and-dime. I might still have it in the attic. You'd make an adorable cowgirl."

Sara was intrigued by this notion. "I could be a cowgirl for Halloween?"

"Certainly," her grandmother said. "I made your father's costumes until he decided he was too old to dress up. There's still a week left to make you one."

"Mommy, can I change my mind about being a princess?"

It was her costume, after all, and I knew that being in this house was making her feel a lot closer to her dad. Naturally she'd want to bask in that feeling. There would always be future dress-up occasions where we could use her princess fabric.

"Sure, I think a cowgirl is a great idea." I glanced at Rose.

"Are you sure you don't mind making it? I'd be happy to sew, if you'd like to, um, supervise." Considering her recent admission of arthritis, I didn't want her to feel obligated.

But her eyes were bright at the thought of making another Halloween costume for a child. "I'll manage. And she will be adorable."

Of that, I had no doubt.

With all the food now prepared, it only took a few minutes to assemble the sandwiches. I buckled Ben into his booster seat and set plates on the table. Rose moved the photo albums to the safety of the kitchen counter, then Sara said grace for us. Ben insisted on taking his sandwich apart and making a mess, but after observing this mealtime ritual, he did eat. In fact, both children cleaned their plates, with considerably less balking than had been exhibited for the Stroganoff the previous night.

The only person objecting was Rose, who grimaced after a bite of her sandwich. "I miss real bacon."

I'd used a low-fat, low-cholesterol, lower-sodium turkey version. And I had to admit, it *wasn't* the same as what my dad used to wake me up with on Sunday mornings, the smell and sizzle of real bacon filling our small house. "I know what you mean, but this is healthier."

She nodded, her gaze wry as it met mine. "I guess we all have to get used to change, don't we?"

Sara stopped suddenly, which jerked me to a halt since she was clutching my hand. "What if no one likes me?" Her dark eyes reflected the same panic evident in her grasp.

I caught my balance on the elementary school steps. "They'll love you. Don't worry, making new friends can be a lot of fun." In theory.

After growing up in a Georgia town where I'd been with the same kids from kindergarten to my senior year, my first year of college had been terrifying. That had changed when I'd miraculously caught Tom Smith's eye, and he'd taken me under his wing...or hunky broad shoulders, in his case.

Kneeling down, I cupped Sara's chin. "You are smart and funny, and the kids here are lucky to meet you. I know it will be tough at first, but you can do it. If it makes you feel better, this will be Mommy's first day, too, meeting new people at work. We can compare notes tonight over pizza."

She twisted her lips to the side, pondering. "I thought Nonna said we were having eggplant for dinner?"

True, but good luck getting the kids to eat it. Besides, life with children often meant flexibility.

"I'll call Nonna, don't worry."

"Okay." With a deep breath, she turned back toward the large building, squaring her orange backpack on her shoulders. She was dwarfed by the flagpole at the top of stairs. Above us, the stars and stripes fluttered in a chilly breeze that made it clear we weren't in Miami anymore.

No one else was out and about in front of the school. Principal Reeves, a lovely woman I'd spoken to on the phone, had suggested I bring Sara in a little late on her first day since a tour would be less daunting if there weren't a few hundred kids in the hallways with us, hurrying to their classrooms.

I held open the front door. "You ready, pumpkin?"

She nodded and my heart squeezed at the look of brave determination on her face.

We walked past some colorful wall murals and a janitor's closet before reaching the administration offices at the front of the building. A long black counter ran the length of the main office, and most employees were busy with computers or phone calls on the other side. Just inside the doorway, a receptionist with curly red hair sat at a welcome desk.

She beamed at us. "Charlotte and Sara Smith? Principal Reeves is expecting you. Go right on in."

Following the direction she pointed, we went through a narrow hall, passing a room where a school nurse filled an ice pack for a sniffling boy. At the end of the hallway, I found an office that read Elizabeth Reeves on the nameplate. An attractive black woman with close-cropped hair stood immediately. She was so tall she probably terrified troublemakers who were sent to see her. But the smile she offered us was warm and reassuring.

"Welcome to Hughes Elementary. I'm Principal Reeves. And you must be Sara?"

My daughter nodded, her expression solemn.

"It's nice to meet you. I think you're going to like it here. You're in Mrs. Zimmerman's first-grade class, and she's one of our best teachers. I'll take you to meet her in a few minutes, okay?"

"Okay."

I shook hands with the other woman across the desk. "I'm Charlie Smith. I've really appreciated your answering all my questions over the phone."

"It's my job. Only part I like better than interacting with the students is getting to know their parents and helping them become involved with the school."

I grinned at the subtly stressed "involved." Not five minutes into our first meeting and she was already laying the groundwork for encouraging participation in bake sales and library volunteering. In Sara's pre-K class, I'd been the room mother, but after the baby and Tom's death... Well, it had been a while since I'd been part of the PTA phone tree.

She focused on Sara again. "I understand from your Miami school that you're quite a reader. Would you like to see our library?" From then on, she had Sara eating out of the palm of her hand.

We toured the library, designated by the doorplate as the Media Center, then went by the cafeteria, where rows of folding tables were spread out before a stage that was hidden behind a thick navy curtain; the music room, where we listened as the teacher practiced scales with a third-grade glass; and the playground, where Sara was dazzled by the number of swings available. I was equally impressed, though I was responding to different criteria than the number of swings.

The school was older than the one Sara had attended in

Florida, but Hughes Elementary was modern enough that everything looked to be in good shape. There were no "portables" on the grounds, which were common in schools where the student population was outgrowing the facilities, and the curriculum was impressively well-rounded. In some districts, there was no emphasis on music, drama or sports until kids reached middle school. Hughes seemed to have everything I would have wanted for Sara, including a beaming, round-faced librarian who said she was always happy to meet eager new readers.

We made our way to Sara's new classroom, where Principal Reeves interrupted just long enough to introduce us to Mrs. Zimmerman, a soft-spoken woman with an intelligent gaze. Her brightly colored sweater set and floral-print skirt made her look cheerful and approachable. She shook hands with me in the hallway, told us to call her "Mrs. Z." and led Sara inside. I hovered for just a second, watching through the glass in the door as Sara was assigned a seat next to a blond girl with long braids. I suppose I should have been paying more attention to the room my little girl would be spending each day in, checking to see if there was a computer station or class pet, but all I cared about was watching to see if that blond girl would smile at Sara. When she did, I exhaled a breath I hadn't realized I was holding and walked with Principal Reeves back to the front of the school.

"She'll do great here," the taller woman said reassuringly.

"Her Miami teacher wrote that she's a smart, sociable pupil, and we have excellent people here."

I nodded. "I'm impressed with what I've seen. It's just that it's been…difficult for her." Tom's death was also noted in Sara's file.

"For all of you, I would imagine." The principal's gaze was sympathetic, but refreshingly free of the pity and curiosity I'd seen in faces of people who had known Tom and me as a couple.

Recalling how the other mothers had suddenly looked at me, I thought it was no wonder I'd stopped going to those bake sales. The questions hadn't been fun, but even when no one had asked, the glances had been hard to take. Here, no one knew me as poor widowed Charlie Smith. No one knew me at all. For all that starting over was intimidating, I suddenly felt relieved and excited. Liberated.

"I'm sure you'll have your hands full," Elizabeth Reeves continued, "moving here and starting a new job, but please consider one of our many opportunities to get involved as a parent. It will help you get to know some people in the community and might ease Sara's transition, as well. We do two school plays each semester. One fall play is for our first through third students, the other for our older grades. The main parts were cast last week, but if she's interested, we can find Sara a job in the chorus or as an understudy. And I know Ms. Cramer, our drama teacher, is still rounding up parent volunteers. Can I give her your number?"

When she'd said "many opportunities," I had nodded along, not expecting anything so sudden or direct. Her request caught me off guard, and the part of me that was most comfortable retreating tried to eke out a quick no. I silenced it. After all, I did want to make this change easier for Sara if I could. And I'd loved drama in high school. While I'd never actually been *in* one of the plays—standing in front of all those people, the heat of the spotlight on me? No, thank you—I'd worked on set design a lot and had stage-managed our lowly rendition of *Pippin*. It had been one of the less popular productions in our small rural school, but you couldn't blame the drama teacher for trying. In the early years of our marriage, I'd managed to drag Tom to some theater shows, but that had never really been his thing.

"Yes," I heard myself say. "You can give Ms. Cramer my number, and if Sara wants to be part of the play, I'll find a way to fit volunteering in around work." They'd love me at the new job. *Shows up for her first day a couple of hours late, immediately asks for flexibility to help with an elementary school play…* Yeah, I'd be Miss Popularity.

These were my thoughts as I drove the fifteen minutes north to the office park where Kazka was located. It wasn't a trendy new complex with shiny awnings and modern sculptures out front. The bulk of the "park" was a nondescript six-story building that had once been a parking garage, converted in recent years to create office space. Next to the structure was a large warehouse with a trailerlike addition on the front. This was where I would be working. The area was clean, though, and located in a part of town being revitalized by productive renovation. Young Princeton elms had been planted, and their yellow leaves added a splash of color to the parking lot.

After locking my car, I crossed the asphalt toward the front of the warehouse, which was probably full of pharmaceutical and drugstore supplies. Kazka contracted with clients who were too small to qualify for the bulk discounts from manufacturers, such as those the national chain stores received; instead, Kazka paid for huge quantities of everything from antihistamine to shampoo, then divvied up the pallets into smaller orders for our customers. We saved them a few bucks and made a few in the process. At least, that was the corporate plan. In the Southeast, we hadn't kept enough customers wanting the same products to make the procedure cost-effective, losing money on the wholesale purchases and eventually closing shop.

But our northern hubs were doing much better, I reminded myself as I approached the door. Maybe it was the chillier weather—higher demand for tissues and cold medicines and cough drops. Martin Kimble had assured me that job security here was high, that growth had even reached a point where they had added a new position to the sales team.

The in-office sales coordinator had become a rep, but I didn't think that particular forward mobility would appeal to me. Sales reps worked long days and traveled frequently within their respective territories—making it kind of hard to rush back if your kid's school called—and a commission-based income wasn't reliable. But I was glad that the last co-ordinator's ambitions had leaned that way, leaving the position free for me.

Though not posh, the front office was warm and tidy. Two desks sat in the open space, facing each other, and the area was livened up by an ornate coatrack, a few potted plants and numerous vendor posters—one explaining why so-and-so's digital thermometer was the best on the market, another showing an illustrated flower that was ten times bigger than the woman sketched beneath it. I was pretty sure it was an ad for allergy medicine, but it passed muster as artwork, in a surreal *Alice in Wonderland* kind of way.

A woman wearing a phone headset over her bleached-blond hair glanced up from one of the desks with a welcoming smile. Her face was characterized by attractive laugh lines that suggested she smiled often. "May I help you?"

"I'm Charlie. Um, Charlotte Smith," I clarified, shrugging out of my jacket. "I'm supposed—"

"You made it!" She shot to her feet and extended her hand. "Wicked glad to meet you. I'm Jess Gillespie, accounts receivable and your phone backup. The general public has little reason to call, so we don't have a receptionist, really, just you. And me, when it gets so busy you need some help catching the lines. It's an easy enough job for two, but now that Claudia's advanced and it's just me up here, the books are sliding into disrepair. Plus, I've been dying for someone to talk to during the day!"

I grinned, unused to anyone but my kids being this happy to see me. "Nice to meet you, too, Jess. And I'm sure once I figure out what's what around here, you'll be able to get back to your accounting."

"Hold on, doll, gotta let the boss know you're here." She leaned forward to press a button on her phone, then spoke into the mouthpiece on her headset. "Don't mean to interrupt, but Charlotte Smith has arrived."

I assumed she was speaking to Frank Carroll, the sales manager. Once he'd finished whatever he had to say, she agreed, then pressed the button again and slid off her headset.

She pointed to the desk opposite hers. "That one's yours, if you'd like to leave your jacket or lock your purse in the bottom drawer or anything. Frank is finishing up a meeting with Claudia right now and wants me to bring you back in a few. Since Claudia's the newest member of the sales team, she still comes into the office on a semi-regular basis to check in with him. The other reps only come through periodically, except for the monthly sales meeting.

"You're replacing Claudia, so Frank asked her to make herself available if you need any training over the next week or two. But I can probably answer most of your questions."

"Thanks."

My amiable new co-worker walked around her desk, professional but comfortable in a pair of twill pants and a cowl-necked sweater that made me feel overdressed in the matching skirt and jacket I'd always called my "interview suit." Oh, well. Better to be overdressed on the first day than under.

"Want a quick tour?" Jess offered. "You'll need a security pass for the warehouse, which is out back. Other than that, we have Frank's office, a conference room, the bathroom and the break room. We've got a couple of vending machines, and I'll show you which one's the worst for stealing money. On Fridays, Frank or Luke usually bring in doughnuts."

"Who's Luke?"

"Luke James, warehouse manager. Nice guy, wicked funny. We had a temp once who didn't know what to make of him because she took him too seriously, but most of the time, he's kidding around. Over here is the supply closet, with your basic assortment of notepads, pens, elastics and paper clips. I'm the closest thing we have to an office manager. I make supply runs when necessary, so let me know if there's anything you need."

"Got it, thanks."

Jess was certainly as friendly as any office companion I could hope for. The same couldn't exactly be said for Claudia Campbell, whom I met a few minutes later.

My first impression of Claudia, when she stood in Frank's office, towering over me in high heels I could never pull off, was that she was gorgeous. But it wasn't a girl-next-door, American-sweetheart kind of beauty. It was sharp-edged and intimidating. Her features were striking, her blue eyes glacial, and her shiny, thick brown-black hair was the stuff of high-dollar shampoo commercials. She was wearing a tailored red jacket and short black skirt that made me feel frumpy in the navy coordinates I'd grabbed off the sales rack at the mall and had convinced myself fit well enough. I gauged her to be in her late twenties, although it was difficult to tell.

"So you're the person they hired for my old job," she said. "I'm Claudia Campbell."

"Charlotte Smith. Everyone calls me Charlie," I added, even though the familiar shortened version didn't help my sudden frump-awareness.

Portly Frank was more personable. "Welcome aboard, Charlie. It's a pleasure to meet you." He pronounced it "pleasha," his accent even stronger than Jess's or my mother-in-law's. "Martin speaks so highly of you, I'm sure you'll be an asset to the team. Claudia and I were just discussing that."

She smiled thinly. Or bared her teeth at me.

Having dutifully shown me to Frank's midsize office, Jess returned to the front, leaving me alone with my two new acquaintances. Frank gave me a standard first-day welcome speech, invited me to approach him with any questions, and assured me that they tried to be flexible with hours and that as long as I put in my forty, they would work with me on days I needed to come in late or leave early.

"Yes," Claudia put in sweetly. "We understand that it's hard to keep reliable hours when you have little ones."

So no point in asking if she was a mother herself, I gathered.

Since all of Kazka's human-resource paperwork, such as health insurance, was run through the Chicago headquarters, I was already on file and only needed to fill out a few new forms. Then, Frank gave me over to Claudia's care.

"You'll learn a lot from her, Charlie. She's a dynamo, this one." His praise drew the first real smile I'd seen from the former sales coordinator. "She'll get you up to speed on all the specifics, and you'll have her cell-phone number if you ever have a question Jess or I can't answer."

Claudia didn't comment on this until we'd left Frank's office. She steered me toward the break room, saying that she wanted a cup of coffee. "If you're as good as Martin says, I'm sure you'll get along fine without beeping and interrupting *my* work every ten minutes."

Her words and tone reminded me of when I'd first met Rose, the way she'd had of sounding condescending and critical without saying anything outright I felt I could protest. Mostly, I'd put up with it because I'd never known exactly what to say in return and didn't want to upset Tom. *Screw that.* I squared my shoulders. The girl who had once trembled in her sandals in the face of Tom's mother was now a forty-year-old woman. I'd been through far more in the last year than a snide sales rep could dish out, gorgeous hair or not.

"Is there a particular reason you dislike me, Claudia?"

Her eyes widened, but she recovered her composure almost

instantaneously. "I applaud forthrightness in a person. All right. I don't dislike you, but let's be clear that just because I graduated from your position to a regional rep doesn't mean there's currently room on the sales team for another move like mine. And I certainly have no intentions of creating a vacancy."

I almost laughed, wondering what in heaven's name Martin had said about me that this woman would feel threatened. But I knew that the sales force could be extremely competitive within its own ranks. There were quotas, competitions, rewards for those who outsold their peers...and if the company took a downturn, those not pulling their share were thinned from the herd. Maybe as the newest salesperson, Claudia used her attitude to hide vulnerability.

"Don't worry," I assured her dryly. "I'm not after your job."

I saw the telltale sag of her shoulders, as she almost let herself show relief before bristling again. "Not that it would matter if you were," she was quick to add. "I'm quite good."

And so modest, too.

When she turned to lead the way back up front, I lagged behind for a second. Partly to process my new environment, partly because I didn't want to trail after her like some flunky. She was headed out of the room just as a slender man with a loosened tie appeared in the doorway. I didn't hear whether or not she murmured a polite "excuse me" as she swept by, but I wouldn't have bet money on it.

The man had a cheerfully rumpled appearance, from his wrinkled blue shirt to his red-gold hair. "You must be the new blood we've been expecting. I'm Luke James. And you've obviously met Claud. Don't worry, she's not really so bad. Of course, no one ever believes me when I say that."

"Maybe it's the overwhelming lack of empirical evidence," I muttered before censoring myself. *Oops*. I hadn't intended to make a grouchy, sarcastic first impression.

But Luke laughed. "I think you're gonna fit right in."

CHAPTER 7

I had just managed to transfer another call without disconnecting it—there'd been a few mishaps earlier with the unfamiliar phone system—when Jess looked up from her computer.

"So what are you doing for lunch, doll?"

Her words made me realize it was after noon, and that, while not exactly starving, I could definitely eat. "I brown-bagged a tuna-fish sandwich." It hadn't taken much effort to make an additional sack lunch for myself when I'd put together Sara's that morning.

My co-worker crinkled her nose. "I hate to think of you sitting here alone on your first day! I'm sure Frank would spring for a coupla spuckies and tonics, but he's headed for the airport in an hour for a meeting in Chicago tomorrow."

"You already have plans?"

"Yup, scheduled an appointment weeks ago." She patted her bobbed hair. "If I miss it, you're gonna start to see roots soon. And Claudia's already headed out. I know she can be a bit high-strung, but I think it's mostly stress. She's planning a Christmas wedding, and between that and wanting to prove herself, she can get tough to take some days. But it's probably temporary."

"Thanks, I'll keep that in mind."

Jess opened the metal drawer of the file cabinet, putting manila folders back in alphabetical order. "You should go to lunch with Luke."

"Who should do what?" a male voice asked as Luke James rounded the corner that led from our office space to the hallway. "I heard my name."

"I was in the middle of telling Charlie all your sordid secrets," Jess said dryly.

He flashed a grin in my direction. "Ignore her, the feds were never able to prove any of that."

"And he wonders why that poor temp didn't know what to make of him," Jess muttered under her breath. "Seriously, I was telling Charlie she should have lunch with you."

"I'm in if she is," he said. When I nodded, he turned to Jess. "You joining us? Two lovely lunch companions, and I'll be the envy of every guy in the place."

"Sorry, can't. But Jerry wants to know if we're still on for Thursday. My husband wants a chance to recoup his losses. We play poker about twice a month," she explained for my benefit. "But Luke cheats."

"I do no such thing! I'm simply a superior player."

"You get me laughing so hard I can't concentrate, and that's like cheating. No dead-parrot jokes next time," Jess insisted.

Making no promises, he smiled at me. "You play, Charlie?"

"Poker? Um, no, not really."

"Oh." He arched an eyebrow. "In that case, you should *definitely* join us."

The invitation, their casual acceptance of me, was heartwarming. And unexpected. It had been so long since I'd felt like I fit in anywhere, even among people I'd known since before Tom had died. *Because* they were people I'd known since before Tom had died.

Although I'd assured Sara this morning that she'd make plenty of friends, I'd had an anxious moment or two myself of "What if no one likes me?" Starting over was terrifying, but things such as Luke's joking were making the transition easier. I knew it wasn't personal; he kidded equally with Jess and temps who apparently had no sense of humor. Still, Dianne aside, most of my acquaintances in Florida had acted as if they'd had to tiptoe around me. God forbid someone say something silly and fun to the grieving widow.

"I appreciate the offer," I told them. In fact, if they knew how much it meant to me, they'd probably think I was nuts. "But I might have to pass. Even though Rose has been gracious enough to keep Ben during the day, she has bridge club and several women's organizations that meet in the evenings. I—"

"Rose is Charlie's mother-in-law," Jess informed Luke. "They live together."

At her prodding, I'd already given Jess a study-notes version of my life story, complete with pictures of the kids. Her smile had turned bittersweet as she'd told me she hadn't even met Jerry until her mid-thirties; once married, she hadn't been able to get pregnant and after a few years had decided maybe it was best not to try.

"You live with your mother-in-law? Ouch." Luke shuddered.

"Oh, you've never even had a mother-in-law," Jess pointed out.

"My sisters do," he countered. "So I've heard plenty of stories."

I laughed. "Rose…isn't so bad." Whatever else could be said, she doted on my kids and was saving me a ton in child care. "You're sure you don't mind my tagging along with you to lunch?"

"On the contrary, I consider it my good fortune that you don't know anyone yet and your options were so limited today. You all set?"

Grabbing my purse, I nodded and followed him outside. Luke opened the passenger side door to his compact car in an old-fashioned gesture that made me wistful. When was the last time a man had opened anything for me, whether it was a door or a jar of pickles? Standing close to him, I was surprised to realize he wasn't as tall as I'd first thought. His slender build added an optical illusion of height, but he was only taller than I was by a couple of inches. What was most noticeable about his appearance were his almost constant grin and the gleam in his hazel eyes.

"You have any strong food preferences?" he asked as we drove out of the parking lot. "There's a deli near here that I can highly recommend, and a pizza joint—"

"Pizza!" I bit my lip, recalling my earlier promise to Sara. "Do you mind if I make a quick call on my cell phone?"

"Don't tell me, just remembered you had a better lunch offer?"

"Not exactly. I remembered that I forgot to change my dinner plans." I was already dialing numbers on the phone I'd pulled out of my purse.

"Hello?" My mother-in-law answered her phone with terse graciousness, the kind of warmth able to cool quickly if the person on the other end of the line tried to sell her something.

"Hi, it's Charlie."

"Oh, good! I've been waiting to hear from you to make sure Sara got settled in all right. Does she like the school?"

"From what I can tell," I said, feeling guilty that I hadn't called sooner. I'd tried so hard to embrace a single-parent mindset that I'd now failed to take into account that there was someone else at home every bit as anxious about the kids' well-being. "Her teacher seemed great, and the principal is already trying to draft me to help with the school play. But Sara and I kind of made an agreement, something she wanted to do to celebrate her surviving the first day at a new place." *Something* she *wanted to do?* As I recalled, the pizza had been my idea. So much for my whole "I am forty, hear me roar" confidence earlier. "Would it be all right with you if we changed tonight's plans and ordered a pizza?"

"Pizza! Honestly, the girl can't eat that seven nights a week," Rose grumbled.

"Very true. But maybe we could make an exception for tonight?"

"Is this because I was making eggplant?" she asked stiffly. "You've never really liked it, have you?"

No, but she kept making it anyway. If I'd been smart, I would've claimed an eggplant allergy instead of politely finishing my dinner on that first visit. I wondered if I could claim it as a late development?

"It was always one of Tom's favorites," Rose said, sounding nostalgic.

I blinked, startled at how well he'd kept this one secret. He'd hated eggplant, but obviously he hadn't wanted to hurt his mother's feelings.

What clandestine knowledge might Ben and his future wife keep from me?

The thought made me want to rush home, hug my baby and tell him he wasn't allowed to date until he was fifty. "We can have the eggplant tomorrow, if you like."

"No, no, tomorrow's *your* night. I can't go off schedule now! I've made plans with women from church to work on Thanksgiving baskets for the needy later this week, and I based my availability specifically on the chart."

"Okay. Then let's do pizza for Sara tonight, and I'll worry about tomorrow." After that, I asked if I could talk to Ben, but she told me he was napping, and we hung up shortly thereafter.

Luke cast a sidelong glance at me. "Not to be an eavesdropper, but if you're having pizza for dinner, how does the deli sound?"

"Great." I dropped the phone back in my purse.

"So…Sara is your daughter?"

I nodded. "She's in first grade, and her brother, Ben, will be two this summer. Be glad you asked in the car, when I can't shove my wallet pictures under your nose and demand you tell me how cute they are."

"I'd love to see pictures later. All kids are cute in their own way."

"You like children?"

He nodded. "I'm the proud uncle of five, but, shockingly, I haven't yet found a woman who's eager to settle down and procreate with me."

I chuckled. "Can't imagine that, especially if you're using romantic phrases like 'procreate.'"

"Yeah, go figure."

Joking with Luke came naturally. His wry cheer was contagious, and, not only was he easy to be around, he reminded me of two guys I'd worked for part-time after getting my associate's degree. They'd been software geniuses who'd shared a small partnership in Miami, but they'd been disorganized geniuses who'd needed me to tell them where various files were and remind them about appointments, along with answering the phone. While I'd worked there, they'd managed to get me hooked on various forms of British humor, and I'd missed them when they'd eventually moved their growing company to Seattle.

One of Tom's co-workers back in those days had asked teasingly over dinner if Tom wasn't nervous about his beautiful young wife spending all day alone with two men. Though a somewhat possessive man by nature, Tom shook his head, dropping his arm around me. "You wouldn't be jealous, either, if you knew the men."

Even though I'd never wanted Tom to be jealous—had in fact gone out of my way to make my adoration clear—his remark had bothered me. Don't know why, really. But I remember thinking that even if Bruce and Larry hadn't been built like studly young football players, they at least understood why I could find surreal comedy about the Spanish Inquisition hilarious. And when I'd been upset about something, they hadn't just told me everything would be okay; they'd either listened or they'd cheered me up with outrageous plans of unlikely revenge.

Luke kept me laughing, too. During our lunch of subs, chips and really bitter pickle spears, he gave me a rundown of the people I'd yet to meet at Kazka—sales reps in the field, men who worked for him in the warehouse. For most of the names he threw at me, which I had no hope of remembering without faces to attach to them, he did humorous impressions. His most endearing quality was how he could make fun of something or someone without ever seeming mean-spirited about it. Maybe because he was so quick to make fun of himself, too.

As someone who'd grappled with depression, I was drawn to his quick smiles and his ability to evoke them in others. When we stood to leave, I realized my cheeks actually hurt from laughing so much.

Without thinking, I squeezed his hand. "Lunch has been wonderful."

His surprised gaze dropped to our hands, then lifted to my face.

I jerked my hand back. Despite his friendly manner, he was still someone I'd only met a few hours ago, and physical familiarity with near strangers might not be welcome.

"Sorry." I punctuated the retreat with a few shuffle steps away from him.

"Don't worry about it."

But I did. After years of being a housewife, I'd had a few awkward moments trying to reacclimate myself to the business world. During my post-baby return interview with Kazka, I'd been horrified to look down and realize one of the nursing pads in my bra had shifted, creating the appearance of a mutant third boob. I doubted that kind of thing happened to polished young women like Claudia with their well-tailored suits and company cars. Though I assured myself that I could be as valuable to the company as a younger, more educated woman, holding hands with the warehouse manager wasn't the way to prove it.

"I just…didn't mean to be inappropriate."

Something unreadable flashed in his eyes, replaced with glints of amusement. "Well, don't let it happen again. I feel violated, you know. You saw her harassing me, didn't you?" He addressed the question to imaginary bystanders.

His exaggerated comical response helped dispel my tension and the knot in my stomach. As we walked to the car, I told him, "You remind me of someone. Well, two someones, actually."

"I get that a lot. Let me help you place it—a cross between Johnny Depp and Pierce Brosnan."

"Not exactly."

"You sure? Look closer, lass, I wager you'll be seein' something of Captain Jack Sparrow," he mimicked.

I grinned, shaking my head. "How did you get so good at doing impressions?"

"Practice. Being considered a nerd in high school, it helped to make others laugh. Kept some of the guys from bullying me and encouraged pretty girls to sit near me. Most of them still said no when I asked them to the prom, of course, but they liked me. Since I spent all my time acting up anyway, my teachers encouraged me to be useful to our drama department."

His nonchalant tone made it clear that he wasn't worried about the teenager he'd once been, but the thought of feeling like an outsider struck a chord with me. What would my college experience have been like if popular, confident Tom hadn't shown interest in me?

"I tried the drama thing myself," I said. "Wasn't very good at it, though."

"Well, you tried, and that's what counts. To be honest, most of my impersonations of people at work aren't really that good. They're only impressive because you haven't actually *met* the guys in the warehouse. Come by this afternoon if you have time, and I'll introduce you. I need to make your security badge anyway."

Because a few of the medicines we supplied to drugstores were strong enough to be prescription and because the public was apparently finding new and ever more bizarrely dangerous uses for over-the-counter meds, no one went into the supply warehouse without an authorized Kazka picture ID.

"Thanks, I'd appreciate meeting everyone."

"No problem. I'd offer to introduce you to people outside work, too, but a lot of my acquaintances are limited to venues like local theater, historical reenactments and the occasional gaming convention. Maybe I didn't entirely outgrow the whole nerd thing."

Despite his self-deprecating jokes, I left work that afternoon knowing that I'd made my first real friends in Boston.

My daughter, however, apparently harbored less warm and fuzzy feelings about her day. She met me on the front porch that night, arms akimbo, mouth twisted into a scowl. I'd no sooner shut my driver's door behind me than she announced, "I want to go home! Not this home, our real one."

Ah, the one I would own into old age if someone didn't show an interest in buying it.

Behind Sara's defiant expression, her eyes shimmered with repressed tears. I wanted to pull her into a hug, but the flat cardboard pizza box prevented that. Rose had told me that the only pizza you could get by delivery in this neighborhood wasn't worth eating, and she'd called in an order for me to pick up on my way home.

Instead of the hug, I settled for empathizing. "You didn't have a good day, pumpkin?"

"Math was hard. And they talk funny. The music teacher called the water fountain a 'bubbler.' And I don't want to be in the stupid play!"

So much for the plan to help her dive right in at Hughes Elementary. "You'll get used to the way your music teacher talks. And if it makes you feel better, Mommy always had trouble with math, too." Principal Reeves had warned me that Sara's class here had a slightly more advanced curriculum than her school in Miami.

My daughter was unappeased. "What about the stupid play? Do I have to be in it?"

Rose appeared in the doorway behind my daughter. "I

We'd like to send you two free books to introduce you to our brand-new series – Harlequin® NEXT™! These novels by acclaimed, award-winning authors are filled with stories about rediscovery and reconnection with what's important in women's lives. These are relationship novels about women redefining their dreams.

THERE'S THE LIFE YOU PLANNED. AND THERE'S WHAT COMES NEXT.

Your two books have a combined cover price of $11.00 in the U.S. and $13.00 in Canada, but are yours **FREE!** We'll even send you a wonderful surprise gift. You can't lose!

FREE BONUS GIFT!

We'll send you a wonderful surprise gift, absolutely FREE, just for giving Harlequin NEXT books a try! Don't miss out —
MAIL THE REPLY CARD TODAY!

Order online at
www.TryNextNovels.com

THE EDITOR'S "THANK YOU" FREE GIFTS INCLUDE:

▶ Two BRAND-NEW Harlequin® Next™ Novels

▶ An exciting surprise gift

YES! I have placed my Editor's "thank you" Free Gifts seal in the space provided at right. Please send me 2 FREE books, and my FREE Mystery Gift. I understand that I am under no obligation to purchase anything further, as explained on the back and opposite page.

EDITOR'S FREE GIFT SEAL THANK YOU

◀ DETACH AND MAIL CARD TODAY! ▶

356 HDL D7VL   156 HDL D7VK

FIRST NAME	LAST NAME

ADDRESS

APT.#	CITY

STATE/PROV.	ZIP/POSTAL CODE

Thank You!

(H-NXT-09/05)

Offer limited to one per household and not valid to current subscribers of Harlequin NEXT. All orders subject to approval. Credit or debit balances in a customer's account(s) may be offset by any other outstanding balance owed by or to the customer. ® and ™ are trademarks owned and used by the trademark owner and/or its licensee. © 2005 Harlequin Enterprises Ltd.

The Reader Service — Here's How It Works:

Accepting your 2 free books and gift places you under no obligation to buy anything. You may keep the books and gift and return the shipping statement marked "cancel." If you do not cancel, about a month later we'll send you 3 additional books and bill you just $3.99 each in the U.S., or $4.74 each in Canada, plus 25¢ shipping & handling per book and applicable taxes if any.* That's the complete price and — compared to cover prices of $5.50 each in the U.S. and $6.50 each in Canada — it's quite a bargain! You may cancel at any time, but if you choose to continue, every month we'll send you 3 more books, which you may either purchase at the discount price or return to us and cancel your subscription.

*Terms and prices subject to change without notice. Sales tax applicable in N.Y. Canadian residents will be charged applicable provincial taxes and GST.

If offer card is missing write to: The Reader Service, 3010 Walden Ave., P.O. Box 1867, Buffalo, NY 14240-1867

BUSINESS REPLY MAIL

FIRST-CLASS MAIL   PERMIT NO. 717-003   BUFFALO, NY

POSTAGE WILL BE PAID BY ADDRESSEE

THE READER SERVICE
3010 WALDEN AVE
PO BOX 1867
BUFFALO NY 14240-9952

NO POSTAGE
NECESSARY
IF MAILED
IN THE
UNITED STATES

asked her not to say stupid. There are more constructive ways to express her feelings."

Probably true. But I'd heard kids not much older than Sara using far more obscene words to express themselves, and considering some of my own slips of the tongue, I was just glad she wasn't saying anything worse.

Ben and Gretchen were both in the foyer, Ben babbling in excitement and ducking the shepherd's enthusiastically wagging tail. Somehow I got dinner to the kitchen without tripping over anyone and sat in a chair to hug both my children.

As we ate, Rose and I managed to coax from Sara some more positive anecdotes. Mrs. Z. was a cool teacher with a collection of books the children were allowed to choose from and take home; there was a pet hamster that Sara had been chosen to feed before school let out. Ginny Trumble, the blond girl who sat next to Sara, was really nice and had shared her brownie at lunch.

"So it wasn't all bad?" I asked. "Because I was afraid we'd have to pack up the van and drive back to Florida tonight! And then you wouldn't get to play on all those swings tomorrow at recess. Or sit next to Ginny at lunch."

"Or help me finish your cowgirl costume," Rose interjected.

I shot my mother-in-law a grateful smile. The reminder that they had a fitting tonight put Sara in much better spirits, and after dinner the two of them disappeared into Rose's room while Ben and I straightened up the kitchen. Well, I straightened. Ben spun in circles, "singing" to himself, then laughing like a hyena when he got so dizzy he fell. And to think of the wads of cash parents wasted on retail toys.

Sara hadn't completely forgotten her apprehension over the play, however. We went through our normal bedtime routine of saying prayers and reading one final story, but she interrupted me during the princess's big rescue.

"Mommy," she said drowsily, "I don't hafta be in the play, do I?"

At least she hadn't called it the stupid play. That was improvement.

During the spring semester of my freshman year in college, I'd signed up for a drama elective, remembering how much I'd loved the productions in high school. But I'd frozen with stage fright during one of the class acting exercises. Tom had said he would support my decision if I dropped the class. "So what if you're not onstage in front of huge audiences? You're rapidly becoming the star of *my* life." No guy had ever said anything like that to me. Possibly because the young men in my small Georgia town hadn't been smooth enough with a line, possibly because they were afraid of my protective father. Whatever the case, I'd melted into a little puddle, staring into Tom's warm chocolate eyes and feeling like the luckiest girl in the world.

But while it had been sweet of him, it hadn't stopped me from looking back with regret. While I didn't for a second believe I would ever have had a career on stage or screen, that wasn't the point. I regretted giving up on myself so easily.

I pressed a kiss to my daughter's forehead. "You don't have to be *in* the play, Sara-bear, but you have to go to a rehearsal. Just one. If you don't like it, we'll tell Ms. Cramer you aren't interested, and they can do the chorus without you."

"But I won't like it," she insisted.

"Maybe, maybe not. But I want you to try."

She scrunched up her nose. "Like asparagus?"

"Kind of."

It had always been my policy that my kids didn't need to clean their plates, but they had to try a bite of everything on it. I obviously didn't instill the kind of awe that caused them to pretend to like a food just for my sake. Then again, I appreciated that Sara was honest with me about how she felt.

"Do we have a deal?" I prompted.

With a solemn nod, she agreed to her end of the bargain, and we returned to our story of the princess, who was rescued in short order and commenced her happily-ever-after. *Good luck with that*, I thought. Ever-afters had a way of turning out differently than one expected.

Late Wednesday afternoon, Sara and I congregated in the cafeteria of Hughes Elementary with other adults and what seemed like hundreds of students but was probably only the same twenty rushing back and forth, carrying on energetic conversations. The children were having their first rehearsal, and Ms. Cramer had followed through on Principal Reeves's suggestion to call me. Reporting for volunteer duty, I took a seat with other parents at the one long lunch table that hadn't been folded and pushed to the back of the room.

I sent an encouraging wave toward Sara, where she stood among a dozen other children by Ms. Cramer's piano, down in front of the stage.

A stylishly coiffed woman with a short shag of chestnut hair walked into my line of vision, making a beeline for me. Her clothes were so hyper color-coordinated—with her blouse, cardigan, capris and pumps all *exactly* the same shade—that I was a little surprised her clipboard wasn't periwinkle, too.

"You must be Charlie Smith!" Her southern twang really stood out among the Boston accents I'd been adjusting to all week, much thicker than my own Georgia drawl, which had lessened during my years in Florida. I guessed her to be a native of Mississippi. "Why, I'm just delighted to meet you! I'm Shannon McCorkle, vice president of this year's Parent-Teachers' Association—I hope we'll be seeing you at meetings!"

It became clear in the next fifteen minutes that Shannon McCorkle was one of those people who spoke with frequent exclamation points. Everything "delighted" her, and she did a lot of heart blessing—most of it sounding genuine instead of the disclaimer for snarky comments I remembered from my own childhood. ("That Delia Clarke hasn't got the sense God gave a june bug, bless her heart!") Shannon was so upbeat and organized, corralling the parent volunteers with enthusiasm and praise for our meager talents, that it was easy to picture her as a teacher here, with her own classroom of kindergartners. But someone, maybe Shannon herself, mentioned to me that she was a stay-at-home mother, a long-held dream she was able to follow thanks to her husband's financial success.

If Tom had come through that angioplasty, cardiovascular health restored, and I hadn't gone back to work full-time, would I have become Shannon, only less dyed-to-match? Not everyone could carry off the monochrome look.

As a young bride, I'd dreamed of raising healthy, happy children with my husband and creating a beautiful home for all of us. Now the dream was over. I lived in someone else's home. Far from the mom who was there every day when her kids got off the school bus, the mom who had time to sew. I'd become the mother who worked and worried about office politics and layoffs. I longed not for matching furniture and homemade accents but a stained, saggy sofa that was such a comfort at the end of a long day. Not that it made any financial sense to transport the eyesore when Rose had a fully furnished living room, but somehow her tapestry-upholstered divan didn't have the same restorative properties.

"Charlie? You still with us, sweetie?"

I blinked, realizing our periwinkle-clad leader had asked me a question.

"Are you a better hand with a needle or hammer? We can still use some help with costumes, and it's always nice to have a few moms working on sets. Men always seem to be more concerned with getting it done quickly and using power tools than how everything looks onstage."

"I can do either," I offered. "I'm not bad with a sewing machine, but I used to help build sets for high-school plays." A long, long time ago.

"Faboo!" Shannon checked something off on her clipboard. "Sets it is! We're so lucky to have someone with actual hands-on experience. I just know y'all are gonna make this one of the best plays Hughes has ever put on!"

The passion with which she spoke about our production was admirable, and occasionally amusing. Our school play was about cheerful orphans who solve mysteries through dance numbers, and it would be performed in an auditorium that smelled like stale French fries. Shannon couldn't be more enthusiastic if we were working with Juilliard-trained actors and a script written by the Bard.

Maybe the French-fry smell would be masked, or blend in, since the play was scheduled to be dinner theater. A local restaurant had donated catering for the night of the performance—which would be given a dry run during school hours—and attendees would pay a per-plate admission to benefit the PTA fund.

When Shannon circled to the other end of the table, rounding up computer-savvy mothers who could design and print the programs, the woman opposite me leaned over and whispered.

"You lucky dog." With her pale freckles and curly blond hair, pulled into a high ponytail, she looked a lot younger than I suspected she was.

I glanced at her adhesive name tag, glad Shannon had insisted we all wear them. Yvette Trumble.

"Are you Ginny's mom?" I asked, recalling Sara's story of the girl kind enough to share her brownie with the new kid.

"That's right, my Virginia's in Mrs. Z.'s class. She plays the part of the youngest orphan!"

Susie McCorkle was lead orphan, which might account for some of Shannon's zeal over the play, except that I couldn't imagine our friendly southern leader as anything other than excited, no matter whose daughter was the star.

I smiled at Yvette, introducing myself beyond the name written in marker and stuck to my shirt. "Charlie, Sara Smith's mother. Monday was her first day, and I really appreciate how nice Ginny's been to her."

Yvette beamed proudly. "Glad to hear I'm raising her right. I hope Sara likes it here at Hughes."

I started to nod, then remembered I still had no idea why she'd struck up conversation with me. "So, how am I lucky?"

"Because you're on set duty," a heavily pregnant redhead interjected from my left, keeping her voice low. "That means Zach Marbury. Hubba hubba. But I'm happily married."

"Oh, me, too," Yvette Trumble added. "Still it's not like you can *not* notice a man like Zach. What about you, Charlie?"

Me? I didn't even know this Zach guy.

"You married?" Yvette prompted.

"Widowed," I answered, trying to keep my voice neutral. I barely stopped myself from overcompensating with a tacked on *but it's no big deal*. Of *course* it was a big deal, I just didn't want to be the reason our friendly chatter suddenly crashed and burned. Instead, I added, "I've had more than a year to cope with it, though."

The pregnant woman next to me clucked her tongue. "You poor thing."

Yvette's eyes met mine, and after an almost imperceptible pause, she bounced back to our topic. "Zach Marbury is father of the third-grade Marbury twins, and our most eligible bachelor. We don't have many single parents active in the PTA, but his wife left him four years ago. If you're interested, you'll probably have to arm-wrestle Louisa Phillips—she owns the restaurant donating food for our little dinner theater. She's been after him since last year's Holiday Musical."

"Oooh." The pregnant redhead sized me up with a speculative grin. "A rumble."

Great, I was making enemies I hadn't even met yet. "I don't think so. I'm not really, um, looking. For a man, I mean." Sure, Dianne had told me to consider the idea, and I would, when things were more settled, but for now...

Yvette chuckled. "Say what you want, but you haven't seen Zach yet."

"That hot, huh?" I appreciated her keeping things light, and was glad I'd met Ginny Trumble's equally friendly mom.

"*Hotter* than that hot."

A few minutes later, I saw her point much more clearly.

CHAPTER 8

"Sorry I'm late, ladies." A man wearing a bomber jacket over jeans and a deep green polo shirt approached us, flashing a deeply dimpled smile. His hair was a rich honey color and his eyes matched his shirt.

When I say that Tom was attractive, it's not bias on my part—my husband epitomized tall, dark and handsome. I'd always been aware, and slightly dazzled, that I was with a head-turner. Nonetheless, Zach Marbury may have been the best-looking man I'd ever seen in person. He had that surreal movie-star quality to him, a charisma that can't even fully be explained. It's just *there*. Around the table, there was a collective feminine sigh.

Unbelievably, Zach zeroed in on me, his lazy smile the kind women write about in their diaries. "I don't believe we've met."

"Nope, she's new," Yvette put in helpfully. "Charlie's a single mother who just moved to the area."

At her subtle emphasis on *single* I shot her a pointed look, not fooled by her innocent expression.

"Zach Marbury." He reached out to shake my hand. "I really appreciate your taking the time to be here. I understand how difficult it can be to balance everything when you're the only parent. How many do you have?'"

"Two," I stammered. The rasp of his calloused hand against mine was having an effect that stunned me. Mostly, I was stunned there was any effect at *all*. That hadn't happened since... "Ben's not in school yet, but Sara's in Mrs. Zimmerman's first-grade class."

I pointed my daughter out among the chorus of kids learning words to a musical number that would be choreographed over the next few rehearsals.

"She's a cutie," he pronounced. He didn't say anything else, but the admiring look he gave me was along the lines of "she obviously takes after her mother."

Was my heart actually beating faster? In my youth I would have found the sensation heady. Now, I just wondered if I needed my blood pressure checked. *You're being foolish*, I tried to tell myself.

Myself wasn't listening. What I felt was good. No longer a teenager who read herself to sleep with romance novels, I was wise enough not to mistake my reaction for anything as poetic as love at first sight, or even a mutual connection. An incredibly attractive man had smiled at me, touched me for a moment, and it had been enough to rejuvenate my pheromones. An unremarkable reaction, if it hadn't been so damn long since my hormones had buzzed to life.

And that's what was so significant to me. I knew that my

warm body and skin prickly with awareness didn't have any deep meaning, but it was somehow…life-affirming. Reassuring and scary at the same time.

Shannon materialized at Zach's side. "How great that you two are hitting it off! Zach, Charlie's had experience with sets before, so she'll be working closely with you!"

"Looking forward to it." He gave me a parting smile as Shannon directed him to the other end of the table for his copy of the schedule. It covered all rehearsals, planning meetings and showtimes and had pertinent phone numbers on it, such as Shannon's and Ms. Cramer's.

Now that Zach was gone, I blinked, trying to regain normal, adult control. I fought the urge to ask Yvette to pass him a note for me during study hall.

She was smirking. "Didn't I tell you?"

"He's handsome, I'll give you that." Charlie Smith, Master of the Understatement. "But I'm really not in the market."

"Fair enough." Yvette sighed. "Never let it be said that I'm a buttinsky. It's a shame, though. You two would make a cute couple, and that Louisa Phillips really gets on my nerves. She's done everything but slap a 'property of' sticker on him since his divorce, barely giving the man a chance to recover from the blow."

"The divorce was his wife's idea?" *Why would you give up a man like him?*

"Yeah. She left him for…another woman."

Oh.

Once we'd all received our volunteer assignments and heard updates on the general information, we broke into smaller groups. Shannon headed up costumers, bringing a couple of kids over at a time to get their measurements. Yvette moved to sit by another mom, and I found myself alone and staring up at Zach Marbury.

"Looks like it's just you and me," he said cheerfully.

"We're the only people working on sets?" That was ridiculous. There were at least three women handling programs, and how hard could it be to select a font?

"No, we're just in charge of it. Maria Reyes volunteered her husband, and so did Amy Powell. I'll meet with the guys later and start building. For now, Shannon wanted us to go to the prop closet in the music room and see if there's anything from last year that can be used or revamped." He held out his hand to help me up.

Still shaken by my earlier reaction, I avoided his touch. I got to my feet, busily brushing imaginary lint from my slacks and looking down. I didn't want to know if his expression proclaimed me rude. Apparently, I needn't have worried. He kept up easy conversation with me as he unlocked the door to the music room, which seemed incongruously silent.

He'd asked whether or not I planned to put Sara in any organizations or team sports now that we'd relocated here. "I coach softball for a youth league in the area, and I'd be happy to give you the names and numbers of some people."

"Thanks. I might just take you up on that. Until recently,

she's been all about princesses and pink and ballet slippers, but she asked not long ago about sports."

"Well, I can't help you if she decides to go the ballet route—my boys have gotten me involved in soccer, softball, karate, football and fly-fishing. But I don't do tutus." A second later, he raised an eyebrow and said sternly, "You had better not be imagining me in a tutu."

"Well I am *now*." Which was a lie because my imagination couldn't quite make someone oozing so much masculine perfection look silly.

"Keep it up and you'll become one of those PTA urban legends," he threatened. "The newcomer who met a mysterious doom in the prop closet when last year's papier-mâché bunny fell on her."

I grinned, thinking absently of Luke. "A killer bunny with huge pointy teeth."

Zach looked at me blankly for a moment then smiled, as if deciding I'd made a joke he should acknowledge even if he thought the punch line made no sense.

Tom and I had often had that reaction to each other, not finding the same things funny. He'd once challenged me to sit with him on the couch through an entire *Three Stooges*. Luckily, we'd been newly married at the time and making out within minutes. A much preferable result to watching Larry and Moe.

There was a flutter inside me, a pooling warmth at the memory of happier, hornier times. When we'd both been young and felt so invincible.

I pushed away the yearning and the sadness that came with it, reminding myself that if we hadn't been invincible, we had still created something lasting, our family. It was for Sara that I was here now, wanting to be involved and stay positive. The last thing she needed were rumors at her new school that her mom was a crazy lady who'd had a nervous breakdown in the prop closet.

Getting back on task and looking around, I saw there was indeed a large rabbit that must have been part of some spring play or school festival. There were also other bizarre and mismatched odds and ends. An artificial Christmas tree, a "magic mirror" from their *Snow White* production, some posters decorated to look like international flags, a few costume pieces, not all of which were readily identifiable… And Zach's cologne, a warm, strong smell. Not overpowering, just confident. Like the man who wore it.

I inhaled deeply, taking a certain guilty pleasure in the scent. My body tingled, but confusion drowned out any more enjoyable sensations. I'd been thinking about my husband two seconds ago—I wasn't honestly lusting after the set designer of my daughter's first play, was I? Was I reacting to a memory or an aftershave? I'd experienced a strange relief earlier, that life-affirming reawakening. But I hadn't quite realized that when your hormones buzz back to life after being numbingly dormant, it's a lot like when you get feeling back in your hand after it's been "asleep." The stinging burn under your skin that hurts. Only this sting was in my heart.

For the rest of the afternoon, I tried to keep my responses casual. Not unfriendly, but not joking and personable, either. I wanted Zach to stay at a safe distance, if for no other reason than I didn't want him to see how neurotic I was. I had visions of being blacklisted by the PTA and it somehow affecting Sara's future.

As I was zipping my daughter into her jacket and preparing to go home, Zach walked up to us, a slip of paper in his hand.

"I'm not one of the 'important numbers' on the schedule," he said. "But I wanted you to have mine. Call me if you have any thoughts about the set or questions about the PTA or those organizations we talked about."

"Th-thanks." Was there a subtext here or would he have made this offer to any volunteer parent? I had no experience with reading men! Not plural. My energy had been focused on one man, and I'd been able to translate his every frown, kiss, chuckle or mutter with ease.

When I reached for the paper, he wrapped his hands around mine. "Or you could just call to talk, okay?"

"We should be going." Once I had my hand out of his, I had the presence of mind to add, less abruptly, "But thank you again, and I'll look into some of those teams for Sara."

In a rare display of restraint, Sara waited until we reached the van to ask, "Who was that man?"

"Another parent. Do you have any homework we need to do tonight?" With that question, the subject was changed, and I was glad that when Sara gave her rundown of the day to Rose, Zach Marbury wasn't mentioned.

I didn't mention him myself, in the e-mail I sent Dianne or during lunch with Jess when my co-worker asked about Sara's first play practice and whether or not I'd met any of the other PTA parents. In fact, occupied with trying to get Sara caught up in math and helping Rose put together Thanksgiving baskets, I put Zach Marbury from my mind.

It wasn't until late Friday that I woke in the middle of the night, my body heated and heavy with the lingering aftershocks of a sensual dream. Hardly the first time I'd awakened from a dream lover to find myself once again painfully alone in bed.

But it was the first time since Tom's death that I could remember dreaming about a lover who wasn't my husband.

The details were fuzzy, but I didn't need a psychology degree in dream interpretation to figure out who the golden-haired, green-eyed stranger had been. For months, after having Ben, after Tom's death, I'd been too numb even to think about sex, followed by a period where I missed it. More specifically, missed having it with Tom. The only man with whom I'd ever made love. I'd never consciously acknowledged my two remaining choices in decisive terms, because I hadn't reached a point where it mattered yet.

Tonight, however, my options were inescapable.

Either give up being held again entirely, being made love to with tender affection, with passion so all-consuming it's a little rough in its execution, with sweet, lazy abandon in the still sleepy hours of the morning…or, for the first time, make love to someone who wasn't Tom. Someone who hadn't kissed me softly the night he'd taken my virginity, telling me he'd always love me; someone who hadn't teased me about my out-of-control sex drive during my pregnancy with Ben; someone who hadn't known my body as well as I did myself.

I wouldn't have that intimacy with anyone else, the bond forged by being together for decades, by making babies together. Even so, a throbbing yearning remained from my dream, and the truth was, I liked it. It felt *good* to want again, to know that my body could. That this part of me hadn't died along with Tom. That I might no longer be a wife, but I was still a woman.

But no sooner had I acknowledged how sweet it would be to be made love to again, guilt hit me in the stomach, so hard I felt sick. In contrast to waking up feeling languid and aroused, I cried myself back to sleep, wondering which was worse—seeing my late husband's face in my dreams, or seeing someone else's.

Weekends were going to be a problem.

Even though I hadn't asked to be the only adult in my house back in Florida, on some level, I'd grown used to it in the year I'd lived alone with the kids. And I could only imagine how much more so that was the case for Rose, who'd had her home to herself for decades, only now to trip over a toddler toy every time she turned around. During the week, when I was at the office, we hadn't been in each other's hair. Even the nights hadn't been a problem, as Rose had gone to bridge club, choir practice and to visit Velda.

But Saturday and Sunday were a different story, as they encompassed a lot of togetherness. In fairness to my mother-in-law, I'll admit to waking up in a bad mood Saturday after a restless, haunted night. The speed with which she offered unsolicited opinions, however, did not improve my mood.

The weekends were when the kids and I bonded, playing and being silly together. While I was singing the ABCs to Ben, Rose interrupted to ask, since we were trying to encourage him to start talking, why not pick a song that had more actual words in it? During Ben's nap, Sara and I made popcorn and decided to watch some girlie movies. When we began clowning around together, I tossed a piece of popcorn to see if Sara could catch it in her mouth. Rose informed me that I wasn't teaching Sara appropriately ladylike behavior.

The criticism annoyed me the most because it had come in front of my daughter and it had disrupted a moment of pure fun. A moment when Sara hadn't been worried or petulant, a moment when I hadn't been stressing over the fact that the Florida real-estate agent had no news to share.

"We were just being silly," I said. "Why don't more people see the value of that?"

Rose scowled. "I have fun with the kids. We play Go Fish,

don't we, Sara? But if this is the kind of goofing off you encourage in the living room—on other people's furniture, no less—it's no wonder your couch looked like something that should go in a garage sale."

The garage sale I hadn't taken her advice on and organized? I missed that couch. I missed feeling at home and not like a permanent visitor. And I hated the way Sara was now nervously looking back and forth between her grandmother and me, her young mind debating whether or not this merited real worry on her part.

I forced a smile for her benefit. "We were done with the popcorn anyway, so let's just all go back to watching the movie." We hadn't dropped any popcorn on any of Rose's furniture, but if we had, I would have cleaned it up. Crisis averted.

By Sunday morning, the tension had increased enough that I was starting to look forward to work on Monday. The children and I were accompanying Rose to church and her visit with Velda, and even the way I drove the van was flawed. Rose shook her head when I stopped at a yellow light, feeling I could have passed before it turned red.

"I don't want to be late to church," she grumbled. "You took an awful long time with your hair this morning."

I'd curled it, for a change, wanting to look a little nicer than usual. I didn't really have a reason, I'd just been more aware of my appearance lately.

The light went green and I accelerated.

"Wait! Hang a left here," Rose instructed.

"At Poplar? This way is quicker."

"Distance-wise, maybe, but there's that big Methodist church and traffic for that will slow us down."

"We have plenty of time." The words came out slowly, through clenched teeth. Next week, *she* was driving. A decision reinforced when a few minutes later, she sniffed. "What now?"

"You don't have to take that tone with me. I didn't say a word," she protested. "But since you asked, it might have been nice if you'd turned your blinker on a little sooner and given that car behind us some notice."

My eye twitched. Did the woman have to control everything? She referred to her cooking and cleaning schedule as if we would plunge into anarchy if we veered from The Chart, and even her major hobby, greenhouse gardening, allowed her some triumph over Mother Nature. Yet somehow, even without Rose having control of the vehicle, we arrived at the church with time before the service started. We crossed the parking lot, Sara holding her grandmother's hand while I carried Ben.

"I'm going to drop Ben off at the nursery," I told my daughter. "Do you want to sit with us during the service or—"

"What do you mean you're dropping Ben off?" Rose asked.

"I thought that would be best for everyone. Helps socialize him so he doesn't become one of those kids who's terrified to leave his mother's side when he's three or four, and keeps him from disrupting the service. An hour's a long time for a toddler to sit still."

"And just how do you expect him to learn, if you don't start working with him at a young age? I can't believe you're just going to hand him over to strangers."

I rolled my eyes—it wasn't as if I'd proposed we leave the kid at a crack house for the next hour. "Rose, you can show your grandchildren off to all your friends after the service."

"We always took Tom with us," she said, preceding me into the church.

I took a deep breath, reminding myself wryly that physically assaulting my mother-in-law on holy premises was just *asking* to be struck down. While Sara and Rose found us seats in the sanctuary, I went to the nursery downstairs and introduced myself to the three smiling ladies who worked in the room for the twelve-to-eighteen-month-old kids. During opening prayer, I expressed gratitude for my job, for new friends and, smothering an internal sigh of exasperation, for Rose's allowing us to live with her. I then asked for patience and repeated my ever-constant request that God help me not suck as a mother. I hoped He wasn't offended by the phrasing.

After church, we went out for lunch. The fried chicken was good, although it didn't quite live up to my own home-cooked recipe I'd perfected while living in the South.

"Should we have taken Velda out to lunch instead of just dropping by the home after we eat?" I asked, wishing the offer had occurred to me sooner.

Rose shook her head. "No, the staff there prepares her

food with her diabetes in mind. And I think she likes the regularity of the menu, knowing what to expect each day. Older people reach a certain age where they're resistant to change or trying anything new. What?"

Until she narrowed her eyes at me, I hadn't realized I was smirking.

"Nothing. Nothing at all."

The retirement home Rose's aunt lived in was one of the best in the city. Though the grounds were fairly barren in the autumn chill, Rose said the landscaping was gorgeous in the spring, flowers everywhere. Each resident had his or her own apartment, and there were even some elderly couples who lived here. Nice meals were served, but a lot of the apartments had their own kitchens, too. As Rose signed us in at the front desk, I looked at the bright paintings on the walls, the recently vacuumed soft blue carpet, and the recreation room where several white-haired women were knitting in front of a wide-screen color television. At the other end of the room, a man played Ping-Pong with a boy I guessed to be his grandson.

Rose straightened, arching an eyebrow in my direction. "Best not be getting any ideas about putting me in a home just yet."

Her comment surprised a laugh out of me. "It didn't even cross my mind."

Ben was alert and interested in the new surroundings, smiling at strangers, but Sara huddled close to me as she walked, as if nervous.

"Everyone's so *old*," she whispered to me. Given what she'd been through, I thought she might have a greater sense of mortality than most children her age.

"Yeah. But they're not that different from younger people," I told her. "Most of them have families, same as you. I bet a lot of them like ice cream, same as you."

She grinned. "With jimmies on top?" To Sara, a serving of ice cream was incomplete if it didn't come with little chocolate sprinkles.

"Absolutely. But I don't think Velda will have any ice cream today, because she doesn't eat much sugar. So don't ask for any, okay?"

"Okay."

We passed a few apartments whose doorways were decorated for Halloween, then Rose stopped to knock at a door at the end of the corridor. A woman called out a greeting and we went inside.

"I brought you visitors." Rose immediately turned to me. "Show her the baby!"

Velda Fiorello, Rose's aunt, was a small, gnarled octogenarian with big dark eyes that dominated her pale face. Sara had met her before, although she might have been too young to remember it now. Unable to travel for Tom's funeral, Aunt Velda had never seen Ben.

I approached the floral-print sofa Velda sat on, her walker within close reach, and dutifully presented my son.

"Cute little fella," she said, her thin lips curling into a grin before flattening again. "Damn shame about him growing up without a daddy."

"Velda!" Rose snapped in reprimand.

At about the same time my daughter declared, "I don't think you're s'posed to say 'damn' on a Sunday."

Velda cackled. "Probably not. But just wait until you get older, you get to say lots of stuff they won't let you say now."

"Really?" Sara climbed up onto the couch next to her great-great-aunt, looking intrigued.

"Really. Being old ain't a picnic, but there are a few perks."

"I thought old was a little scary," Sara confided. "But Mommy said the people here were nice, and that they liked ice cream."

"Most of them are very nice, but I don't blame you for being scared. Mr. Angelino across the hall can take out his teeth. Now *that's* scary."

Sara ran her tongue over her bottom front teeth. "I lost two this summer, but new ones grew in. See?"

Velda leaned down to get a closer look. "Yep, those are some adult teeth all right! You're such a grown-up girl. What are you, twelve? Thirteen?"

Sara giggled. "Six."

"Old enough to trick-or-treat tomorrow. You have your costume already?"

While Sara and Velda talked about Halloween and her new school and various other topics, I mostly followed Ben around the small apartment, gently moving his hand away whenever he reached for a glass-encased picture frame or one of the porcelain cats Velda collected. At the conclusion of our visit, Rose asked if Velda would like us to walk her to the center's library before we left.

"We've got plenty of free hands to help you carry books back," my mother-in-law said, "and Sara might like to see it. She loves libraries."

"Thanks, but no." Velda wrinkled her nose. "When it's warm, the residents spend lots of time out on the grounds, but now that it's turned cold, everyone's stuck inside reading. All the good books are already checked out, and there's nothing left on the shelves but moldy old classics."

"What do you like to read?" I asked her. "Maybe we could bring you some books on our next visit."

Her eyes lit up at this suggestion. "Something *hot*. You know, lots of love scenes. Get to be my age, it's the only kinda nooky a body can get."

I coughed, hoping Sara would just ignore the new word. "Well, we'll see what we can do."

"Good." She glanced from me to Rose, then back. "Probably too late for her already, but if I were you, I'd make sure to get enough sex while you're young."

"Velda!" Rose looked outraged. I wondered if it was because her aunt had suggested I get some or because she'd ruled Rose out as already being too decrepit.

I had a startling realization—to the best of my knowledge, Rose had never dated anyone after her husband had died.

Twentysome-odd years ago. Had she really gone that long without…um, being held? I didn't make it a habit of wondering such personal things about my mother-in-law, but lately I'd had a vested interest in this subject myself. And while Rose and I might not have had the smoothest weekend together, maybe she was someone I could talk to about my feelings. Someone I could ask about her own decisions.

Bemused, I hugged Velda goodbye. "We'll be seeing you soon."

"You just make sure you bring these beautiful children back with you," she ordered, kissing Ben on the cheek when I held him close enough.

Back out in the hall, I grinned at Rose. "She's as feisty as ever."

My mother-in-law looked pained. "Indeed."

Sara had skipped on ahead of us and glanced back to tell us her throat felt scratchy and she was sure ice cream was just the thing she needed to make it feel better. "I was real polite and didn't ask!"

Surprisingly, both Rose and I came to quick agreement. We took the long way home, stopping in a shopping center where we all enjoyed ice cream, then strolled through a small pet store. Ben and Sara oohed and dating the mrs. smithshed over the tanks of fish as though we were at the New England Aquarium. Rose and I exchanged a smile over Sara's enthusiasm for that rare and exotic favorite, the goldfish.

I realized that it was a lot easier here, anywhere that

wasn't Rose's house. Although Rose had voluntarily made the offer—insisted we stay with her permanently, even—I'm sure the situation was as awkward for her as it was for me. It had been her home once, where she'd been someone's wife, someone's mother. And now it was where I was raising my own children, displacing her. Literally. The woman had given up her own bedroom!

I thought about asking her if she was sorry we'd moved in, but the question would have insulted her. She would have taken it as an indictment of her hospitality, would have deemed me ungrateful for the dinners cooked, the days she'd watched Ben. In the past, Tom had been, if not the mediator, then at least the buffer between us. Now we needed to fend for ourselves.

She'd coped admirably with the loss of both her husband and son, and I'd left Florida behind, driven up the coast with my kids and started over. After Rose and I had accomplished all that, how difficult could it be for the two of us to learn to talk to each other?

CHAPTER 9

There was a small office party on Monday, not because it was Halloween but because Claudia closed a major deal with a new customer. Frank took her out to lunch and they came back with jack-o'-lantern paper plates and deli goodies for the rest of us to enjoy in the break room as we toasted her with fizzy ginger ale. The young woman was smiling and looked more relaxed than I'd seen her on any of her previous visits to the office.

She sidled up to me as I sipped my drink. "Your little ones are probably trick-or-treating tonight, aren't they?"

I nodded, a little surprised. Unlike Luke, who had an anecdote about one of his nieces or nephews every time I saw him, kids weren't a normal part of Claudia's conversational repertoire. "Sara's going as a cowgirl and Ben will be a football player."

"Well, if you need extra time, you know, to get them all dressed up and ready before it gets late, you should leave early. You worked really hard last week, and…and did a great job."

She'd been snippy over the phone last Wednesday when I'd said I had to leave for Sara's play rehearsal, but I'd more than made up for the time by being in the office early every morning. Good to know my effort had been noticed.

"Thank you, Claudia. I might just take you up on that suggestion."

Having accomplished her unspoken apology, she nodded and moved off to accept the congratulations of another salesman who'd been in the area today.

"Looks like you survived that unscathed," Luke remarked. He had plates in each hand and offered one to me.

"Thanks." I accepted it, but was surprised that no manic need gripped me when I saw the chocolate cookie. Truthfully, I wasn't really in the mood for anything sweet. Although I was now eating more Italian food than ever before, I had at least stopped mindlessly downing baked goods from the neighbors or fast food that tasted like cardboard and had five-digit calorie counts. Some of my pants were even fitting a little looser.

"Yeah, you were right about Claudia not being so bad. I think when I first got here, maybe she just…"

"Felt insecure?"

"We didn't mesh." There seemed to be a lot of that in my life right now. Maybe it was me. "Maybe I'm uniquely un-meshable."

He laughed, leaning against the counter. "Why would you think that? Because of Claudia?"

"Not just her. Rose, too."

"Your mother-in-law?" Jess joined us, popping a pretzel into her mouth. "How's it going with her?"

I sighed, trying to be objective about the situation. "She's been great with the kids and letting us stay with her, but I swear sometimes—well, she has a way of making me feel like I can't do anything right. And of course six hundred suggestions on how to do everything better."

Jess laughed. "You just described my relationship with my mother. Cheer up, Charlie. They interfere because they love you."

"She couldn't find someone else to shower with this particular brand of affection?" I muttered.

"There's an idea," Jess said, her eyes bright with enthusiasm. "Find her someone else to love."

"You mean like a pet? Because we have the dog, and Gretchen already likes Rose much better than me. I think she senses I'm a cat person."

Luke nodded. "I—"

"Not a pet," Jess interrupted. "Focus, people. I was talking about a man. Finding Rose someone to love, literally. Maybe she seems overbearing because she's a little lonely."

I blinked. It was the second time in as many days that someone had brought up romance, or its lack, in Rose's life. "I don't know…"

Jess shrugged. "Just a thought. If she had someone else she was preoccupied with, she'd be out of your hair more, right? Not as prone to standing over your shoulder and giving her opinion on everything."

"Theoretically. But I don't know if she *wants* to date. How do you put yourself back out there after twenty years? And she loved her husband so much."

"Like you." The quiet statement didn't come from Jess, but from Luke. Meeting my gaze, he continued. "You loved your husband very much, right?"

My throat tightened. "Very." We hadn't talked much about how or when Tom had died, but I wouldn't have been surprised to learn Jess had filled him in.

"And do you think you could ever date again?" he asked.

"I'm not sure." I thought of Dianne joking that I needed a hot young guy in my life, of the way I'd felt when Zach Marbury had shaken my hand, of Velda telling me to make the most of my romantic opportunities while I was still young. "But this isn't about me, anyway."

"No. Of course not." His green-gold eyes were far more serious than I was used to seeing them. "I just thought, if you want to bring this up with her, maybe you could use some of your own feelings to get the conversation started. Then again, I'm a guy and getting in touch with emotions isn't really our thing. I could help Rose pick out a great car, though."

I laughed. "Either of us needs wheels anytime soon, you'll be the first one I call."

"But for dating advice, you turn to your female friends, right?" Jess demanded. "Because I've got ideas. There was just a write-up in the local paper about a senior center that's started to do speed-dating. Maybe you could talk Rose into that."

"What the heck is speed-dating?" I asked.

Luke snorted. "It's where men and women pair up, talk for five minutes, then move on to someone else, trying to determine who in the room is their most likely match. All the awkwardness of a first dinner date, but without the convenience of actually getting to eat something."

Trying to repeatedly make the best possible impression in short, artificial installments? No pressure. "I think I can safely say Rose would not enjoy speed-dating." But maybe it wouldn't hurt to find out what she thought about the regular kind.

Halloween costumes were different in Boston than Miami. Our first holiday here didn't see a lot of scantily clad "Christina Aguileras" such as I'd distributed candy to in years past. No bare-armed gladiators, either, in plastic chest plates and warrior skirts made more macho by the likes of Russell Crowe and Brad Pitt. One year in Florida, we'd had an eighty-degree Halloween and an all-time low in creativity. Some kids had shown up claiming their swimsuits were their costumes.

"I'm a surfer," a sixteen-year-old had told Tom, defending his right to candy.

My husband had told me later that he thought it was silly for teenagers to be trick-or-treating. "After all, don't they know this is the perfect night to watch scary movies with girls?" He'd pulled me close with a grin. "Great make-out opportunity."

I'd teased him about being a juvenile delinquent when he was younger, the type of teen parents warned their daughters about. It had been a pretty hot night, even more so than the eighty degrees warranted.

Damn. I came back to the present with a jolt, realizing that I'd spilled the bag of mini candy bars across the kitchen counter instead of into the oversize orange-and-black plastic bowl. Pandora was definitely out of the box. After so many months of not really thinking about sex, now that I'd started again, my thoughts frequently strayed in that direction.

The doorbell rang, creating a not unwelcome distraction. Since Rose was upstairs helping Sara get ready, I answered.

A little boy with a long robe over his clothes held up a sack. "Trick or treat."

From the scarf and empty black eyeglass frames that were too large for his face, I assumed he represented the heroic Harry Potter. His mother stood with him, carrying a baby bundled up in sweatpants and a faux leopard-print coat with a fuzzy hood. Someone had drawn black whiskers around the baby's nose. Our trick-or-treaters had just left when my daughter bounced down the stairs, ready to be told how wonderful her costume was.

"Yee-haw, cowgirl! You look great." I raised my head to include my mother-in-law in my smile. "Nonna did a really great job."

Sara's dark hair was parted in the middle and split into two braids beneath her red costume cowboy hat. Rose had sewn a fleece-lined vest made to look like black-and-white cowhide and a black denim skirt. Sara was wearing tights beneath the skirt and a red turtleneck under her vest. She was well-covered, but still, it was dark and chilly out, a far cry from the sunny climate to which she was accustomed.

I bit my lip. "You probably need a coat, though, okay?"

Instead of the protests I expected, Sara lifted a conspiratorial grin toward her grandmother.

"We saved the best for last," Rose said, with a rare glint of mischief in her eyes. She retreated up the stairs and returned with a black duster, one of those long cowboy-style trench coats seen in western movies with the flap in the back, down over the shoulders.

Sara shrugged into it, obviously feeling pretty cool. She was adorable, and the jacket was a work of costuming art.

"You made that in just a week?" I asked Rose.

"You like it, Mommy?"

"It's great, bear. Your daddy would have loved it, too." Sometimes my instinct was to shy away from mentioning Tom, lest it upset her, but Rose brought him up constantly. I had to admit, it didn't seem to be hurting Sara any.

However, I had mixed feelings about how Sara gazed adoringly at his football trophies and had abandoned all mention of a pink room with princess accessories. There'd never been much of a reason for me to go into Rose's room—and I respected her privacy, a place untouched by our presence—but

I wondered how many of the mementos from her old bedroom she'd simply rearranged downstairs. I was all for preserving a loved one's memory, but there was something almost disturbing about imagining my daughter at eight, ten or twelve, still surrounded by her father's memorabilia. I wanted to make sure she was creating and celebrating her own memories.

Had Rose been creating her own memories over the past few decades, or just tending old ones? It was disquieting to think about now…perhaps because it made me wonder what my life would be like at sixty.

Lonely?

I swallowed. "Okay, I think we're all ready. Just let me grab Ben's helmet."

My son was looking at board books in the sunken living room and already dressed in a preschooler's football costume. Since it was a couple of sizes too big, it worked great over clothes, giving him a bulky, faux-muscular look. I knew he'd be warm enough, and the finishing touch was a heavy felt helmet that would cover his ears, assuming he didn't pull the thing off every couple of minutes.

"Did you get film for your camera?" Rose asked me.

"It's digital, so I don't need film, I just download the pictures to my computer." My PC, while older and slower than top-of-the-line models, was one of the few household possessions that had traveled with me and now sat on a small table upstairs. Rose had scowlingly resisted my attempts to show her how to use the Internet or set up an e-mail account.

We got a shot of the kids sitting in the foyer, the bucket of candy between them. I took one of Rose and Sara, then asked my mother-in-law to snap one of me and the kids. But after four tries, I was still headless in all but one picture…in which Rose's thumb took up most of the frame.

"Never mind," I said. "We should head out before it gets any later."

"Maybe just one more?" she asked. "We could take a really cute picture of Ben with some of Tom's old football trophies."

Probably because I'd already been feeling uneasy with living among all the reminders of the past, her suggestion made me irritable. "We already have cute pictures of Ben, and we need to get a move on. Tomorrow is a school day, after all."

Rose slanted me a look as she shrugged into her jacket. She didn't press the issue, but as we walked to the first house, she reached over to pat Ben's cheek. With all the time they spent together on weekdays, the two of them were growing really close.

"Such a handsome little man," she said proudly. "I can just imagine what you're going to look like in a real football uniform."

"*If* he wants to play," I stressed, watching Sara skip up the steps to the front door. She'd insisted she was grown up enough to ring the bell by herself.

Rose's expression was quizzical. "Well, of course he will. Don't most little boys?"

Maybe, but I wasn't stupid enough to believe she was making an assumption based on *most* little boys. She was specifically referencing Tom, and my son was not a replacement for hers. My anger was somewhat irrational in nature but every time we turned around, we were hearing what had been Tom's favorite pastime, Tom's favorite food, how he might've wanted his children raised.

"I'll support my kids," I told her evenly, "if they want to star in school plays, if they want to hide in the back row of the audience. If Ben wants to play football, I'll drive him to team tryouts, and if he'd rather join the chess team, I'll cheer him on. But I want them to make their own decisions, be their own people." I didn't want them pretending to like certain foods or making life plans they thought appealed to me.

For all that Tom had liked to play college football, he'd never said a word to me about going pro. Instead, he'd recounted the destruction he'd seen as a child, when his parents had taken him to Orlando months after a hurricane and many places had still been in ravaged disrepair. He'd loved to build, and construction had been a natural fit. When Rose talked about him, she sometimes made it sound like he'd been cheated out of his Super Bowl ring.

"Their own decisions? Newfangled liberal parenting," she muttered. "Parents are *here* to help guide their children. If Sara informed you she was staying up until two in the morning every night because she'd decided she was a night owl, would you let her?"

Because Sara had turned back toward us, I didn't respond. Obviously I wasn't going to let my children start making destructive decisions if I could help it. If. What Rose rarely seemed to acknowledge was that, eventually, there were some things beyond our control.

I'd say this for her, though. Unlike so many of my friends who'd started treating me with kid gloves after Tom's death, Rose treated me the same way she always had. Even if she was critical, in a warped way, I appreciated her consistency.

As we progressed through the cul-de-sac, Sara glanced between me and her grandmother. "What's wrong?"

"Nothing, pumpkin." I resolved not to bicker anymore with my mother-in-law tonight. She and Sara had worked hard to put together a very cute costume, and my daughter had been looking forward to this night. I wasn't going to ruin it for her. Sara deserved happiness, the kind of fond childhood memories you don't even realize you're creating until you look back in later years.

Why limit it to childhood? If you stopped creating memories, moving forward, as an adult, what was the point of life?

I shifted Ben on my hip, glancing toward Rose as we threaded our way through a group of pint-size goblins moving the opposite direction on the sidewalk.

"What?" Rose's spine was as stiff as her tone.

"I was wondering…if I could ask you about something?"

Her eyebrows lifted, but she nodded. "Of course. I've always wanted you to feel welcome to take advantage of my wisdom."

I chose my words carefully. "I know that you loved Thomas Sr. very much. As I loved Tom. But…they would want us to be happy, don't you think? Cared for? I know Tom used to take great pride in looking out for me, being there when I needed him."

"Yes." There was pride in her gaze. "He had a good heart. He looked after me until he went to college and you know how he always fussed over me when he came home. With his 'Mom, I can cut the grass,' or 'Mom, don't stand on that ladder! I can change the lightbulb.'"

Suddenly her expression changed, becoming unexpectedly mischievous. She looked ten years younger with that twinkle in her eye. "Who, I wonder, does he think took care of his poor, feeble mother when he was in Florida?"

I laughed, thinking of a few times when Tom had insisted he deal with the mechanic so I didn't get fleeced and other instances where he'd protected me and I'd indulged him with a loving "Yes, dear, whatever you think is best."

The unexpected camaraderie bolstered my courage. "I did need Tom, truly, in many ways. But that doesn't change the fact that…"

"He's gone now?"

I nodded, surprised she'd been the one to voice it.

"I know. I still miss his father, but he's never coming back, either." Her words were raspy with emotion, but she got them out. It couldn't be easy for her to discuss the two men she loved most, not from this angle. She talked about both of them constantly, but in the context of their lives. A song she and Thomas Sr. had danced to at their wedding, a city they'd all seen on a family vacation, a Christmas present Tom had particularly loved as a child. She rarely talked about their deaths.

"Then, given that—" I swallowed hard "—would it be so terribly wrong if you—or I—found love again? Maybe not even love, but companionship at least."

"You mean *sex*? That Velda! Is—" She broke off suddenly when Sara came running toward us to show us her haul and tell us she'd seen some girls from her school and wanted to know if we could cross the street and say hi.

We did, Rose and I nodding hello to the parents managing the throng of mermaids, pirates and barnyard animals.

Quietly enough that no neighbors were privy to the conversation, I addressed Rose's question. "Companionship actually meant companionship—I mean, one step at a time here. It wasn't a euphemism."

"Oh." She mulled it over. "I suppose it would depend on the man. The circumstances, in general."

"But you're not...opposed to the idea?"

Her eyes met mine, but her gaze was unfocused, as if she were looking inward. "I'll have to think about that."

So would I.

* * *

On Wednesday afternoon, there was another play rehearsal, with certain parent volunteers showing up to help with their respective committees. Zach Marbury and I, along with two fathers who were helping, placed set pieces onstage, "blocking" them to make sure Ms. Cramer liked our intended layout. The pieces were still mostly unfinished and unpainted.

To my embarrassment, Zach seemed to be finding ways to maneuver the two of us together. When I looked at him now, instead of seeing the face of a god, I mostly just equated him with post-fantasy shame. There wasn't exactly a handy way to work that into conversation, though. *Actually, Zach, what if you and Roger carry the boat, and I'll help Paul with the forest backdrop. Because, frankly, I had an orgasmic sex dream featuring you and would rather avoid you now.*

When he asked me if I wanted to walk out to his SUV with him and carry in some supplies, I couldn't think quickly enough of a reason to say no.

As we walked through the parking lot, he smiled down at me. "I don't want to sound like a loser who was waiting by his phone, but I had sort of hoped to hear from you."

Wow, I hadn't expected the direct approach. I should feel flattered, but mostly I just felt clammy. As if my entire body were one big nervous palm. "Um. Sorry?"

"Don't be." He lifted his key remote and aimed it at a red SUV. "Giving you my number was an invitation, not an obligation. This is just my clumsy way of…would you like to go out sometime?"

"No!" The word shot out in a burst of panic and could no more be recalled than a cannonball that had been fired. "God, that sounded awful. I didn't mean anything by it. I just think it's still too soon after my husband died, you know? I realize you weren't asking for a major commitment—"

"I was thinking more along the lines of getting coffee," he said ruefully, "but I understand. Especially the not-being-ready part. After my wife left, I was pretty soured on women for a while, then a little hesitant to put myself back out there. I wasn't even sure if I remembered how—we don't have as many single parents in our PTA as current divorce statistics might lead you to expect. You seemed nice, so I decided to take a shot. This was the first time I've asked someone out since the divorce was final."

I winced, regretting the staccato refusal. "Oh."

"Don't worry. I'm just glad I did. Gives me hope for the future, you know?"

"Trust me, I know. And I'm sure down the road, when I am ready, I'm going to kick myself for this. You seem like a great guy, and a great dad to your kids." I couldn't find a tactful way to add that he was also a major hottie. "Lots of women are going to want to go out with you."

"Thanks." He smiled. "And you have my number, should you ever want it. In the meantime, do me a favor? I'd appreciate if you didn't mention this to Louisa Phillips. She's a nice lady, but she's been a little, er, assertive in her attempts to console me since the divorce. If she thinks I'm ready to start dating again…"

"Say no more."

It wasn't until we were back inside the building that I realized Zach's asking me out had been as much a milestone for me as for him. The last time a man had asked me out, I'd still been Charlotte Wagner, college student. Charlie Smith, mother and widow, had just received her very first offer of a date.

I wasn't sorry I'd said no—whatever pheromonal reaction I'd had to meeting Zach was tainted now—but the fact that he'd asked felt kind of…nice.

CHAPTER 10

After rehearsal, Sara and I joined Yvette Trumble and her daughter Ginny for dinner. The four of us had a great time, but I noticed Sara didn't eat much. Maybe she'd just been too busy chattering with her friend. By the time we got home, however, she was irritable. I attributed her mood shift to the math test she had tomorrow morning. She'd been doing a great job on her recent homework, but it would never be her best subject.

She surprised me when we got home by saying she wanted to go to bed early. Rose volunteered to help me get both kids ready. I asked if she wouldn't rather just take some time for herself, since she'd been alone with Ben all morning, but she shook her head cheerfully, flashing a sly grin.

"No, I want to help you get the little ones settled. And then maybe we could talk."

Intriguing. From her demeanor, she seemed like someone with a happy secret she was impatient to share. I couldn't think of what it might be. It crossed my mind that we'd recently talked about her dating again, but surely not even Rose with all her stubborn determination could have accomplished that so soon? A boyfriend wasn't like a carton of milk—you didn't just make the decision you needed one and run out to the nearest corner market.

Of course, you probably also didn't call them boyfriends past sixty. A beau, maybe? Gentleman callers? *This is Rose, not Scarlett O'Hara.*

Once the kids were in bed, Rose and I went to the kitchen, where she put on a kettle of water to make hot tea. "Charlotte, dear. I know we haven't always been the picture of harmony, but I never had a daughter. And you were born without knowing your mother." This is where anyone else might have said she loved me like a daughter. Rose did not, but the implication touched me nonetheless. "I want you to know that I heard you the other night. Loud and clear. And I've been thinking about it."

I returned her grin. "So this *is* about dating?" Aha!

"Yes, and I'm touched you wanted my blessing."

"Bl-blessing?"

"To date. All those things you said, about Tom taking care of you, asking if he would want you to be happy again. Wanting me to tell you it would be okay."

Oh, that was so not what I had been trying to get at.

She reached her hand across the table, laying it on mine. "You were absolutely right about all of it. So how better for me, his mother, to honor his family than to help you?"

"Help me?" I'd come into the kitchen expecting her to tell me she'd decided to take ballroom dance or play bingo at the senior center, and meet people her own age. Instead—and my dizzy brain couldn't quite process this—my dead husband's mother wanted to help me land a man? Once again, she'd taken an idea and run too far, too fast with it. In the wrong direction. "That's...really good-hearted of you, but there have already been so many changes in my life, in the kids' lives. We haven't had time to adjust to them all. Heck, we haven't even sold the house. I don't think the kids are ready for the shock of Mommy dating on top of everything else."

"It's because of the kids that this is such a perfect idea, dear! Don't you think they should have a father? Obviously no one can replace Tom, but they could still be raised by a good man. He would have wanted that."

Egad. She wasn't just talking about dating, she'd zoomed clear on to *marriage*. "Rose, I need to take things really slowly right now. When I brought this up the other night, I was talking about you."

She drew back in her chair, eyes wide. "Oh, I couldn't."

"Why not? You're encouraging me to try it."

"You have the children to think of. And you're so young." She stood, going to the stove to remove the kettle.

Opening the cabinet where she kept the teacups, she arched an eyebrow in my direction, but I shook my head. It seemed so dignified and healthy to drink herbal tea, but try as I might, I just couldn't stand the stuff. Neither of us spoke as she stirred her beverage.

When she came back to the table, she looked sad. Wistful. "Tommy was a good son right from the beginning, a quiet, alert baby. Thomas Sr. made a good living—obviously left me well cared for—and the three of us traveled often. I've never lived anywhere but Boston and never plan to, but I liked going, knowing that home was waiting for me. Once Tommy started school, he and I stopped traveling with his father so much. Alone, while he was in classes, I thought it was a shame we'd never had another child, but by then, I couldn't imagine ever loving another one as much as I already loved Tom Jr. He and his father, they were my world.

"When I lost my husband, Tom was old enough to help me through it, and I was able to stay strong while he was here, telling myself it was for his sake. But when my son went away to college, I fell apart." She took a deep breath, staring at the teacup clutched between her hands. "Lost it completely."

"You?" I couldn't imagine it.

"I tried to keep Tom from ever knowing, but yes, I was a wreck. Went for days without even changing out of my bathrobe, avoiding my friends' calls, until I finally had to snap out of it enough to go to the market because there were no groceries left in the house."

My heart squeezed with sympathy. I knew how awful depression could be—thank God Dianne had been there to help see me through mine. "I'm so sorry."

She shrugged. "It's behind me now, and not something I dwell on. What finally jolted me out of it was a mistake I made. One I also don't care to dwell on. A man who had been a friend of the family invited me to dinner. I was trying to force cheer I didn't feel, and I behaved recklessly. Drinking more than my usual single cocktail, flirting with him in a manner that wasn't sincere, although the poor man didn't know that. He confessed that night to having long-held feelings for me, and was overjoyed that I seemed to return them. I didn't, but I…went home with him anyway. It was awkward and awful, and I hated myself the next morning. The shame of what I'd done kept me from even thinking about dating, about men, for a long time to come."

Recalling my own guilty reaction to Zach Marbury, and knowing what a turn-off that guilt was, I could understand what she must have felt. Still, I hoped she wasn't beating herself up all these years later. "It was a mistake made a long time ago, Rose. I'm not trying to minimize your feelings, but don't you think that maybe now…?"

"I feel the same way about loving another man as I felt about a second baby. By the time I thought to have regrets, I also realized that things had probably worked out for the best. I honestly don't know that I could ever love another man the way I did Thomas Sr. And the last thing I want to do is be unfair to someone else, offer them only a small part of my affection. Use them. Besides, I've been alone too long. I'm not sure I can make the compromises relationships require anymore. That's why *you* shouldn't wait, dear. You should find someone else, and I can help you."

So she'd mentioned earlier. "Help me how?" I had horrific visions of that speed-dating Jess had mentioned. I couldn't be enrolled without my consent, could I?

"I'm delighted you asked." She stood again, color returning to her cheeks as we redirected the topic.

I was surprised and strangely grateful that she'd shared such a personal piece of her history with me, but I suspected she'd rather drop the subject than have me thank her and share my own recent emotions.

On the counter underneath the wall-mounted phone, Rose kept a spiral notebook with flowers blooming on the cover. She returned to the table with the book and flipped it open. One entire page was filled with columns of inked-in information. I saw names and phone numbers. *Many* names and phone numbers.

"What is that?" Maybe I should have had some tea, after all. To soothe the rising hysteria.

"This is what I spent today collecting and organizing," Rose answered, obviously quite satisfied with her work. "Names and life details of potentially suitable young men."

I glanced in horror at the carefully categorized abundance of information. *New, from the woman who brought you The Chart—it's the Daddy Auditions.* Now I almost wished she had enrolled me in a night of speed-dating. That would have been one quick evening out of my life and maybe some funny stories for Luke and Jess. This was...

"You made a list of men?" I asked.

"I had help. I called friends."

"Right. Even better."

My lack of rampant enthusiasm seemed to be getting through to her. "Charlie, on Halloween, you sounded as if you were all in favor of finding someone."

"For you," I stressed. "Finding someone for you."

"And if I'd been interested, how would we have gone about it—trolling bars and asking people their astronomical signs?"

"Astrological," I corrected with a chuckle. "And of course not. I just thought you could…to tell you the truth, I hadn't completely thought it through yet."

"Well, my method is more thorough. I've put asterisks by the men who would be my first choices for son-in-law."

If I ever got married again—and that was a big if—I didn't think Rose would have any official relation to the man, much less be his mother-in-law. But it tugged at my heartstrings that she would consider herself such. It apparently also tugged at my sanity, temporarily dislodging it. "Let me see your list."

Beaming, she shoved it toward me. "It's alphabetized."

I stared.

"You're thinking of having me medicated, aren't you?"

"You know, Tom wasn't nearly this…organized."

"Why would he be?" She smiled absently. "I took care of the details so that neither my husband or son had to worry about them. It was one of the things I liked about you. I knew he'd have someone to take care of him."

"But, it was really the other—" I broke off, thinking. Who'd been the one who'd known the pediatrician's number by heart, made sure everyone was eating from all four food groups, and that when you opened a dresser drawer, there would be clean laundry inside? Me. Tom had taken care of me in other ways, but Rose was right. The details had been my province. I just hadn't alphabetized and cross-referenced them. "It's nice to know there was something you liked about me. When Tom and I got together, I mean."

"You weren't what I'd envisioned for him, I'll admit, and I hated that he settled in Florida and never moved back, but the two of you loved each other very much."

Remembering just how much made it tough to look at her list. But what if that kind of happiness was out there again and I missed it because I was afraid to look? Would I end up like Rose, alone in my sixties and feeling it was too late? I glanced down, noticing a good number of surnames were Italian, probably from families Rose's family knew. A few names even looked familiar.

"Do I know Michael Barber?" I asked her.

"You met his father at church. Michael's a good man, never married. That unfortunate gambling problem was an obstacle for a while, but I'm told he got help and it's under control. As long as you don't honeymoon in Vegas, you should be fine. That was a joke," she added helpfully.

"Uh-huh. What about Dean Keller? I know I recognize that name." And he had an asterisk. The information she'd compiled in Dean's column said that he was forty-two, divorced and owned a hardware store.

She lowered her gaze. "He may have been at your wedding. Nice man with a little boy just a year younger than Sara, but the mother has custody. Stable income, good with kids."

Apparently, I'd been wrong. Men *were* like cartons of milk. You just let Rose know whether or not you were interested in skim, butter or chocolate and she diligently set about getting it for you.

I closed the notebook. "I appreciate your trying to look out for me, Rose, but I can't just call up one of these guys and explain to him that he was on my mother-in-law's recommended list. I couldn't even call up Zach Marbury, and he asked me to."

Though she didn't have any visible antennae, I could feel them going up nonetheless. "Who is Zach Marbury?"

"One of the few eligible bachelors in the PTA. But I'm not interested in dating him, either."

Either she heard the finality in my tone, or my mother-in-law had mellowed since I'd first moved in, because there was no argument. Only thoughtful silence.

She steepled her fingers under her chin. "Would you give it a shot if I did? Dating, I mean. I really think you finding a nice man to help take care of you and the kids would be a good thing. But it's hypocritical for me to push you toward something I avoided. The least I could do is…consider it."

I grinned. "Does that mean I get to compile a list for you? Maybe Velda and Jess could help."

"I suppose you think the list is silly. These are just sons and grandsons of people I know, so I could introduce you to any of them if you were interested. I warned you I'd been out of the dating world for a long time. If I'm really going to think about meeting men again, you'll have to help me figure out how these things work nowadays."

"Sure." Just as soon as I figured it out myself.

In the morning, Sara was grouchier about getting out of bed than usual.

"I don't feel good," she croaked.

"Does this have anything to do with your math test?" I asked. For someone so young, she'd already demonstrated a fair amount of stress over her grades. I empathized, since I'd worried from an early age about letting down my dad.

"No. My throat hurts."

Rose stuck her head in Sara's room. "Breakfast's ready, you two."

Sara had pulled on the clothes I'd given her, but she crawled fully dressed back into bed. "I don't wanna eat."

"Too much of that Halloween candy this week," her grandmother predicted.

Maybe not. To the best of my knowledge, a little candy corn had never resulted in swollen lymph nodes. I prodded gently beneath Sara's chin. *Not again.* Parents don't like seeing their kids miserable, and Sara's health problems, while not major and worrisome, had been frustrating for both her and me.

"Charlie?" Rose's voice echoed my own weariness. While we hadn't spoken frequently when I'd lived in Miami, we'd talked enough that she knew Sara had seen several doctors for recurring throat infections. *Looks like it's time to take her to see one more.*

I conjured a smile for my little girl. "Good news, I don't think you'll have to take that math test today after all."

"I was thinking about asking if you wanted to have lunch today," Luke said, leaning against my desk. "But I'm not sure I want whatever you and Jess are passing back and forth. First you Friday, now her."

My co-worker had called in sick this morning. "It wasn't actually me who was ill last week, it was Sara."

"Oh, I hope she's feeling better."

"Enough that she went back to school today. But I'm waiting for her pediatrician to call me."

Luke's eyes searched mine. "You're concerned."

"Some. They did throat cultures, promising to get me lab results, but went ahead and prescribed antibiotics in case it turns out to be strep. She fought off tonsillitis several times last year and I thought she was finally free of it. If it's not strep and is the same problem as before, we might have to schedule a tonsillectomy."

"I know this won't stop a good mother from worrying about her kid, but my nephew had a tonsillectomy a year and a half ago and didn't even stay the night. Home the same day, no big deal."

"Nice to know." I tried to give him a grateful smile, but failed, and felt stupid for being this anxious. Tonsillectomies generally weren't considered a big deal; plenty of kids, including myself, had survived them just fine with zero complications. Then again, angioplasty was a low-risk, same-day procedure, too. Suppressing a shudder, I reminded myself that the two things could not be less connected and that my fearful reaction was irrational.

Not that fear has to be logical to wield power. And logic or no, I wasn't in a big hurry to see anyone else I loved wheeled away from me on a gurney.

Luke crossed to the coatrack, grabbing my jacket. "Your pediatrician has your cell-phone number, right? Let's get you out of here, and I'll buy you lunch. Tell me which vendors are ever rude to you on the phone, and I'll mock them with very bad impressions. It'll be fun."

I laughed. "Thanks. But why does it feel like you're always feeding me? Between doughnuts on Fridays and lunches during the week, I'm gonna have to watch my weight around you."

His gaze slid from my face over my body—not insulting or inappropriate, but when his eyes met mine again, there was a hint of masculine appreciation. "Nothing to worry about as far as I can see."

"Well, not yet, maybe. It's the future I worry about."

With his typical chivalry—he claimed his sisters had drummed it into him—he helped me into my jacket. I experienced a little ping at stepping so close to him after the once-over, then told myself I was being a nut. The quick way my breath caught was undoubtedly the subconscious byproduct of my recent dwelling on sex and talking to Rose about dating.

"Like seafood?" he asked as we walked to the car.

"Love it."

As he drove, we talked about the office bridal shower being arranged for Claudia, the fact that Ben had added *choochoo, no* and *kitty* to his vocabulary, and an overhyped movie that was coming out at Christmas, making predictions as to how bad it would be.

Luke's gaze skated from the road toward me. "This won't be your, um...never mind."

"What?" His uncharacteristic hesitance made me curious.

"I was just wondering about the holiday season." His tone was apologetic. "It's not the first, is it? Since you've been widowed."

"No. Last year." I glanced out the window, watching chilly pedestrians hurry toward one of the subway stations used by Boston's T lines. The first serious cold snap of the season had come in, and even inside Luke's car, I shivered at the memory of the wind. It had a bitter edge to it that promised the weather would get far worse before it got better. Even though I was almost as eager to see snow as Sara—I'd lived in the South long enough to consider the white stuff an exotic treat—part of me just hoped I didn't freeze before spring. "It was hard, but to be honest, kind of hazy now. I'm hoping to make new memories this year."

He nodded. "Your first holiday season in Boston is the perfect time to start some traditions and enjoy ours. The Boston Common tree lighting, shopping on Newbury Street… Oh, have you taken them to the Children's Museum yet? It's great any time of year, but they schedule special holiday events. My niece Karen has two favorite places in the city—the Children's Museum and the *Make Room for Ducklings* garden, with the statue."

I smiled. "I've read that book to the kids. Along with about a zillion others, although Sara is getting old enough that she reads some of them to Ben herself."

"How's she doing with her play? Showing any signs of stage fright, or is she looking forward to the performance?"

"Definitely looking forward to it. She has two songs memorized cold, and Ms. Cramer has actually made her an understudy for another little girl. Sara's thrilled, but between you and me, I'm afraid she's actually hoping the other girl will suddenly move out of town or something."

He laughed. "Not an uncommon sentiment for an understudy. Speaking of plays…I mentioned that I'm involved in a community theater? This weekend, we'll be finishing a run of our latest production. Would you have any interest in going to see it with me?"

The invitation was unexpected, but a night at the theater, even a small local one, sounded great. Assuming that Sara was still feeling better, it would be fun to get dressed up and go out for the evening. Would Luke pick me up? I stole a glance at his profile, surprised when my stomach did a little somersault. He wasn't the kind of man who drew all women's eyes when he walked into the room; he was the kind of man who, the more a woman really looked at him, the more she liked what she saw.

"I didn't mean as a date, of course," he added.

"Oh." I felt presumptuous…and deflated.

"I just thought it might be something you would enjoy. If you can get away for an evening."

"I'll have to see. With any luck, Rose's social life will be blossoming soon, so I should probably start investigating other babysitters."

He pulled into a parking garage. "You talked to her about her social life?"

"She's going to consider dating again, on the condition that I consider it, too."

He did a double take. "Really? I got the impression you weren't interested in exploring that. Are you seriously considering it, or just striking an agreement?"

"Too soon to tell." Five seconds ago, I'd been considering it—but an evening at the theater with a man I knew made me laugh was different than randomly picking a stranger off a list of men Rose and her bridge club deemed suitable. "What about you? Jess talks about Jerry like the two of them are still newlyweds, but I've never heard you mention anyone special."

"The last someone special moved to L.A.," he said. "We'd been together for a long time, had kicked around the idea of actually getting married, but she made it clear she was shopping job markets outside of Boston."

"And you don't want to leave?"

He turned off the ignition. "A few years ago, my oldest sister, Jayne, was diagnosed with Hodgkin's. She came through it and continues to do well at all her checkups, but it really drove home the importance of family. One of my other sisters lives in Connecticut, the only one of us that far away, and she was a wreck the whole time. For now, since I'm the only one without kids, I was able to do things for Jayne no one else could because I didn't have as many responsibilities. I would hate to move now, especially with my folks getting up there in years. So, no, when push came to shove, I didn't want to leave."

"I don't blame you. I don't have much in the way of family, but if I did, I'd want to be close to them."

He grinned. "Can't get much closer than living with them. Is Rose your only family now?"

"Pretty much." And I couldn't even remember if she advocated mashed potatoes or sweet potatoes at Thanksgiving,

A star or an angel on the Christmas tree. This year, I'd try to combine some of her traditions and some of ours, and to make new ones for all of us.

We walked through the bracing cold and approached a small, wooden structure that I wouldn't have guessed a restaurant if I'd just been driving by.

"I know it looks like a hole-in-the-wall outside," Luke said as he opened the door. "But the food is fantastic, trust me."

Inside, the owners had kept the navy-and-bronze decor simple. No cluttered nautical theme or walls full of pictures. Just a friendly open space that seemed larger than it had from the outside, filled with warmth and the savory smells of clam chowder and broiled shrimp. We were shown to a booth where Luke recommended his personal favorites, and service was prompt but unobtrusive. Luke had barely started telling me about the latest poker night at Jess's house when the waitress brought out our soups.

Luke and I were having a great time, but conversation was interrupted by my cell phone.

No strep, the nurse from the pediatrician's office reported. Some parents would have been happy to hear that, but the doctors had confirmed what I'd already suspected. Sara suffered from chronic infections, which might recur and worsen unless we considered a tonsillectomy.

"Why don't you come in tomorrow for a consultation?" the nurse asked. "You and Dr. Abrams can discuss all the options, and he'll refer you to a good otolaryngologist."

"We'll be there at nine," I said, just before disconnecting the call.

"Not the news you were hoping for?" Luke asked afterward.

"Nothing awful, they just want us to see an otolaryngologist."

"Now there's a fifty-thousand-dollar word. Good thing it doesn't come up in more casual conversation, since it's damn near unpronounceable."

The observation dredged a wan grin from me. "She'll probably need her tonsils out, which will be good in the long run if it keeps her from getting more infections and missing more and more school as she gets older."

"But you're not overjoyed at the thought of your little girl going under anesthesia," he surmised, his eyes kind. "Charlie, no parent would be. Would it be helpful if she talked to my nephew? Maybe we could grab Happy Meals or check out that Children's Museum, and he can tell her what it was like. From a kid's perspective. I don't know if she'll be nervous about it, but maybe that would help."

"Thank you." This was light-years better than sitting inside my office alone, worrying about things that were out of my control. "Jess often says the discount meds are the best perk of this job, but there's a lot to be said for who I get to work with, too."

"The feeling's mutual."

I worked twice as hard that afternoon, knowing I'd have

to miss tomorrow morning. When I arrived home, Sara was upstairs sleeping.

"She was running a low fever after school," my mother-in-law said, "and looked like she could use some rest. I told her we'd wake her up for dinner."

"Dinner!" Damn. "It's my night, isn't it? I forgot completely."

"Don't worry, I put some soup on. I thought it might be easier on her throat, since she was complaining that it hurt to swallow." Rose flashed me a sudden grin. "See, I can stray from The Chart."

Impulsively, I threw an arm around her in a quick hug. Had I ever done that before? Just hugged her? Surely I had, in twenty years of knowing her, but all I could remember were the stilted, obligatory goodbyes at the end of Tom's and my visits with her.

When Rose pulled away, her eyes were suspiciously bright, and I felt like a heel. Even on my darkest day this past year, I'd had two babies eager to snuggle and express their affection for Mommy. I doubted Rose had experienced much of that unconditional warmth until we'd moved in. I was suddenly very glad to be here, and not just because I didn't know how to pay for a second place when I still hadn't unloaded our house in Florida.

"Oh, and you got a phone message," she told me. "From that scandalous friend of yours I don't approve of." Her tone was more teasing than censorious.

"You mean Dianne? Is everything okay?"

"Everything's fine. Said her cruise ship's in port for a few days, and she wanted you to call when you had a chance, so that the two of you could catch up. Why don't you run upstairs and do that, while Ben and I take care of the dinner preparations?"

Until I heard Dianne's voice on the other end of the phone, I didn't realize how badly I'd missed her. After we'd exchanged greetings and she'd given me a brief overview of life onboard, she demanded, "Tell me all about you! About Boston and how the kids are doing. What's new?"

My life. It was all different, I was different. Making new friends, adjusting to a new environment, trying to rethink the role men played in my life after being a married woman for so long. Trying to reshape my relationship with Rose.

I took a deep breath but was unable to organize the jumble of thoughts that spilled out. "Sara might need surgery— just a tonsillectomy, but still!—and she turned into a cowgirl, not a princess for Halloween. Ben was very cute as a football player, and I think Rose has graciously stopped trying to plan his future NFL career. Work is going great, especially now that I no longer think my mentor hates me. Meanwhile, I could have seriously embarrassed myself when I thought a guy was asking me out today, but wasn't, and I turned down the only man who has, the most desirable single father involved with Hughes Elementary."

"Well." There was a long pause as she processed my bizarre,

stream-of-consciousness summary, deciding what to tackle first. "Just how desirable is this single father, and does he know about your gorgeous best friend who's terrific with children?"

CHAPTER 11

It's amazing how balanced talking to a good friend can leave you. For days after my conversation with Dianne, I felt more chipper, more grounded. That lasted until the doctor told us Sara indeed needed a tonsillectomy and due to scheduling around the holidays, the best appointment they could give her before spring—by which time she may have missed more class days—was immediately after Thanksgiving. Frankly, we were lucky they'd found a spot to squeeze her in. She could check in that Friday, have it done and, barring complications, go home. It would give me the weekend to spend with her during recuperation without missing tons of work.

Unfortunately, it meant she wouldn't be singing in the school play the following week. Just because she might be able to go back to school after a few days didn't mean she was cleared for belting out show tunes. Her throat would be raw after the procedure.

Sara had turned stony at this revelation and wouldn't talk about it at all. I didn't even know if she was nervous about the operation, but I knew she was mad.

That Sunday, Rose and I took the kids to see Velda, and Rose pretended not to notice when I handed the older woman some romance novels with suggestive titles and racy covers.

From the rapid rate at which Sara relayed stories from the life of a first grader, I deduced her throat wasn't bothering her today as much as it had most of the weekend. I was surprised, though, when my daughter asked if Velda could come see her in the play.

"So you've decided to take Ms. Cramer's suggestion?" The music teacher had first said she'd be happy to give Sara some sort of role, like ticket-taker or an honorary official duty. Then she'd suggested that Sara could get in costume and lip-synch with the rest of the class and that, as well as she knew the words to all the songs, no one in the audience would ever know the difference. Sara had flatly responded that it wasn't the same.

Had she changed her mind?

"I want to sing," she said, looking past Velda at me. "And I want Velda to come hear me."

I bit the inside of my cheek. "We've talked about this. You're not going to be able to sing that night."

"But Velda will be coming over for Thanksgiving," Rose put in with determined cheer. "Several people are. It will be like a party, with lots of food and we can even put up a Christmas tree that night if you like."

When I'd asked Rose about her traditions, I'd been surprised to learn that she used a fake tree. Here I was, up where Christmas-tree farms abounded, and we were still going to get an artificial one. On the other hand, it meant we could put it up as early as we liked and not worry about it drying out or shedding between now and New Year's.

Sensing that Sara was not going to be appeased by the mention of the holidays, I thought it best to get the kids out of here before a potential blowup. "Velda, we'll see you soon. For now, we'll go, so you can get some rest."

"Rest." She snorted. "Plenty of time for that after I've cocked up my toes. For today, I plan to read some of these books you brought me. You earned yourself a prominent spot in my will, young lady."

When Rose asked if I wanted to take the kids for ice cream, I glanced expectantly at my daughter, who informed me she wasn't hungry. She kept up the silent treatment during the ride home, but once I'd put Ben in his crib for a nap, I knocked on her door.

"I'm tired," she answered. "Go away, so I can sleep."

Apparently, she hadn't realized that my knock had just been a formality and that I was pulling Mom rank. I pushed the mostly closed but not latched door the rest of the way open.

"We need to talk, pumpkin."

She was curled up on her bed, clutching Ellie and facing the wall. "After my nap."

"You don't usually take naps."

"I'm tired."

I sat on the edge of the mattress, running a hand over her hair. "You have been tired a lot lately, and not feeling very well. It'll be so much better after your tonsils are out. I have mine out, too, you know."

"I know. You told me. Did you have to miss *your* play?"

I sighed. "Sara—"

"It's not fair!"

Well, that much was inarguable. And if I was still trying to cope with the life-isn't-fair concept at forty, how could I expect her to fully accept it? "You're right. But this is what's best for you, and you can try out for the play next year."

"You made Daddy go to the doctor, too," she said, still not looking at me.

My blood chilled at the unexpected accusation in her tone. "What?"

"You were fighting because he hadn't called somebody, didn't want to go to the doctor, but you made him. Then he had to go to the hospital, and he didn't come back."

"Oh, Sara-bear. No, Daddy and I weren't fighting, not really. I was just worried he might get sick, and he thought it was silly for me to worry. But he was sick, and the doctors wanted him to go to the hospital to see if they could make him all better. I'm so sorry they couldn't. You're *not* sick like that, though, and your father would want you to have this tonsillectomy. It'll be okay."

"That's what Daddy said, too. When I didn't want him to go."

Tears stung my eyes and stupid, meaningless words bounced around inside my skull. How could I reassure her?

What promise could I give that she'd believe, and did she, somewhere deep inside, blame me for Tom's death? That possibility had never occurred to me, but now it twisted in my gut. Parenting was a sly, tricky business that kept one humble. The second you thought you knew what you were doing, made the mistake of feeling competent, something like this hit you with the force of a brick falling from the clear blue sky.

"Sara...are you mad at me because Daddy went to the hospital?" I held my breath, not wanting to influence her answer but wondering if I could take her response.

"No." She rolled over, blinking up at me as tears spilled out of eyes that reflected her father's. "I'm mad at Daddy. For lying to me."

I felt a tear slide down my own cheek, then. "He loved you very much, I promise. And he never would have left you if he'd had a choice."

"But I still get mad," she admitted, her voice barely audible before the tears came in a rush.

I couldn't think of anything to say to her but the truth. "So do I, sometimes." I hauled her and Ellie into my lap, and we cried. There's a time to be strong for your kids, but there's a time to grieve together, too.

I took Luke up on his offer for his nephew to talk to Sara. The Saturday before Thanksgiving, we planned for Luke, his nephew Kevin and his five-year-old niece to meet us at Rose's house. Then we could all ride together in my van to a nearby children's pizza restaurant. The food there was rumored to be an abominable grease fest, but there were games galore and even a toddler zone Ben could enjoy.

Rose told me over breakfast that she was going to use some of the time alone to wrap Christmas presents.

"You mean you've already started your shopping?" I asked, impressed.

"Started? I'm almost finished, dear."

"Oh." I hadn't given it much thought at all, telling myself that it was more fun in December, when you could truly get into the spirit of the season.

I was upstairs, trying to help Sara find the barrettes she wanted, when the doorbell rang.

"Charlie, I believe your young man is here," my mother-in-law called up the stairs.

I started to call down that he was not in any way mine, but since I heard her opening the front door and greeting Luke, decided against it.

When Sara and I got downstairs, we found Rose pleasantly grilling my co-worker in the front parlor. She'd apparently clarified with him that the two children in tow weren't his, that he had no children, and had in fact never been married.

"Really, dear? And how old did you say you were?" she asked, her warm smile never faltering.

"Thirty-seven," Luke answered. "How old did you say *you* were again?"

She raised an eyebrow at his question, but I thought the corner of her lips twitched. "I didn't mean to pry," she lied. "I just found it interesting that a man your age has never settled down."

"Oh, I plan to," he returned. "The last few years were chaotic for my family, and I spent a lot of time helping them."

"So family is a top priority for you?" Though her tone was approving, I decided the interrogation had gone on long enough.

"Luke! Good to see you. You've met Rose, obviously."

His gaze met mine and he grinned. "Uh-huh. Of course, I felt like I already knew her, after all I've heard you say."

Now it was my turn to get Rose's lifted eyebrow and I felt the beginnings of a blush. For the most part, I had little negative to say about my mother-in-law these days, but there had been a few times I'd needed to vent. I suspected that after five minutes with her, Luke had a better idea of where I'd been coming from now.

"So, where are the kids?" I asked him.

"Out back, playing with Gretchen," Rose told me. "Luke's nephew agreed to keep an eye on Ben."

Luke smiled at my daughter. "You must be Sara."

She nodded.

"I'm Luke, and I work with your mommy. You like pizza, Sara?"

"I love pizza!" Her shy smile widened into a grin of anticipation.

"Me, too. Wanna help me round up everyone so we can go get some?"

They headed toward the back of the house and Rose came to stand next to me, watchful.

"It's nice that he's doing this," she said.

"Well, Luke is a nice guy."

She harrumphed. "A little cheeky, but he has potential. Should I add him to the list?"

When I realized what list she meant, I laughed. "No, that's all right. I don't date co-workers, especially younger ones." Although, there had been almost three years between Tom and me, too, so why should it matter so much who was on which end of those years?

"Hm." From the look Rose sent my way, I suspected that the minute we left the house, she was going to jot his name down anyway.

Thanksgiving was a cheerfully hectic gathering. One of Tom's cousins I hadn't known very well came to Rose's for the day, bringing her three children and two pies. Apparently, her husband would be working a night shift and was using the peace and quiet to sleep. Rose told me she had also invited two of the women from her bridge club and their respective spouses. Amid the flurry of arrivals, I drove to the retirement home to get Velda, leaving the kids to watch the televised Macy's Day Parade and Rose to covertly add seasonings to my homemade stuffing. I didn't think she was any less territorial about cooking than she had been the day I'd met her—but she was less overt about it, so she got points for making an effort.

When Velda and I got back to the house, another car had parked alongside the curb, the second couple she knew from bridge, I supposed. The Carmichaels had arrived earlier.

I helped Rose's aunt up the porch steps and was reaching for the knob when the front door opened and Rose peered out. "There you two are!"

Had we taken longer than she'd anticipated?

"Happy Thanksgiving," Rose told her aunt, taking Velda's elbow and steering her into the foyer. "Thank you so much for picking her up, Charlie. I think everything's well in hand for dinner now, so we have a few minutes if you want to run upstairs and spruce up."

I glanced down at what I was wearing. "I need sprucing?" I hadn't realized this would be a dressy dinner. Granted, Rose wore a nice sweater with black slacks and pearls, but Rose would wear pearls to get the oil changed on her car. I was wearing dark jeans and a maroon pullover. "I suppose I could change."

Rose beamed at me. "Wonderful! You know, that navy wrap skirt of yours always looks nice."

Alarm bells dinged distantly in my brain. On the one hand, Rose had never been shy about voicing an opinion on my appearance—or anything else, for that matter. Also, now that I stopped to think about it, this holiday was a bit more formal than the ones the kids and I had endured last year. We'd had a rotisserie chicken in place of a turkey, and I'd cried when I'd remembered that Tom had always carved. Dianne had been there, but no one else. And I'd felt as fragile as the china I would have used if I'd had the heart to pull it from the cabinets. We'd eaten off paper plates, instead. This was different.

On the other hand, Rose's cheerful manner seemed to have an anxious undertone, and was I imagining things, or was she standing squarely in the foyer, not letting me past? Velda had walked by her to mingle with the other guests, but Rose was herding me toward the stairs with all the subtlety of an Australian shepherd.

"Rose, is there—"

"Rose, where is that crystal you wanted me to use for the relish tray?" A tall woman with silver hair and a regal face approached my mother-in-law from the kitchen. "Dean was able to get those pickles open, but I thought we should let the olives marinate a bit longer. Oh, hello."

This last part was directed at me.

"Hi, I'm Charlie. I don't believe we've met."

"Not officially. Emily Keller, from Rose's bridge club." She beamed at me, but then her gaze slid down over my sweater and jeans. "Oh, dear. Is that what she's wearing, Rose?"

Clearly Bostonians had definite ideas about holiday apparel. Then the penny dropped.

"Did you say Dean?" I asked her.

Emily bit her lip. "Um…I should really get to work on that relish tray." She bustled off, leaving me with Rose.

"Dean isn't her husband, is he?"

"Her son," my mother-in-law said. "She and her husband were invited, and of course they weren't going to leave their son alone on a family occasion like this one."

"Uh-huh. He would be Dean Keller? I seem to recall that name from your list." Along with an asterisk, if I wasn't mistaken.

Unlike Emily Keller, Rose was unflappable. "I can certainly invite friends to my home on Thanksgiving, can't I?"

"Absolutely. Just as I can wear whatever I think is festive on the holiday." I brushed by her, deciding I didn't want to go upstairs and get all dolled up for some guy I'd never met. Was he aware of Emily and Rose's attempt at matchmaking, or was he, as many men often are in these matters, clueless?

"Mommy!" Sara rushed at me, hugging my legs. "I set the table. Aren't I a big helper?"

"The best," I told her, scooping her up as I glanced around the living room.

Dean wasn't hard to spot, especially since he and I were the only adults under sixty in the house. Good-looking, with the exception of the pained expression on his face. One glance at his air of resignation told me that he knew perfectly well what his mother was up to. And that he didn't want to be here.

I was glad I hadn't changed and could instead greet him in my casual clothes. I hoped the jeans made it clear I wasn't part of the plot to make me the future Mrs. Keller.

Behind me in the kitchen, Emily cleared her throat delicately. I'm sure she was sending pointed glances in her son's direction. Rose was looking more subtle by the moment.

Dean rose from the ottoman, running a hand through his dark hair. A solidly built man, I thought. Probably right at six feet, he'd aged well, stocky without his muscles going to fat.

"Dean Keller," he said, holding his hand out to me. "Sara and Ben were kind enough to keep me company while the more experienced cooks worked on dinner."

I set my daughter down, then straightened to shake his hand. "Charlie Smith. Nice to meet you."

His smile was rueful. "We've actually met before, but as the bride, you had a lot going on."

He'd been at my wedding? No surprise that I didn't remember since I'd only had eyes for one man that day. "Well, it's nice to see you again."

To fit all the guests into the dining room, Sara and the three other children sat at the folding card table Rose used for bridge, while the adults and Ben gathered around the polished oak table. Unsurprisingly, it somehow worked out that Dean and I sat next to each other. I imagined that each guest had quietly been assigned a seat long before Rose ever announced the food was ready.

He was a pleasant man, obviously fond of kids, and as the dinner wore on, he seemed more tolerant of our being forced together. As we cleared the table, he shot me a smile. "Would you like to go for a walk around the neighborhood? I would've suggested going for an ice cream or something, but I doubt anything's open today."

Plus, I would be surprised if I felt like eating again any time this month. I glanced out the window, debating. The sun was shining, but the chill in the air was unmistakable, making itself known whenever one got too close to a door or window.

Dean grinned at me. "We might as well humor them. If we don't, do you really think they're going to give up peacefully?"

I had a sudden image of Dean joining us for Christmas Eve service and helping ring in the New Year. "I'll get my coat."

In a remarkable display of restraint, Rose didn't ask about our walk or what I'd thought of Dean until all the guests were cleared from the house that evening and the children were ready for bed.

"He's very nice, don't you think?" she asked as Sara brushed her teeth.

"I'll admit you have good taste," I told her, "but for future reference, I'd prefer not to be ambushed."

"You're sure? Isn't it better just to meet someone casually in a friendly environment than to be all nervous about it beforehand? I'd think this way was better."

I filed that away for future reference.

"So will you be seeing Dean again?" she asked.

"No. No, I don't think so." For the first few minutes of our walk together, he'd shared anecdotes of people who'd come into his home-improvement store needing advice because they'd tried to fix something and made it worse. Then we'd talked about our kids—he missed his greatly but would have them for Christmas. Then, as we talked about getting back to the house to watch football, the conversation had turned to Tom, a friend of Dean's until they'd parted ways for college. Even then, they'd kept in touch. Apparently, we'd been unable to attend Dean's wedding but had sent a lovely gift. I was quite sure I'd been the one to pick it out and sign the card, as those tasks had always fallen to me.

By the time we'd returned to Rose's, it was clear that Dean had begun to see me primarily in the context of his buddy's widow. Going out with him would be awkward.

"Oh." She looked disappointed, but, to her credit, didn't push the issue.

Together, we tucked in Sara, who was showing some eleventh-hour anxiety about her upcoming tonsillectomy. "Promise me that I'll be okay, Mommy?"

I knew she was happily stuffed and should be drifting off to sleep, but little shadows of worry haunted her eyes. What a bizarre irony that more than anything, kids wanted their parents to tell them everything would be all right, and more than anything, parents wanted to give them exactly that. Even when it wasn't in our power.

"I promise." Although I didn't have the medical expertise to make such a guarantee, I could give her the peace of mind she needed to get some rest.

Her eyes closed, the anxiety smoothing out of her face. But she wasn't about to go to sleep without making sure we all remembered she'd been wronged. "I wanted to be in my play."

Ironic, since I'd had to talk her into participating in the first place. I wondered if I should regret doing so, considering the turn of events, but she'd blossomed too much during practices among her new friends. "I know."

"Life's not fair!"

"No." Her grandmother answered from the doorway, her arms folded underneath a fringed shawl. "But it's not all bad, either."

Sara accepted this. "Can we do something when my throat's all better? Something special to celebrate?"

I exchanged wary smiles with Rose. When Sara made a request like this, you never knew whether it would be sparkly lip gloss or a pony.

"What did you have in mind?" I asked.

"Getting my ears pierced."

"Absolutely not!" Rose said. "You're too young for that."

I raised an eyebrow.

"Er, well, I suppose we'll have to see what your mom says, but I vote you're too young."

"Duly noted," I said before turning back to my daughter. "Maybe in a few years. What if after your surgery, you and I go have a girls' day of beauty? We'll get haircuts, have our toes painted. Sound glamorous?" Not as much as the pierced ears, perhaps, but it was the best offer she'd be getting tonight.

And she knew it. "It's a date."

A lump caught in my throat. They were the words her father had frequently used when she'd begged him to do something—have a tea party after work, help her organize her sticker collection. As he'd leave for the office, she'd say very sternly, "Don't forget tonight, Daddy. You promised!" And he'd wink at her, tell her it was a date.

I knew how much he'd loved the kids, how fiercely proud of them he'd been. Would he have judged the job I was doing with them a good one?

Rose trailed me to just outside my room, hovering unexpectedly in the doorway.

I'd just sat at the chair in front of my computer.

"You aren't going to bed yet?" she asked.

"Thought I'd check e-mail." Although I wasn't expecting any PTA updates on a holiday, there were several ex-co-workers I kept in touch with from Florida, and messages from Dianne were always a day-brightener.

Rose stepped in the room, regarding the computer with bemused interest. "Can't believe what people accomplish with these things. Emily told me you can even play bridge with other people on your computer!"

"Yep. And Jess keeps hinting you can actually date online. Rather, meet people to date."

"Through your computer?" Rose looked appalled. "That sounds horribly impersonal. And dangerous. And a little… icky, as Sara would say."

I laughed. "Well, it's not for everyone, but other people swear by it."

She sat on the edge of my bed, frowning. "Do you just put your name on some site somewhere and tell people you're trying to find someone?"

"I've never actually tried it, so I'm not an expert. But I imagine you'd put your first name, or a nickname, and talk about the things you like to do, the kind of person you might be interested in. Then hope to hear from someone who meets the criteria."

"Definitely not for me," she said after a moment's consideration. "But I suppose it's easier to meet someone to date when there's a vast pool of strangers out there, someone who doesn't know me from Eve. I realized at church recently how long I've known most of my friends, and none of us are getting any younger. I seriously doubt any man I've known for forty years is going to suddenly ask me for drinks."

She had a point. "You could ask one of them."

"I'd rather try that computer dating," she said with a grimace. "I'll tell you the truth, dear. I feel old."

A few months ago, the admission would have shocked me,

but Rose had been more open about her vulnerabilities lately. Now, I just wanted to help. "You should come with Sara and me when we have our day of beauty." I regretted that it hadn't occurred to me to invite her originally. "We'd love it if you joined us, and a little change might be just what you need."

"I don't know. But I appreciate the invitation, Charlie."

"I won't twist your arm, but maybe all people need to see you differently is for you to see yourself a bit differently, too. Wouldn't you rather have a makeover than sign up for computer dating?"

She shot a look at my PC, glaring at it as if it might turn evil like one of those computers in the movies, trying to take over the world or kill the astronauts as in *2001: A Space Odyssey*. "All right. Sign me up for a makeover."

CHAPTER 12

We were pretty cranky when we got to the hospital—Sara because she wasn't really a morning person and hadn't been permitted to eat breakfast, me because my daughter was having surgery. The bright primary colors did little to soothe me, but I kept a smile in place anyway. Though Yvette Trumble had been gracious enough to stay with Ben, part of me wished he were here. I was overcome with the maternal urge to squeeze both my children tightly to me. Sometimes I wasn't sure if hugs were meant to comfort them or the other way around.

At check-in, Rose kept Sara from sheer boredom by asking what my daughter wanted for Christmas, a list that could take a while. In the meantime, I filled out all the usual paperwork, experiencing twitches of déjà vu—registering in the maternity ward, excited that Sara would soon have a baby brother; Tom and I signing our names on medical releases when he'd come in for his procedure; the documents I'd had to sign later, for the hospital, for our insurance company, for… Damn, I didn't want to be here. I knew hospitals represented something good, people trying hard to do good, but that didn't make them pleasant to visit.

Soon, Sara was wearing the standard-issue bracelet and gown. A bag of her belongings sat on a green guest chair, along with Ellie, who'd made the ride with us. Jess and Yvette had both said they'd be here in spirit and had asked me to call afterward, when she was in recovery, and let them know she was doing well. I think they were less worried about Sara and her minor procedure than they were about me. Ironic that I was so concerned about something so simple—when I'd checked Tom in, I hadn't been that concerned. I'd mostly been glad that the doctors had caught his arterial problems so early, when angioplasty was still an alternative instead of going straight to bypass. I'd been annoyed that he'd waited so long to have a checkup and had been feeling vindicated.

When the doctor had come out to tell me what had happened, I'd been looking for a private place where I could use a breast pump, since it was the first time I'd been away from our newborn son for any stretch of time. Utterly absurd. One minute, I'd been thinking that I hated breast pumps because they made me feel like I belonged in a dairy farm, the next, my place in the world had been yanked out from beneath me.

Prior to Tom's surgery, the doctors had outlined potential risks, of course, but I hadn't been alarmed. After all, in the medical releases I'd had to sign to give birth at the hospital just weeks earlier, there had been some mention of "dismemberment or decapitation," and you rarely saw news stories of women who'd been beheaded in the maternity ward. Tom hadn't shown any concern at all, had told me in his usual bluff, confident manner that it would be fine. Like Sara, I'd believed him.

So, even though I knew odds were slim to none that anything harmful would happen to my daughter today, I wasn't so quick to make assumptions. Maybe, in part, that wasn't such a bad thing. Maybe instead of sitting out in the waiting room feeling bored or bickering with my mother-in-law, which I well could have done a couple of years ago, it was better to be more cognizant of how much the people in my life meant to me.

Though it was mostly nurses and other hospital staff who directed us to the room and prepped Sara, Dr. Jonathan Leonard, the capable specialist we'd met with, stopped by to see if we had last-minute questions. He was a handsome man with a reassuring grin, his dark hair streaked with just enough silver to make him look distinguished and safe. Exactly the person you would want taking care of your child in these circumstances.

It was the first time Rose had met the doctor, and when he'd left the room, she turned immediately to me. "You didn't tell me he was so good-looking! Do you think he only does pediatric surgeries? I didn't mention it before, but my throat's been a little scratchy."

My daughter giggled at her grandmother's joking, which had probably been the intent.

When the nurse came to tell us it was time to roll Sara to the operating room, Rose dropped her hand below the level of the bed, where Sara couldn't see it, and squeezed my hand. I appreciated the encouraging gesture. Feeling bolstered, I kissed Sara's forehead and told her I'd be here when she woke up.

We escorted them to the doorway of the room, but the nurses had told us this would be the best place to see her off, since we couldn't go near the operating area. Sara was only a few feet away when she lifted her head, eyes frightened, and called, "Mommy! I want to give Ellie a kiss."

The nurse looked expectantly at Rose, who shook her head. "Her stuffed elephant. Give us just a moment."

The woman sighed, not looking nearly as cheerful as her brightly patterned smock would lead one to expect. "I really need to get her—"

I moved faster than I'd realized I was capable of, reaching the nurse's side. I could have darted into the waiting room and grabbed the stuffed animal already, only I'd been half-afraid that if I broke visual contact, the impatient nurse would have wheeled my daughter away. "She wants to give Ellie a kiss."

"Is there a problem here, ladies?"

Looking over my shoulder, I saw the attractive Dr. Leonard, his eyes the color of chocolate as he met my gaze. "We were just asking Nurse Patterson to give us a second so that Sara could give Ellie a kiss for luck."

Rose had already ducked into the room and was now walking toward us.

"Naturally, we do everything we can to make a patient comfortable." He gave his associate a pointed look. "Don't we, Nurse Patterson?"

I smiled, absurdly grateful. "Thank you."

Sara got her wish and handed Ellie to me for temporary safekeeping. Then there was nothing to do but wait.

"You know she'll be fine," Rose said gently as I paced in one of the small waiting areas of the hospital. "Do you want to watch television? Look at a magazine?"

No and no. But I took some women's journal she handed me, anyway, leafing through it as I walked. I caught sight of one of those lists women's magazines always have. I'd never checked to see if men's publications had them, too. Did they worry about things like Five Ways to Thrill Her in Bed, or Seven Surefire Exercises to Tone Your Abs before Swim Season? I doubted it.

This list was the Ten Most Stressful Events in a woman's life. Getting married and having a baby were near the top, joyous but stressful. Menopause was right under them and, on another day, I would have laughed at the juxtaposition. Funny how none of your girlfriends throw you a shower for *that* rite of passage. Changing jobs, moving, losing a parent, losing a spouse… Sobering, I dropped the magazine to one of the tiny square tables, not wanting to read anymore. They could have just called the damn thing Charlie, This Is Your Life.

I stopped, studying Rose. I wanted to ask her if it got easier, this worrying about your children, wanting to protect them all the time and hating that you couldn't. But considering what she had gone through with her one and only child, I couldn't.

"She looked scared," I said finally.

"Yet she shows no fear about letting some high-school dropout at the mall poke holes through her ears," Rose marveled. "Don't worry, she's brave like her mother."

I laughed. "The one who's pacing the waiting room and swearing at women's magazines?"

"The one who packed up her kids, drove cross-country and started over." Rose glanced down. "I never would have had the courage. I've lived within the same fifty miles my entire life. Friends told me I should sell the house that was really too big just for me, but I couldn't. I couldn't imagine leaving, trying to piece myself back together somewhere else."

"It's lucky for us you didn't get a smaller place. Where would we be?"

"I don't know, but you would have been fine. You have a way of looking at things…" She cocked her head to the side, as if searching for the words to describe whatever quality she saw in me. "It can be grating at times. Irreverent, but it serves you well, and you take care of your children. That's what matters."

"You did well by your son, too."

She shrugged. "*He* took care of *me* those first years after his dad died. Maybe I didn't need it as much as he thought in recent years, but what kind of mother does that make me, that I wasn't stronger for him when he'd just lost his father?"

"I know Tom. Thinking that you needed him gave him a reason to be strong." I sat next to her, thinking that strength was unpredictable and revealed itself in a variety of ways. "You know where I draw my strength from? The people around me. I was so lucky to have met Tom, lucky to have friends like Dianne, now Yvette and Jess. And I'm very lucky—the kids and I are lucky—to have you."

It wasn't the same as being needy, I realized. Having loved ones didn't mean you couldn't be independent, they just boosted your confidence to do so. I didn't think Rose saw it that way yet. She always wanted to be the one who was helping, not understanding that sometimes needing others *was* helpful.

Instead of arguing my point, I gave her a compliment I knew she could appreciate. "Sara's been happier than I've seen her in a year, and her grandmother's love is a big part of that. Thank you for everything you've done for us."

Rose smiled at me, her eyes misty. "Careful, dear. I might get the impression you like me."

Sara came through the surgery with flying colors, and Dr. Leonard came out to talk to me afterward. He teased that he'd almost sent Nurse Patterson to look for us, but that she was afraid of me.

I smiled sheepishly. "You think it was silly that I was so adamant about a stuffed animal?"

"You were adamant about your daughter," he corrected. "I admire that. The irony of being a pediatrician is that I spent so many hours in med school, interning, at the practice, I haven't actually married and had my own kids. But I love working with them and seeing parents who truly care. I give you high marks for parenting, Mrs. Smith. See the nurse on your way out for a sticker and a lollipop."

Laughing, we scheduled a follow-up appointment for Sara to see Dr. Leonard in a few weeks. Rose heckled me about it in the van, as we took a groggy Sara home to rest.

"I think the good doctor likes you," Rose said. "Wear something pretty to the follow-up."

I rolled my eyes, hanging a right into our subdivision. "Rose, you can't assume a man is attracted to you just because he's nice." I thought of Luke, who'd been quick to assure me his invitation to the theater wasn't a date. The day we'd had at the loud, sticky, overly bright pizza parlor had been fun, too, but completely platonic. "Trust me on this."

"We'll see."

I grinned at her. "Is that just a general expression, or should I expect to come home one night and find out you've invited the doctor and his parents for dinner?"

She sighed. "I already told you that wouldn't happen again."

Never hurts to make sure.

Once I stopped the van, Sara's eyes opened and she glanced around with a yawn. "Are we home?"

"Yeah, baby. We are." *Home*, not just Rose's house. Though I couldn't exactly pinpoint the moment it had happened, my feelings were very different than when the kids and I had first pulled into this driveway almost two months ago.

Friendships had also been made in that time, and my friends came through for me in the next few days. They fussed over Sara and helped take her mind off the play she was about to miss. Jess sent flowers, Yvette and Ginny brought over get-well brownies and even Luke came bearing gifts.

"I thought she could learn to play poker early," he told me, handing Sara two separately wrapped boxes the size and shape of card decks. "She'll be the best bluffer on the elementary playground."

"And I'll be getting calls from Principal Reeves."

"Relax." He grinned. "I'm just kiddin' ya. See?"

Sara had unwrapped Go Fish and another popular children's game, thanking him in her temporarily raspy voice.

"So did you get to keep your tonsils in a jar?" he asked, looking around the room.

"Eww." Sara glanced at me, rolling her eyes. "Boys are gross."

Luke laughed. "You just keep that in mind, princess. Stay far, far away from them until you're at least, oh, twenty."

I walked Luke to the door and thanked him for his thoughtfulness.

He shrugged it off. "You'd do the same for me, right? If I ever had a wife, who bore us a daughter, who then needed a tonsillectomy. By the way, I had one other present. Rose put it in the freezer for me when I came in."

I raised my eyebrows.

"A gallon of the best ice cream in Boston," he said.

"That's sweet, Luke, but the doctor said that whole ice cream thing is a myth. Something about dairy and phlegm production, it's not really good for a recovering throat."

"You're going to stand there talking about phlegm and Sara says I'm gross?" With a laugh, he took the porch stairs two at a time, turning at the bottom. "The ice cream was for you, Charlie. I considered booze, but wasn't sure what you would like, or if Rose would approve. The last thing I want is to get The Eye from her."

"You're safe, she seems to like you so far. And thank you for the ice cream."

"You're welcome. I wanted to do more, but it's not confirmed yet. I'm working on a surprise for you and the princess."

"What kind of surprise?"

He gave me a knowing grin, the kind that said, "If I told you, it wouldn't be a surprise," then walked toward his car, whistling, obviously pleased with himself.

I found out what he was up to the following week, at

work. While I was in the process of updating a vendor spreadsheet, Luke's hand, holding what looked like a half-dozen little red tickets, appeared in front of me.

He spun me around in my chair, so that I was facing him and could see his ear-to-ear grin. "How much do you love me right now?"

I laughed. "Jess, do you have any idea what this man is talking about?"

"Not the slightest," she returned.

"All right, I bite. What are the tickets for?"

"A play your daughter will be in," Luke said proudly. "Or will be, for one night only, if her mother says it's okay. The theater's next play starts soon, and it's a western piece. Bandits have come through the town, and when the good guy rides through, asking if anyone's seen them, the townspeople are too afraid to tell the truth. Until a little boy steps up and admits which way the bandits have gone, eventually leading our hero to the hideout. It's only one line...and there's no real reason a little girl can't do it. I talked to Kevin, who technically has the part, and to the director, who has grandchildren of his own. They'd be happy to let Sara take his place for a night. So I picked up enough tickets that she can have her own private fan club there to cheer her on. Sound good?"

"Good?" I shot to my feet, the chair rolling hard against my desk. I heard what was probably a coffee cup of pens fall over as I engulfed Luke in a tight hug.

"Okay, okay." His voice was half laugh, half protest, but his arms came up to hug me back.

If it wasn't the kind of behavior that normally went on in the front office of Kazka's Boston location, still there was nothing torrid about the embrace. But as I started to pull away, having decided that smothering the man to death was not a fitting thank-you, I paused, and our gazes connected. Luke had really nice eyes. Hazel, twinkling with merriment and goodness.

And something more?

I didn't know. I had no experience reading these eyes, so unlike Tom's dark gaze. Did I want there to be more?

"Ahem." Jess cleared her throat. "While *I* understand that there's nothing going on here, it might be harder to explain to the six salespeople due for a meeting with Frank in half an hour."

Luke and I sprang apart. Mumbling an "I'll see you later," he disappeared. I merely sat in my chair, feeling shaken. That hug had been the most physical contact I'd had with a man in over a year. Maybe that's why my insides felt so fluttery, my skin flushed.

"Interesting."

When I blinked Jess into focus, she was smirking.

"Not that interesting," I protested. "Just really nice. Luke is a nice guy."

"And haven't I said you need a nice guy in your life?" she asked reasonably.

"He's already in my life. W-we're friends. And co-workers. You don't go out with co-workers."

"You can as long as neither of you directly supervises the other. For instance, you and I couldn't date Frank, not that his wife would stand for it, anyway. And Luke couldn't date anyone who works in the warehouse for him, not that any of them are the right gender. But, hypothetically, if one of us wanted to date Luke…"

"I don't think he's interested in me like that." Funny, what I'd meant to say was that I wasn't interested in him, or anyone. Was I? "Plus, he's younger than I am."

She waved a hand dismissively. "Not by enough to matter. Besides, you should have seen what his family went through when his sister was sick. There's a lot of depth beneath the occasional goofy joking."

The joking was one of the things I liked most about him, but Jess was right about the depth. He might kid around, but that didn't stop him from noticing when things were serious and being there for the people he cared about.

"I'm just saying," Jess added. "Hypothetically."

Right. Hypothetically.

Never go to a salon with loved ones, I decided Saturday afternoon. They lend you courage and you get cocky, do stupid things. Rose had impressed me by turning herself over to her stylist and saying she was willing to do something new.

"Like body glitter?" Sara had asked. "Or orange toes? What about a different hair color?"

Eyeing the doorway as though she might bolt for freedom at any moment, Rose shook her head. "Not *that* new. But maybe we should tone down some of the gray? And I've always worn it so long, but maybe…"

The stylist threaded her fingers through Rose's hair, considering. "We could do long layers, lose some of this length without giving you short hair. It'll take twenty years off your appearance."

Rose grinned at me. "Wanna pass for sisters?"

Inspired by Rose's courage and Sara's vivacious youth, I told my stylist to cut my hair short, to give me something fun and modern. Unbeknownst to me, the weight of my hair had apparently been balancing out the curl created by that last pregnancy. There had been a lot more curl than I'd realized. Because once the stylist had hacked off about four inches, my locks exploded into a clownlike poof around my head.

The stylist hovered at my elbow, looking as if she might try to throw herself between me and the mirror, but it was too late—I'd already seen my reflection.

"Don't worry," the woman assured me. "A new cut just requires new product. We'll tousle in a little gel and tame it into the look you like best."

We tried tousling techniques for about ten minutes, but as far as I could tell, we only angered the hair.

"I am calling in sick Monday," I muttered to my newly stylish mother-in-law as we got in the van.

"But you're not sick," she pointed out. "You can't call in bad hair."

"Wanna bet?"

From the back seat, Sara said, "If I'd had a bad haircut, you'd still make me go to school and take a math test."

This was true. "But your hair looks adorable, Sara-bear." It was a short pixie cut that highlighted her features so well that I caught glimpses of what she would look like down the road, the young lady she'd be before I even realized the time had passed. She looked so much like her father.

And Rose looked so much…different. The stylist may have been exaggerating about the twenty years, but the cut definitely gave her a more vibrant appearance. Or had it just given her new confidence and a new outlook, thus providing the sparkle in her eyes?

I caught her turning her head slowly from side to side, checking out her reflection in the rearview mirror. "Thank you for inviting me, dear. I wouldn't have thought to do this otherwise. And your hair…will grow out."

Since Rose was right about my not being able to call in sick on Monday, I went into work, where Jess stared at the new me.

"You got your hair cut," she said, staring.

"I'm aware. And trust me, I've tried to forget."

She bit her lip, looking caught between horror and laughter. "It's different, isn't it?"

I dumped my purse into my lower desk drawer, wishing I had a hat. "If by different you mean more curl than Little Orphan Annie, then, yeah."

"Oh, doll, don't worry. It's lively. And it'll grow out."

When Luke came through the room a little while later to pull some files and cross-check an inventory report, he stopped, tilting his head as he studied me. Great. He had to be the one man on the continent who noticed when a woman changed her hair.

"I got my hair cut," I said, making a preemptive strike.

He nodded. "Clearly."

"And it looks like a poodle died on my head." I resisted the urge to run my hands through it, since that might encourage the riotous chaos.

"It's not that bad," he said. "Besides—"

"It'll grow back?"

He shut the drawer. "No, I was going to say that your face is so beautiful, who's going to pay all that much attention to your hair?"

"Oh." The compliment wasn't surprising, since Luke had a knack for saying just the right thing, but the way he said *beautiful* was shocking. As if he meant it. As if it was a foregone conclusion.

As he left with the file he'd come for, I noticed Jess smirking.

"Don't," I warned her.

"I didn't say a word."

* * *

I couldn't feel my nose. Unfortunately, I could still feel my fingers, which were getting soggy as the snow eventually seeped through my gloves. I didn't think I'd ever been this cold in my life.

"Sara, I really think we should go back inside now." This had been the first snow of the year and I'd been all for coming outside to play in it, but, in retrospect, the snow angels had been a bad idea. Even through the layers of clothes, my butt was numb. Rose had already come outside to rescue Ben when his teeth had started chattering.

"But I'm not cold," my blue-lipped daughter protested.

"We're not staying out here any longer because the last thing I need is for you to get sick again! Besides, you should pace yourself, or you'll be sick of snow by spring."

Mumbling that she'd wanted to make a snow friend for her already completed snowman, she nonetheless followed me inside. Compared to outside, the house was a sauna, warmer than usual because Rose had been baking. She was taking baskets of cookies to a women's shelter later. Between the cinnamon smell of the spice cookies and the Christmas music she had playing, it was very festive in the Smith home. We'd even put up a tree last night, although it would have been clear to any outside observers that Rose was accustomed to putting up decorations by herself. Ever organized, she'd wanted to place the ornaments symmetrically, with the larger ones on the bottom and smaller toward the top.

Then she'd tried to show the children how to take the silver tinsel icicles, one at a time, and hang them on individual branches.

I'd sat back with my spiked eggnog, laughing silently as she'd tried to show my one-year-old how to hang a single strand at a time. Finally, Rose had caught my grin, asked me to pour her a glass, and watched as the kids threw clumps of tinsel at the tree.

After playing in the snow, we all warmed up with soup for lunch, and then Rose and I suggested a trip to the mall. The kids had yet to see Santa and I had shopping to do.

"Why don't you drive?" I asked, extending the van keys to Rose. "You have more experience driving on snowy days than I do."

"I'm less worried about the roads than I am the mall parking lot," she said. "Going this close to Christmas? We're risking life and limb. That's why I shop early."

But by the time we'd been inside the crowded mall for fifteen minutes, she'd already spotted a dozen items she wanted to buy. Mostly for my children.

"You don't think Sara would look adorable bundled up in that coat?" she asked me out of the side of her mouth as Sara admired some sparkly shoes on display in the girls' department.

"I'm her mother, it's my job to think she'd be adorable in anything. But don't you think you've bought her enough presents already?" I asked gently.

I didn't want my kids to be spoiled rotten, and no matter how well Thomas Sr.'s investments had paid off, leaving Rose a large nest egg, she was still living on a fixed income.

"I suppose you're right, but…I'm so excited to have you all here this year."

Even though neither of us said it out loud, we both wanted to make up for our last abysmal Christmas, when we'd all been missing Tom so much it had hurt just to speak to one another.

"Well." I glanced at the rack of clothing. "It is marked down. And she could always use another jacket, right?"

"Exactly what I was thinking! Let's go find Santa, and I'll sneak back here to make my purchase while the kids are distracted."

Sara needed no prodding to visit the jolly man in red; in fact, she was impatient to get to the front of the line. An older gentleman sat patiently on a throne framed by giant candy canes, patiently taking requests while garishly dressed elves took pictures. The man's glasses and white hair looked as though they belonged to him, but I suspected the beard had come with the velour suit.

When it was my daughter's turn, she went through a list of toys, starting with dolls and accessories, continuing on to games and ending with books she wanted. Her instinctive categorization made me laugh and I shot a look at Rose.

She returned my glance owl-eyed. "What?"

Then it was Ben's turn, but he was less willing than Sara.

Judging by the shrieks and the way he clung to my shirt so tightly I expected to hear fabric ripping, I'd say he wasn't willing at all.

"Maybe I could try," Rose said, frowning.

"Be my guest, if you can pry him out of my arms." I was aware that others were waiting behind us.

She leaned in close to Ben, humming something and speaking softly. I didn't want to traumatize my son, but if Rose could settle him down, framed pictures of the kids with Santa would make a nice stocking stuffer for her.

Ben let her take him, but he held on to her with a death grip.

Santa, who must see a dozen screaming kids a day, was watching Rose with a smile. "What if you just came and sat next to me? The three of us could have a picture together." He winked at her. "Consider it a personal request from Santa."

"All right." It was awkward for her to perch on the arm of the throne, but with Santa's good-natured help and laughter on her part, she managed. "This is my grandson, Ben."

"You look awfully young to be a grandmother."

I blinked, realizing Santa was flirting with my mother-in-law.

After a second, Rose returned both his smile and his playful tone. "Well, I was a child bride."

Safe and content in his nonna's arms, Ben reached out to play with St. Nick's beard and laughed at the feel of it.

When the elf snapped the picture, all three subjects were beaming.

Santa gave Ben and Rose tiny candy canes. "So, have you been good this year?"

"Aren't you supposed to know that already?" she asked.

They chatted for a few more minutes, until harried mothers behind me began to glare at Rose. Afterward, the kids and I got snacks in the food court while Rose dashed into the department store to snag a jacket for Sara. She returned carrying three bags.

"That looks like more than just one purchase," I observed.

"I was caught up in the holiday spirit," she defended herself with unrepentant cheer.

"Nonna, how come you were smiling at Santa Claus like that?" my daughter wanted to know.

When Rose flushed, I told Sara, "Nonna was just putting in a good word for you and your brother."

Actually, as I watched the extra lift in Rose's step for the rest of the afternoon, I thought to myself that the few minutes of fun conversation with a man she didn't know had been her gift to herself this year. And I doubted I'd be able to find anything at the stores to top it.

For Sara, Christmas came early, in the form of Luke's favor. Though the shabby little theater might not have been the Boston Opera House or the Colonial, tonight it was both of those rolled into one for my daughter. She was onstage in a real theater, surrounded by adult actors, with an actual spotlight shining on her as she delivered her single, but crucial, line. "I saw 'em, and unlike these yella bellies, I ain't afraid to admit it, mister—the men you're looking for headed over them hills toward the Painted Lady Mine."

Well, Luke had never promised it was a well-written line. Still, Sara delivered it in a clear, brave voice that made my throat constrict with pride. As soon as the play's hero rode off, closing the first act, the people seated around me— Yvette and Ginny, Jess and Jerry, Rose and Ben—erupted into applause, cheering as if she'd delivered a Shakespearean soliloquy or belted out an Andrew Lloyd Webber solo. Ben clapped his hands together, but mostly he found his introduction to the theater boring and fidgeted in my lap.

During intermission, Luke, working tonight as a stagehand, came to find me. I'd stayed seated while others made trips to the restroom and concessions, and Rose took Ben to throw pennies into the small but pretty lobby fountain. It was unfortunate that Velda couldn't have joined us tonight, but she tired early, and wasn't up for the evening show. Sara had signed a copy of the program, however, and I was tucking inside it a picture of her in her costume and makeup. We'd deliver it during our Sunday visit.

"She did a great job," Luke said. "Caught her cue better than that marshal in scene two. I told her she could come sit with you for the rest of the play, but she'd rather stay backstage if that's all right."

"Absolutely."

"And the director has invited you all to join the cast party afterward."

"Luke, thank you again for this. It means the world to her, and I'm sure her classmates will be hearing about this for many show-and-tells to come."

He reached out to tuck a strand of hair behind my ear. "Don't mention it."

Strange. He'd made the gesture before, and it hadn't felt personal, just amicable. *Things change.* I almost laughed at the thought, which summed up my life in two words.

Luke noticed. "What are you grinning about?"

"Nothing. Just…happy."

There were still a few minutes left before people would be returning to their seats, and I felt suddenly shy about meeting his gaze. I glanced toward the stage, angling my chin. "There was a time I wanted to act. Not professionally, or anything, but something like this would have been fun. I loved the theater, loved stories. When I took drama in college, I choked pretty badly and that was that."

"You should try again," he goaded. "After all, you're a long way from college."

I narrowed my eyes. "Was that a crack about my age?"

"I should really get backstage now and help out." He said it with all seriousness, but I heard him laugh as he left.

The second half of the play wasn't as spellbinding to me, since Sara had no part in it, but it was still entertaining and passed quickly. Everyone was game to stay for the cast party afterward, particularly Ginny, who happily told anyone who listened that she was friends with "one of the stars."

Luke met us in the lobby after the final bows and escorted us backstage. There was one large central room, with tiny dressing rooms off it, and everyone had congregated in the main area, where deli trays and a cooler of beverages waited. Some actors were still in costume, others in street clothes, still others in a bizarre combination of the two.

"The theater owns some stock costumes," Luke told me, "and people are quick to change out of those since replacing and repairing them can be expensive. Most of the people still dressed are wearing costumes they own." Sara had wanted to wear her red cowboy hat from Halloween, but they'd explained that it didn't quite fit the rugged aesthetic.

While Luke introduced some of my friends and family to actors and stagehands, I carried Ben through the crowd to congratulate his big sister. She was sitting and talking to a lovely young woman who had portrayed the town madam. Her more provocative outfit had been replaced by baggy jeans and a pink T-shirt with an Asian character printed on it. She was explaining to Sara that it meant "peace" when I came up beside them.

Sara bounded to her feet. "Mommy, did you see? Was I good? Could you hear me from where you were sitting?"

"Every word," I assured her.

"Luke said that the theater might try to do *The Sound of*

Music this summer, and I could try out to be one of the von Tramp kids."

"Von Trapp," I corrected.

"I told her she could *ask her mom* about trying out."

Turning, I found Luke holding several brightly colored plastic plates with food. He handed one to me, one to Sara and one to the young lady in the peace shirt.

"Thought you might like a bite," Luke told me. "Then I can introduce you to Gregory, the director. He's a great guy."

"Nonna likes him," Sara chirped.

I followed my daughter's gaze and saw that her grandmother stood not far away, talking to a tall gentleman with silver hair, a strong jaw and commanding presence that not even the slight stoop of his shoulders diminished.

"That's Gregory?" I asked Luke.

He nodded. Before he could say anything, an unfamiliar sound reached our ears. Rose *giggled*. I'd heard her laugh, but this was something else entirely.

Luke's eyes met mine and he lifted an eyebrow.

Well, well, well. It didn't look like Rose Fiorello Smith needed my help meeting anyone, after all.

CHAPTER 13

"So…it looked like you and Mr. Scott hit it off," I observed on the ride home.

"We had some things in common." Rose's tone was breathless despite her matter-of-fact words. "He was very admiring of the bouquet we brought for Sara, and impressed that I grew the flowers. He's supposed to be quite the gardener himself but doesn't have a greenhouse."

"You should invite him over to see yours," I said, trying to sound very casual about the idea.

"We'll see."

I didn't want to push, and Sara was eager to rehash her own glory, so we dropped the subject and let Sara talk about her stage debut. Half-expecting her excitement to keep her awake all night, I was surprised when she fell asleep almost before her head hit the pillow. We were in the middle of saying prayers when her breathing suddenly deepened, evening out to long, relaxed inhalations.

With both my children in bed for the night, I retired to my own room and was surprised to find my mother-in-law sitting on the edge of my bed.

"Is it okay that I'm in here?" she asked, her expression oddly vulnerable.

"Of course." I was touched that she even asked, considering this had been her bedroom for decades. "I just thought you were downstairs. Did you want to talk about something?"

She sucked in a deep breath, as though fortifying herself for a painful task. "I have a favor to ask."

Her grave manner made me wonder how serious a request this was going to be. "What do you need?"

"I know Friday next is your office Christmas party, and I was going to keep the kids, but do you think we could find someone else to babysit them?"

I laughed. "Is *that* all?"

"Well, I did give you my word, which isn't something I take lightly."

But mostly, she just hated to ask anyone for anything, even though it was about time. She wasn't even technically asking me for a favor, just letting me know she couldn't do the one I'd asked of her. "I'll find someone. So. Does this mean you have plans for Friday?"

She blushed. "Gregory will be directing a production at a small local college next week, a different play than tonight's, and he invited me to watch it. After I explained to him what a theater buff I am."

Theater buff? Before tonight, I wasn't aware of a single show she'd seen, but there was no way I would laugh at her stiffly delivered words. She was feeling sensitive about her new acquaintance and the last thing I wanted was to discourage her.

"That's wonderful, Rose. And don't worry, I'll take care of Friday night."

Luckily, Yvette agreed to let my kids spend the night at her house Friday. She came to pick them up, leaving Rose and me to get ready for our respective evenings. I'd lived in an all-girls' dormitory my first two years of college and tonight reminded me of being back in that dorm; Rose had come upstairs twice to ask me about her hair.

"I'm just not sure what to do with this new cut," she said. "It's not all the same length and doesn't pull up into my usual bun very well."

"You got the cut because you wanted something different than the bun," I reminded her. "Why don't you wear it the way you did at the play? Gregory seemed to like that. Now, since you're here...which of these dresses do you like better?"

When the pealing doorbell announced that Gregory had arrived to pick her up, I stayed upstairs. I didn't want to make Rose more nervous by overseeing her departure, and I needed to finish my own primping. It was the most effort I'd put into my appearance in a long time.

Because the Christmas party was being held in the ballroom of a rather nice hotel, I could rationalize that as my reason for dressing up. I wore a rayon-and-silk oversize button-down shirt, a burnished red with patterns in muted purple and gold. It reminded me of an old-fashioned Christmas ornament. I wore the shirt over a black skirt, covering up a stomach that had carried two babies but showing off legs that didn't look half-bad for a forty-year-old broad.

And I was starting to get the hang of the new hair. Ironically enough, curlers helped. At least then I had some control over which direction the crazy spirals were pointing. I added makeup while waiting for the curls to set, then, when everything was finished, put on earrings and my wedding band, on my right hand, instead of the left finger where the indention had finally faded from notice. During my marriage, there had been so many nights like this one, when I'd dressed up with a sense of breathless anticipation, waiting to show Tom and see his reaction, knowing that I was going through the trouble for him.

Tonight, I was decked out for *me*. I needed to know I could still look like this when I wanted to, that I could catch a glimpse of myself in the mirror and see an attractive woman, not just the widowed Mrs. Smith, a woman who had grown heavy and despondent in the months following her husband's passing. I'd lost ten pounds since moving to Boston, but I thought there were other reasons I felt lighter, as well.

This was the first office party I'd ever attended alone, but the second I walked into the ballroom, my trepidation eased. Jess called out a hello, and a man I recognized as one of the warehouse workers smiled in greeting and told me I looked nice. I had friends here and it was easy to feel festive in the ballroom, decorated with fake snow, miniature Christmas trees and red-and-white balloons.

"There's an open bar," Jess told me when I joined her and Jerry at a table. Sparkling silver confetti snowflakes had been tossed on the white linen tablecloth. "And a not bad buffet. Jerry promised that after he's eaten, he'll take me out on that dance floor."

A small band was currently playing a lively version of "Jingle Bell Rock."

"Did I hear someone say dance floor?"

I turned at the sound of Luke's voice. "You know how to dance?" Most men I knew actively avoided it.

"My sisters had to practice with someone," he said, smiling. "And I've been to enough of their weddings to have the basics down. I wouldn't mind a drink to bolster my courage before I go out in front of an audience, though. Can I get you anything from the bar while I'm there?"

"Hm?" I was rather distracted by Luke's appearance. I wasn't the only one dressed up tonight. He wore a black jacket over a white shirt, and the lack of a tie seemed more formal than the slightly crooked, loosely knotted ties he was always tugging at in the office. He'd had a haircut this afternoon, too, I'd noticed. Jess and I had joined him for morning doughnuts, and his hair had been a little shaggier. He was more debonair now. Even his smile seemed more sophisticated.

"Charlie?" he asked, that smile widening.

"Uh, an amaretto sour would be great."

He nodded. "As the lady wishes. I'll be back in just a minute."

The first amaretto sour went quickly and I was glad I wasn't drinking anything stronger. Since I hadn't yet eaten, one drink and the way Jerry spun me dizzily around the floor during the dance Jess urged me to accept were enough to soften the edges of reality. I returned to my chair, watching as Jess and her husband stepped out onto the floor for a waltz.

"Do you want anything to eat?" Luke asked.

I shook my head, feeling shy but not hungry. There were butterflies in my stomach. "No. Thank you."

"Well, if you're sure…how about another turn on the dance floor?" he invited, holding his hand out to me.

I took it, noting the warmth of his skin. "All right, but go easy on me. Jerry got a little carried away there at the end and I felt like I was getting off that ride at Disney where you spin around in the giant teacups until you want to heave."

"No problem. We can go as slow and gentle as you want."

His answer made me blink, and I couldn't think of a response. So I found myself wordlessly tucked into his arms, tracing lazy circles around the floor. It was odd, dancing with someone so close to my own height, almost alarmingly intimate. With taller men, a woman can lay her head against a chest or shoulder, averting her eyes. In Luke's arms, his gaze, his face, his mouth, were so close to mine. My pulse accelerated and I had a moment's worry that my palms would go damp in his. Nothing more ladylike than sweating on your dance partner.

"You look great tonight." His voice sounded deeper than usual. It wasn't, not really, but it was missing the teasing note I was used to hearing.

"Th-thank you. So do you. I was almost a little surprised when you first walked in."

His laugh rumbled through him, vibrating against my body. "Because I'm normally such a slob?"

I exhaled in a gust of frustration. "I'm not good at this."

"At talking to me? You've always been fine at it, Charlie."

True. Conversing with Luke had felt natural since the day I'd met him. Until now. "You haven't really changed that much—a haircut, new jacket. So how can you look so different?"

He was silent for a minute, leading me around the dance floor with subtle mastery. He'd been modest when he'd said he knew the basics. "Maybe you're just seeing me differently."

"Maybe I am." I swallowed. "How would you feel about that?"

Pulling me closer, he murmured, "Pretty good."

After our dance, I switched to ice water. My head was already swimming; I didn't want to risk what alcohol would add to that.

Later, when Luke was dancing with Claudia and Jerry was

getting more drinks, I admitted to Jess what she'd been bad-
gering me about for weeks. "You were right. I do like him."
Like? I felt stupid using such a juvenile term, but I wasn't sure
what else to say. I didn't love him, I wasn't sure I wanted to
sleep with him—sleep with *anyone* yet—and it would be coy
to say I wanted to get to know him better. I already knew him
pretty well, and what I knew, I…liked.

It was enough for Jess.

She raised her hands toward the ceiling. "And the light
dawns ova Mahblehead—hallelujah! Don't look so anxious,
doll. He feels the same way."

After the dance with him earlier, I was inclined to believe
her. Still, it didn't entirely put me at ease.

"I don't know, Jess. It feels…"

"Strange. And new," she guessed. "Because it is. But what
about all those things you told me you said to Rose? About
moving on, about Tom wanting you to be happy? About living. Didn't you mean them?"

I nodded. "Yes, but there's a difference between telling
yourself you're ready and actually being *out* there." I wondered if Rose was having a good time tonight with Gregory,
if she felt as jittery as I suddenly did.

"You sure you don't want one of the boys to get you something stronger than water?" Jess asked shrewdly.

I laughed, the sound catching in my throat when Claudia and Luke walked back to the table. Even before they
reached us, his gaze had already locked with mine. And I'd

told Jess that Luke and I were "buddies"? Dismissed the idea that I could be attracted to him? I was an idiot. A nervous idiot. Would he ask me out before the night was over? I didn't want to go to work on Monday with this hanging over us, this unspoken suggestion of something more, some new place I hadn't imagined going. Not with him, anyway.

"Did you want to dance some more?" he asked me.

"Not really."

"Want to go out on the terrace and look at the view? I know it's chilly tonight, but it's supposed to be pretty."

"Okay." At least out there, if I was trembling, I could attribute it to the cold. "I guess we should get our coats."

After we'd both slid into our jackets, he draped my cream-colored scarf over my shoulders, then flipped it playfully across my throat.

"After you," he said, pushing open a balcony door. A gust of cold air met us and I shivered instinctively against him. My knees turned to water. The feel of a man's body pressed against mine was something I'd missed. Badly. Even if it had made me feel guilty to admit it. My throat went completely dry.

Move, I ordered my feet. They did, but in graceless, awkward steps that made me feel as if I were wearing cement boots. Despite all the times I'd joked around with Luke, I couldn't think of one clever or funny thing to say.

I leaned against the ornamental railing at the top of the

steps. Beyond the partially enclosed balcony, there was a wide staircase that led down to a private patio used for outdoor events in warmer weather. "I have no experience at this. What do we do now?"

He ran a hand through his hair. "You're really nervous, aren't you? We can go back inside. The last thing I want is to make you uncomfortable."

"No, I...I wanted to be alone. With you." I made the admission to my shoes, knowing that my face would ignite in a poinsettia-red blush if I tried to meet his gaze. Why was this so hard? I was a grown woman. A woman who'd had babies and made love plenty of times, under plenty of conditions.

But only with one man. And Luke wasn't him.

"What if—" Luke cleared his throat. "What if there was mistletoe hanging in this alcove?"

My gaze immediately shot upward, my heartbeat thundering in my ears as I looked above us. "There's not." Was I relieved or disappointed?

"I know that." He chuckled softly. "It was a hypothetical question."

"Oh." Could I kiss a man when my mouth had lost all moisture and my tongue was glued to the roof of my mouth?

"If there were..." he cupped my face in his hands, somehow making me feel delicate even though he wasn't exactly a hulking presence "...would you let me kiss you, Charlie?"

My yes came out as a breath against his lips, which closed gently over mine. *Oh.* My heart was skipping erratically, and

I wasn't sure when or how his arms had folded around me, but they felt good there. He felt good. It had been so, so long, and to be touched… Except it wasn't quite right. There was a foreignness, a hesitance, as if he were somehow seeking permission I thought I'd already given. The more self-conscious I felt, the more I froze up. My eyes fluttered open.

Perhaps because I'd gone still in his arms, his eyes opened, too. And then we were just looking at each other, awkwardly, both struck by the absolute wrongness of that kiss.

Luke dropped his arms and took a large step back, leaving me in the cold. "Um…I'm sorry. I shouldn't have—"

"No, I wanted you to," I answered, my fists clenched at my sides in balls of frustration. "I just…it wasn't…"

His expression softened. "You aren't ready, are you? I knew from the way you first mentioned him that you still loved him, it was why I never intended to ask you out. I should have stuck with my original gut feeling."

"No, Luke. That's not it. I—"

When Tom had first kissed me, it had been one of those storybook moments. Tender passion and a sense of rightness. Did that happen twice in a lifetime? Tears pricked my eyes. There had been a spring in my step when I'd left the house tonight, but maybe it was only the echo of something I was trying to recapture. Right now, I felt every minute of my forty years and quite a bit beyond.

"I think I'm just going to duck inside and grab my purse,"

I said. "If I miss anyone on the way out, tell them I said good-night, won't you?"

He grabbed my elbow lightly as I passed, but I didn't turn. "Charlie, it really is okay."

Easy for him to say.

The entire time I drove home, I tried to blot out the embarrassing memory of what had happened. Maybe if I got well and truly into denial tonight, by morning I could pretend it was a bad dream. At the house, I called out to announce my presence, but there was no answer from Rose, which was for the best. I wasn't really in the mood to talk.

After washing my makeup off, I crawled into bed, staring at the dark ceiling. A few months ago, I would have cried myself to sleep. There were no tears now. Only the vague sense that I was standing at some sort of crossroads...and needed to figure out what in the hell I was doing so I could move forward soon.

CHAPTER 14

I ducked out of the house early the next morning, leaving a note that I was taking advantage of the stores' extended holiday hours to buy a few last-minute gifts before picking up the kids from Yvette's. Mostly, I just wandered the nearest mall, trying not to think and wanting to be alone. When that accomplished nothing, I went to get Sara and Ben, which was better. Their happy chatter drowned out the recriminations in my head that silence had only heightened.

I couldn't believe the vocabulary Ben had now! He tried, through one-word sentences and excited gesticulations, to tell me about their time at Yvette's house. In addition to Ginny, the Trumbles had a preteen daughter—Yvette's husband's from an earlier marriage—and she was old enough that she thought helping take care of the "baby" was cool. She doted on Ben, leaving Ginny and Sara free to play. I planned on doing some Christmas baking and putting together a nice basket for the Trumbles. We stopped by the grocery store on our way home, and I asked Sara if she wanted to help me make some goodies.

But by the time I rolled into the driveway, Sara was asleep

in her seat. No doubt the girls had been up half the night. Rose met me out on the front porch, frowning. "That Jess you work with has called four times today. I don't know why she doesn't believe me when I tell her that I'll have you call back. No sense in pestering *me* every five minutes when you aren't even here. Want some help with those bundles?"

"Thanks." I handed her a couple of grocery bags, knowing Jess would want to talk about Luke. I was in no hurry to do so, but I might as well get it over with so she didn't pounce on me when I walked through the door Monday. I didn't want to discuss it at work.

After unfastening Ben from his car seat, I let him trail Rose into the house. He reminded me of a duckling, but he was getting taller all the time and his gait more steady. He wouldn't be my baby much longer. Then I turned to his sister, who was out like a light. Carrying her upstairs gave me a good excuse to cuddle her close against me and pretend, for just a moment, that she was still my baby girl.

When I came downstairs, Rose was putting away the perishables I'd bought. Other items like baker's chocolate and cookie cutters, she put on the counter. "You planning to use these today?"

I nodded. "If you don't mind." Ben was coloring at the table. As long as he was in one of his quieter, more manageable moods, he could even help stir the batter. "So, you want to tell me how your evening went last night?"

Rose blushed, smiling girlishly. "Dial your friend back

first, we'll talk later. Just don't be on the phone too long. I'm expecting Gregory to call."

As I'd thought, Jess wanted to talk about Luke—she and Jerry had been on the dance floor when I'd gotten my purse and had left for the evening, and she said Luke hadn't stayed much longer than that, either.

"I'm guessing by his grim expression you didn't both leave separately so that you could meet up for an illicit rendezvous with no one at work any the wiser? Are you gonna be okay?"

"I've survived worse," I reminded her with a grim laugh.

"Of course. I just meant at work. Will it be awkward?"

Probably.

But it turned out to be a nonissue. I didn't see much of Luke the following week. I'd never realized how much we went out of our way to see each other before, me walking back to give him forms or messages that I could easily e-mail or leave on his voice mail, him coming through the front of the building every day when he could just park in the loading lot that was actually closer to his office. Jess was sensitive enough not to mention his conspicuous absence.

Luckily, I had plenty else to occupy my thoughts and time. Christmas itself was a joy this year. Sara was bouncing on the foot of my bed before the sun was even up. Bleary-eyed, I woke up Ben who, even though he didn't technically understand the significance of the day, had caught his sister's contagious enthusiasm. Rose was already awake and brewing coffee.

"I couldn't sleep, either," she admitted. "I was too excited."

Though I'd nagged Rose about her extravagance when it came to gifts for the kids, the excitement on their faces cheered me. Toys from Santa were piled beneath the Christmas tree and both kids were squealing in delight. Rose nudged me with a rectangular box.

"This one's for you, Charlie."

"Thank you. I have some for you behind the tree." I'd picked out some of the figurines she liked to collect, as well as some gardening supplies, which hadn't been easy to find in the dead of winter.

Sara found a box with Rose's name on it, then sat next to her grandmother on the divan as Rose unwrapped it. Meanwhile, I opened my own box, pulling aside gauzy tissue paper to find an absolutely beautiful sweater. The thick material was soft and lush, and the color was exactly what I would have picked out for myself.

I held it up against my cheek, touched. "Thank you. This is gorgeous."

Rose smiled knowingly. "Well, I've had a chance to get to know you more over the last couple of months."

Later in the day, Rose went to pick up Velda while the kids and I played outside on our first-ever white Christmas. It wasn't enough of a fall to make snow people, but it satisfied us. When Velda arrived, she shared with me the news that her center's librarian had taken a new job and had been replaced by a man in his late sixties.

"I think he winked at me last week," she said. "Of course, he's far younger than I am, but I think that's the secret. We should all see if we can't get hooked up with younger men. *They* can outlive *us* for a change."

Well, it did have a certain logic to it.

I didn't know Gregory Scott's age, but he dropped by that afternoon. He refused to come in, claiming he wasn't going to disturb a family holiday but that he had a gift he wanted to drop off. He left Rose with an adorable gardening ornament for the tree. She glowed for the rest of the afternoon, not even minding Velda's slew of ribald suggestions for furthering the romance.

That night, as I snuggled under the comforter, I found the cold outside cozy. I slid toward sleep, suddenly jolted with the realization that I hadn't thought much about Tom today. Even more surprising was the feeling that it was okay. He'd loved the holidays and he would have wanted Sara and Ben and me to spend the day exactly as we had, as a family, joking and eating and showing one another we cared. Nowhere was it written that I had to be miserable on every future holiday because he wasn't there to spend it with me.

After that thought, I sighed, then fell into the deepest sleep I'd had in weeks.

The day after Christmas was Sara's follow-up appointment with Dr. Leonard. The office was mostly deserted, except for one nurse working the front desk. Jonathan was trying to talk her into taking the rest of the day off when Sara and I walked in.

"Ah, merry Christmas—a day late," the doctor greeted us. "Did Santa bring you lots of toys, Sara?"

She nodded, giving an exuberant description of her haul. It might have been more detail than he was looking for, but she spoke at such a rapid-fire pace, it didn't take long.

He gestured across the empty room. "I think we can skip the ceremonial waiting period today, don't you?"

Sara and I followed him through the door that led to the examining rooms. Usually a nurse collected all the vitals, but today, Jonathan did it himself.

"Did you have a good Christmas?" I asked, as he wrote on Sara's chart.

"Good, quiet. I spent Thanksgiving with the whole family in Vermont, so stayed here for Christmas. Mostly, it was me and the dog."

I frowned. "That's sounds…quiet."

"I guess it sounds sad out loud," he said, laughing. "But the uncharacteristic peace and quiet was like my gift to me. At least I have the dog. Last year it would have been just me."

"We have a German shepherd," Sara told him. "What's yours?"

"A mutt. Showed up on my doorstep in the spring, half-starving. I took her in just until I could find a good home. My hours don't make me the perfect dog owner, but she's been there ever since."

Dr. Leonard completed Sara's checkup, asking both of us questions about how she'd felt since the tonsillectomy and the different symptoms he'd cautioned us to watch for. "Everything looks great," he told Sara. "Bad news for you, you might not get to miss any school days at all next year."

She grinned at this. "I did miss a play, but then it was all right because Mom's friend Luke got me a part in another one."

He patted her shoulder. "See there? Everything tends to work out. Unfortunately, now that you're so healthy, I probably won't be seeing you anymore. Dr. Abrams, your regular pediatrician, will take good care of you, though."

Sara looked disappointed. I think she liked Dr. Leonard, and it was easy to see why. He was handsome and charming, with a reassuring, authoritative air.

I stood. "Well, I'm sorry our paths won't cross again, Dr. Leonard, but thank you for making her all better."

"It's what I do." He paused for a moment, shoving his hands into the pockets of his long white coat. "Mrs. Smith, er, Charlotte, I hope you don't find this inappropriate, but since Sara won't be my patient any longer, would you like to have coffee with me sometime?"

Luke's face flashed in my mind, and my gut reaction was to say no. But then I thought of Rose, how happy she looked whenever Gregory called. Just because things hadn't clicked between Luke and me, did that mean I should give up and never try again?

"Sure," I told him. "I'd like that."

He grinned, handing me his business card after scrawling his personal number on it. "Terrific! It's a date, then."

When I told Rose about Jonathan's invitation to coffee, she was thrilled. "He's such a nice young man! A doctor. They can support families."

I dumped a load of Ben and Sara's clothing into the washing machine. "I think it's a little premature to think about Dr. Leonard supporting anyone. It's just coffee."

"For now. But I have high hopes. He just seems so right for you, dear." Then she bit her lip. "Do you think you might want to have dinner with Gregory and me? A double date, I mean."

Double dating with Rose. The idea was bizarre. "You're sure you want to do that?"

"You'd be doing me a favor." She glanced down at the kitchen table. "Gregory wants to take me to dinner soon, and I accepted, but I'm not sure it's such a good idea for us to be alone. I've already grown so fond of the man, and it's moving, um, faster than I'd expected. It would be good to have a chaperone."

I laughed out loud, unable to contain it. "So I'll be there to make sure you don't do anything rash?" Rose Fiorello Smith, slave to passion.

"Never mind. Forget I asked."

"No, no. I'll call Jonathan and see if we can make it dinner instead of coffee. I can't guarantee he'll say yes, but I'll ask." I was strangely calm about calling the attractive doctor and asking him out. Why wasn't I the wreck I'd been when I'd gone out onto that balcony with Luke?

"Charlie? Is everything all right?"

"Hm? Sure. I was just thinking…there's really not a full load here. Do you have anything you want to add?"

"And *mix* our clothes in spite of the allotted washing time?" From the twinkle in her eye, I knew it was a joke. Two months ago, it might not have been.

Either Rose was really nervous about her upcoming date with Gregory or she was really pleased by the idea of me dating Jonathan, who agreed to join our foursome as long as we could wait until after New Year's Eve. We made a reservation at a nice restaurant, and I hired a woman we knew from the church to stay with Sara and Ben. Nancy was a new grandmother herself and often worked in the church nursery. She arrived early so that she could feed the kids a dinner of frankfurters and macaroni while Rose and I got ready. My mother-in-law surprised me by the way she fussed over me.

"Your hair would be just long enough for a lovely French braid," she said. "Do you ever wear it that way?"

"Not unless I want it to be crooked. I'm much better at braiding Sara's hair than my own."

"How about I do it for you? Let me get dressed, and I'll meet you upstairs, see what we can do about your hair."

Though we'd grown much closer over the past month, the offer still seemed unlike her. I wondered if she wanted a distraction from her own nerves or really wanted Dr. Leonard to like me and didn't trust my own styling skills. Whatever her motivation, the result was pleasant. I sat in a chair in front of my vanity mirror, as she secured the braid in place. When the doorbell rang, she went to look out my bedroom window.

"Gregory's here! And it looks as if Jonathan has just pulled up, as well."

I got to my feet, but Rose shook her head, admonishing me with a smile. "No need to rush right down. It won't hurt them to wait for just a moment, will it?"

I supposed not, especially with Nancy to keep my kids on their best behavior. Except that Nancy popped her smiling face into my bedroom a few seconds later.

"My, but you two are the lucky ones," she said, fanning herself with one hand. "There are a distinguished director and a handsome doctor waiting downstairs."

Rose flashed a grin that was almost giddy—however nervous she might be, her happiness exceeded it. "Only the best dates for the Mrs. Smiths, right, Charlie?"

We went downstairs, to where the children had cornered Gregory and Jonathan in the front parlor. Ben was trying to share his apple juice with Gregory and Sara had sat Ellie next to the doctor.

"Of course I remember her," Jonathan was assuring my

daughter when Rose and I walked into the room. He rose to his feet. "Good evening, ladies. I was just renewing my acquaintance with Ellie here."

Gregory had stood, as well, and crossed the room to give Rose a kiss on the cheek. "You look lovely tonight."

She flushed. "Charlie, Jonathan, we still have a few minutes—would you mind terribly if I showed Gregory the greenhouse very quickly before we left?"

We assured her that we didn't, although I noted with humor that *we* hadn't been invited. She was already ditching her self-appointed chaperone.

Instead, we stayed in the parlor with the kids while Nancy cleaned up the supper dishes in the kitchen. Jonathan had been wise to go into pediatric medicine, because he was very good with children. He acquiesced to Ben's demands for a game of horsey, bouncing Ben on his knee, all the while letting Sara know that he was listening to her as she told him about her classroom and the things she'd missed over the Christmas break. She was looking forward to going back to check on the class pet and to see what new books Mrs. Z. might have added to her private library.

Everything was going smoothly until Sara came to a stop, only to demand, "Are you going to be my new daddy?"

Jonathan coughed, losing his grip on Ben. I caught my son before he could slide off onto the floor. Whether Nancy had heard the question or just the resulting spluttering, she hurried around the corner, her voice just a little too cheerful and high-pitched.

"Kids! Let's go run your bath now. Won't that be fun?"

When they were gone, I laughed at his still-stunned expression. I grew more accustomed to Sara's little bombshells every day, but I imagined they could come as quite a shock to someone who'd never had any children.

"I bet they're a lot easier to deal with when they're under anesthesia, aren't they?" I kidded sympathetically.

He looked appalled by this, so I made a mental note not to joke anymore about drugging children or him being less than perfect with them. Other than that, we had a very nice evening. It was decided that we should take Jonathan's car, a decision I was grateful for since I thought Gregory and Rose would be much happier in the relative intimacy of the back seat; Jonathan and I were not at that stage.

He pulled my chair out for me at the restaurant, and everyone loved the food. There was a comfortable, familiar quality to the evening. I couldn't quite place it, but there was none of the stomach-churning anxiety that had gripped me at the Kazka party. It was nice to feel so calm and to be on such friendly terms with Rose. She and I had turned out to be much better roommates than I ever could have hoped.

She was animated and vivacious at dinner, laughing at Gregory's jokes and offering him bites of her food. But I saw her stiffen once or twice when he dropped his arm around her or touched her leg. I wondered if this was what she had meant by their moving too quickly. Was he pushing her beyond her comfort zone and she didn't know how to tell him? But I'd never known Rose to be unable to tell anyone anything, and besides, she'd been the one to drag him off to the privacy of the greenhouse and snuggle up to him on the ride here.

When Jonathan started talking about med school, the conversation regressed to his college days and the fact that he'd played football. It startled me to realize they were discussing it because I hadn't noticed the change in topic. My mind had wandered and, feeling guilty about it, I forced myself to pay better attention as Rose shared a story about one of Tom's UF games. It had been his one and only Gator Bowl. She hadn't actually been present for it, but Tom had excitedly filled her in on the win against Iowa. She told the story almost as well as if she had attended…until the end. I blinked in surprise when she credited her son with the winning touchdown.

That's not how it happened. But it certainly wasn't an important enough detail to correct her in front of her new boyfriend. She'd probably just remembered it wrong, which was understandable considering how long ago it had happened. But it bothered me enough to keep me distracted for the remainder of the evening.

After we reached the house, Gregory walked Rose inside. Wanting to give them their privacy, I asked Jonathan if he'd like to have some hot apple cider with me out on the front porch. He agreed and we sat outside talking some more. He asked me a little about Kazka, which led to him discussing some new prescription medications that were in development right now. As a physician, he was pretty excited about them, but I had to fight to stay awake. When the front door shut, I jumped.

"Didn't mean to startle you," Gregory said cheerfully. "But I'm headed home. Hope to see you again soon, Charlie. Jonathan, it was nice to meet you."

Once he was gone, I stretched. "It's probably getting late."

Jonathan nodded, leaning toward me as he prepared to stand. "Late enough that I should be going, too. But thank you for the dinner invitation. I had a wonderful time."

Either because of my distracted state tonight or simply because he was fairly suave about it, he was kissing me good-night before I even knew it. It was…nice. I kissed him back instinctually, having learned the hard way that stopping mid-kiss was awkward for everyone. This felt cozy. Nonthreatening.

But did I really want kisses that were analogous to comfy gray sweat socks and flannel pajamas?

I extricated myself, realizing that my mind was wandering. "Good night, Jonathan." I stood there watching as he walked to his car, relieved that he drove away without making mention of calling me. Aside from what had to be a hectic schedule for him, I wasn't sure I wanted to go out again.

When I got inside, I found Rose in the kitchen, humming. She had changed into a nightgown and was trimming some blooms she'd brought inside from her greenhouse.

"Oh, did Jonathan leave then?" she asked when she saw me. "That was a lovely evening, dear. And the two of you make such a cute couple."

No, we made a *familiar* couple. The similarities might not be quite so on the nose as to be psychologically disturbing, but the fact was, the comfort I felt when I was around Jonathan was because he was a little like Tom. Tall and darkly handsome, the type who took charge of situations and took care of others, deferential to Rose, with even similar hobbies and outlooks. I suppose it made sense that I would be attracted to him. Jonathan was "my type." Or should have been.

I sat at the table, loosening the braid and running my fingers through my hair. "Rose…that story you told about the Gator Bowl? You know Tom didn't win that game, right?"

She paused, giving me a quizzical glance. "Certainly UF won. I'm sure of it."

"We did. But *Tom* didn't."

"Well, it was a team effort, but I know he did his part."

I bit the inside of my lip. It was late and the details were unimportant. Why was I arguing this with her? "Rose, you rarely say anything negative about Tom. Or his dad."

Her eyebrows shot up. "What reason would I possibly have for disrespecting either of their memories? And to what negative qualities are you referring? They were both very good men."

"The best," I agreed softly. "But still just men. We should preserve their memories, not canonize them."

I thought of Sara's tears before Thanksgiving, when she'd admitted that she was mad at her father. She meant for leaving us, for dying, but there had been moments since moving here that I'd felt annoyed. And then felt I didn't have a right to that annoyance. Well, why not? Why should I have to pretend that Tom had been perfect and that he and I had never clashed? Any healthy relationship was going to have disagreements, bumps.

When Rose didn't respond, I added, "I want my kids to grow up knowing their father as well as they can, under the circumstances, but we don't have to make him sound like something more than he was. What he was is plenty to be proud of. Why lie to them and set them up for disappointment? Why set an impossible standard to follow? Isn't it better for children to know people don't have to be perfect to be well loved?"

Rose just stared at me, stunned, and I was beginning to think my words had been a bad idea. Then, she smiled faintly. "See, I *told* you that you were a good mother."

She slumped into a chair, staring out the window into the dark yard. We were silent for a long time, and Gretchen padded over to the table. She laid her head on Rose's thigh and whimpered once.

"Good girl." Rose rubbed between the dog's ears. "I love you, too."

The dog's tail wagged a staccato beat against the air. *Whoosh, whoosh.*

Finally Rose said, "Thomas Sr. chewed on pens. Made me nuts. When we first met, he was a smoker. Back then, doctors, or people claiming to be them, did radio ads for cigarettes, if you can believe it. But even before smoking started to fall out of fashion, he became unhappy with his growing dependence on them. Perhaps you noticed that people in the Smith family can be an independent, stubborn lot? He quit with little fanfare, but from then on, he always chewed on the ends of pens and pencils. I'd go to write a grocery list and pick up something mangled by his teeth marks."

"Thank you," I said. Maybe it was a weird response to her random anecdote, but she'd let me know that she'd heard what I was trying to say.

She shook her head. "Thank you, Charlie. It's a lot less scary to go into a new relationship when you aren't afraid the man won't measure up against a perfect memory. When you realize that maybe it's okay to let yourself fall."

Let yourself fall.

Was that why I'd been a nervous wreck with Luke and so calm tonight, because there was a chance I was already falling for the compassionate man with warm eyes and the doctor didn't trip any of those internal sensors?

I was reading to Sara when the phone rang the next day. Since I assumed it was probably Gregory making one of his daily calls to Rose, I didn't budge from my spot on the floor, where Sara and I had just reached the part about the princess getting rescued.

"Next time we're in a bookstore," I decided, "we are finding you a book about a princess who rescues herself."

Sara frowned, pondering this. "Can she still ride off with the handsome prince?"

"It's entirely up to her. Heck, maybe she could rescue him from something."

"Like a dragon," my daughter said with a giggle. "A pink one. What do you think?"

"I—"

"Phone for you, Charlie," Rose informed me, handing out the cordless. "It's a Jason Anders."

I drew a blank. "Who?"

"Your—"

"Real-estate agent." It came rushing back to me. "Right. Did he say why he was calling?"

She nodded. "Someone's made an offer on the house."

Shock flooded me. I didn't know if it was because I'd given up hope of selling the darn thing or just because, here lately, I'd forgotten about it. I took the phone.

"Hello, Jason."

"Charlie, great news!" He outlined all the details, then concluded with a hearty, "I think you should take it."

Of *course* he did. It was the only serious offer we'd had since the house had gone on the market. But considering what the couple was willing to pay, along with things they could have asked for and didn't, I had to agree. It was a good offer and I authorized him to accept it. Plenty could happen between now and the time someone with my specified power of attorney signed the papers at closing, but it felt final, as if the house were sold. Tom's and my house. Part of me was relieved, part of me was sad.

By that evening, Jason called back with the closing date, saying the buyers were happy to have such a quick acceptance. When I tucked Sara in that night, she didn't have much of a reaction to the news, except to say that she liked it in Boston and would hate to move away from Ginny.

I had trouble sleeping, though. On a subconscious level, I hadn't let go as well as I'd thought I had. Some part of me, knowing that the house was still there, had held on to the past. Tom and I had made a lot of good memories there. *Bad ones, too.*

Recalling my advice to Rose, that we force ourselves to remember things as they were and not just the way we wished they'd been, I thought about the pregnancies that hadn't gone full-term, the fight Tom and I had had when I wanted to go back to work as Sara entered preschool, the way he'd insisted we should have a dog but had not once, in my recollection, been the one to feed her. I'd loved him very much, but he hadn't been perfect. Neither had I.

I mulled it over most of the night, but by the time we left for church the next day, I could honestly say I was happy someone wanted the house. I was ready to move on in a way

I hadn't been back in October, even as Rose and I had packed up the house and I'd moved anyway. I'd done what I needed to do, for me and the kids, but I hadn't been particularly glad about it.

Now, I was happy. We were making friends, all of us, changing and growing. Maybe we weren't the same people we'd been, but I liked who we were becoming. The Tom I'd met at eighteen had been the perfect man for Charlotte Wagner. But Rose hadn't been looking at the full picture when she'd said Jonathan Leonard was a good date for me, Mrs. Smith. I'd already been Mrs. Smith and wasn't looking to replace the wonderful husband I'd lost. If I began a new relationship, it should be with someone who fit this new Charlie. That didn't negate who I'd been before, and it wasn't a betrayal of what Tom and I had shared. The realization was so sharp it was almost a pain in my heart, just for a second, then it was gone.

I really was ready to move on.

By Monday morning, I bordered on giddy, the result of two almost sleepless nights—the first because I'd been up worried about the house, the second because I'd been thinking about my love life. Rather, deciding that it might not be so bad to have one. Eventually. But first, there was someone I needed to talk to and, with any luck, he'd come to work habitually early.

I opened the door to the warehouse. The overhead lights were on, of course, but I was more concerned with the small corner office with mini-blinds closed over the window. Were lights on in there?

Yes.

Increasing my pace, I hurried past metal shelving units, my heels echoing on the concrete floor, hoping to get to that office before my courage deserted me. Then I rapped my knuckles across the closed door.

"Come in," Luke's familiar voice called, reminding me how much I'd missed it the past few weeks. When I opened the door, his eyes widened and he sagged against the back of his chair. "Charlie!"

"I was thinking," I began, "about what you said about auditions for the community theater. I'm sure I missed whatever play you specifically meant, but I just wanted to let you know, I want to try out for something. Soon. It doesn't need to be the lead or anything, but I do want to be onstage, not just designing the background."

Tom had told me once that I was the star of his life. It had been sweet, and I was grateful for the way he'd cheered me up at the time. But now, I needed to star in my own life.

Luke walked around the cluttered desk, then leaned against the front of it. "That's great, Charlie. I'll bet you're a lot better at it than you think. You're a lot braver than you think."

Was I? That was the question I'd asked myself all night, and there was one surefire way to find out. I leaned forward, grabbed his shirt by the collar and kissed him. I'd been so tense last time, and it had been so awful. I had to know if that could be improved on, if we could erase that memory.

For a second, Luke stood stunned and I had a flashback to the kiss that wasn't. But that passed quickly and his hands came to my waist as his lips met mine. He traced them with his tongue, nipped at my lower lip with his teeth and kissed me so deeply I wondered why I'd let him get away from me at the Christmas party. Heat sparked through me, a wave of long-repressed sensation rolling through me, tingling and undeniable. *I remember this. This is good.*

But it was also different, and that was good, too.

When Luke drew back, still holding me against him, his eyes were dazed. "Well. That was certainly an improvement."

I sighed, recalling that botched mistletoe incident. "I'm really sorry for before. I think the fact that it had been so long since I'd been kissed put a lot of pressure on me, on the moment. And, I was dealing with some…"

"Issues? Charlie, it's understandable that you'd have some things to sort through. I felt like a heel for rushing you."

"But you weren't. You thought I wasn't over my husband—wait, I don't actually like the way that sounds. I spent half my life with him and I see him every day in Sara's eyes and hear him in Ben's laugh. He won't be something I get 'over.' But I always knew that he'd want me to be happy, even if that meant finding someone else. I guess I just thought it meant having to find someone like *him*. You're so very different, Luke. Admitting that I might be attracted to you seemed too much like acknowledging there were ways my husband of twenty years was a bad fit. And that hurt."

"Charlie." His voice was as tender as his touch as he caressed the side of my face. "I don't know what to say."

"That you'll be patient? That you're interested in seeing if this might go somewhere?" I smiled hopefully. "That you'd be willing to kiss me again?"

"I can manage that."

And he did.

I hadn't anticipated celebrating Valentine's Day again anytime soon, but a lot had changed. That seemed to be the constant in life.

Luke took the kids and me back to the obnoxious pizza place where the food was overpriced, and the main attraction was an assortment of electronic games and rides with flashing lights. We had a blast. I was pleased to see that he didn't let Sara win at air hockey. She got frustrated when she lost the first time, but he told her that she'd get better at it and that, in the meantime, learning that things don't always go your way was an important life lesson. She informed him that she liked life lessons about as much as she liked math, and he laughed.

Rose had a more eventful Valentine's Day, although she and Gregory spent the night at a bed-and-breakfast so I didn't find out about it until the next morning. She came home early Wednesday, having assured me she'd be back before I left for work to watch Ben. She and Gregory burst into the kitchen, both grinning, and she waved a modest ring under our noses. We celebrated the engagement over oatmeal.

"I'm thrilled for you," I told her, hugging her close. "I'm a little surprised, though. Gregory's great! I just wasn't expecting anything like this yet. Not too long ago, you were worried about 'moving too fast.'"

She shrugged. "Neither of us is getting any younger, so why waste time on a long courtship?" They wanted to be married in April.

I was excited for her, seizing the day. Me, I wasn't in a hurry to seize anything just yet, but it was nice to take things one day at a time and see what happened.

"I wouldn't have had the courage to say yes to Gregory's proposal before," Rose confided in the corner of the kitchen. Her betrothed was answering Sara's questions about whether or not she should start calling him grandpa and when she'd get to meet his grandchildren. "I've said before that I've been on my own for a long time. I wasn't sure, if I found a man who was worth it, whether or not I could still compromise. But I did find that man, and I figured if I could get used to living with *you*..."

I laughed. "I know what you mean."

"Speaking of living with people. Eventually Gregory will move in here. While we're making changes anyway, I thought—" She broke off, and I waited while she found the words and the strength to voice them. "I thought maybe

Sara would like to redecorate her room. Something more feminine, perhaps?"

I was almost too touched to respond. But if she could manage, so could I. "Actually, I've been thinking about that, too. I'm ready to move on, Rose. Naturally, we'll stay close, and we'd like to see you as often as possible, but it's time. And I can afford it once the sale's closed on the house in Florida. Besides, you newlyweds might want your privacy."

Her only answer was a broad grin.

"If I might ask you one favor, though," I added. "Since you already have the fenced-in yard, and she has such a rapport with you—"

"Why don't we just call Gretchen a wedding present?" Rose suggested.

"Good idea."

"Well, you don't get to be my age without gaining a little wisdom, dear." She patted my hand and joined Gregory and the kids. Ben and Sara were holding hands and jumping up and down. Gregory was smiling and doing his best to make sure they didn't fall and crack their skulls on the dishwasher.

An April wedding.

Spring was coming. It might not seem like it now, with the days so bitingly cold, but it would be here before we knew it. And summer would bring the kids' birthdays. They were growing so fast, it was hard to believe, but I was incredibly proud of both of them. I was also looking forward to my summer visit from Dianne. I'd have so much to tell her during our spa day! She'd love shopping with Jess, trying Yvette's homemade fudge.

Then, in the fall, I'd be forty-one. Maybe *that* would be the age where I had my life figured out. Okay, probably not, but the future certainly looked promising.

And that was enough for now.

eHARLEQUIN.com

The Ultimate Destination for Women's Fiction

For **FREE online reading,** visit
www.eHarlequin.com now and enjoy:

Online Reads
Read **Daily** and **Weekly** chapters from
our Internet-exclusive stories by your
favorite authors.

Interactive Novels
Cast your vote to help decide how these
stories unfold…then stay tuned!

Quick Reads
For shorter romantic reads, try our
collection of Poems, Toasts, & More!

Online Read Library
Miss one of our online reads?
Come here to catch up!

Reading Groups
Discuss, share and rave with other
community members!

For great reading online,
visit www.eHarlequin.com today!

Holiday to-do list:

- wrap gifts
- catch a thief
- solve a murder
- deal with Mom

Well-respected Florida detective Maggie Skerritt
is finally getting her life on track when a
suspicious crime shakes up her holiday plans.

Holidays Are Murder
Charlotte Douglas

The colder the winter, the sweeter the blackberries will be once spring arrives.

Will the Kimball women discover
the promise of a beautiful spring?

Blackberry
WINTER
Cheryl REAVIS

Kate Austin makes
a captivating debut
in this luminous tale
of an unconventional
road trip…and one
woman's metamorphosis.

dragonflies AND dinosaurs

KATE AUSTIN

HARLEQUIN®
Next™

HN24
Available December 2005
TheNextNovel.com